Returning

Returning

J.T. McDaniel

Riverdale Books
Dublin, Ohio

Returning

For information, please contact:

Permissions Department
Riverdale Books
PO Box 3716
Dublin, Ohio 43016

This book is a work of fiction. Names, characters, places and incidents are either the product of the author's imagination or are used fictitiously. Any resemblance to actual events, locales, businesses, or persons, living or dead, is entirely coincidental

ISBN-13: 978-1-932606-45-4
ISBN-10: 1-932606-45-9

Library of Congress Control Number: 2017936012

Riverdale Books is an imprint of Riverdale Literary Holdings, Inc.

For Zebidiah and Zahara

Contents

One

CAPTAIN KIMEWE ROMIWERO LEANED FORWARD, her hands resting on the weathered stone balustrade bordering the stone-flagged terrace of her family home, looking out over Tufaria Bay. The moonlight reflected off the gently-undulating waters. In the distance, she could see the lights of the great naval anchorage of Koril Harbour. Once, it had been the main anchorage for the Eastern Sea Fleet. Now, after 139 years of peace, it was more museum than anything else. The great capital ships were carefully maintained, but seldom left the harbour, unless it was to participate in some mock battle for a motion picture.

Even that was rare now. It was easier to recreate the battles in a computer.

Behind her, the party noises grew suddenly louder as someone opened the terrace door. She heard soft footsteps approaching. Romiwero straightened and turned. An attractive, middle-aged woman, wearing a dark-green party dress, was making her way across the terrace.

"I thought I'd find you out here," her mother said. "You always used to come out here when you were little, any time you wanted to get away from people."

"I like the view," Romiwero replied.

"Having second thoughts, Kim?"

"Not exactly. Just thinking about all the things I'll be leaving behind. All the people." She smiled wistfully. "You and Dad, for instance. For thirty years, you've always been there for me, and in another day or two you won't be, ever again."

Korasi Romiwero nodded. "We're astonishingly proud of you, Kim," she said. "You, and everyone in your crew. You'll see things the rest of us can only imagine."

"I know."

She thought of her ship, *Warrior*, parked in orbit some 400 kilometres above them. The lead ship in a class of three, she was 5.2 kilometres long, with a 450-metre beam. Her range was presumed to be essentially unlimited. No one knew for sure. Jump drive technology had been developed 40 years ago, and first tested in 486, with a relatively modest jump of five light years.

In 496 they had discovered two things. That the jump drive worked, and that it worked only if you were aboard the ship using it. The crew reported enthusiastically of being instantly transported to a point five light years from Barzak, spending a week exploring the vicinity, and then being instantly transported back to where they'd come from. They'd been away for a grand total of seven days, six hours.

They had been a bit taken aback to discover that, so far as everyone on Barzak was concerned, they'd been gone for ten years. The light speed barrier, it seemed, remained unbroken except in a temporal bubble around the ship, where time simply ceased to exist. In jump space, the ship travelled precisely at the speed of light, so time stopped for everyone aboard, but continued for the rest of the universe.

Even that shouldn't have been possible, Romiwero thought. Griisniskirian Physics argued that an object gains mass as it approaches the speed of light, and at the speed of light its mass becomes infinite. That shouldn't have allowed travel at light speed.

Avigor Arkhgaizim, until 497 head of the physics department at the University of Balin, had found a way around the problem. The jump drive he developed might move the ship at exactly light speed, or it might simply draw one location in space-time into proximity with another location lights years away, allowing the ship to pass instantly from one to the other. Either way, the ship had traversed the distance, but the same amount of time had passed in ordinary space-time.

Romiwero knew what was planned for *Warrior*. In another two days, the ship would leave orbit, travel a safe distance from the planet, engage the jump drive, and make a 200 light year jump. When the ship emerged into normal space, everyone they'd left behind on Barzak would have been dead for more than a century.

They could return to the planet, but never to the people they knew.

Her mother looked up. "Is that yours?" she asked, pointing.

Romiwero raised her head and looked. The shape was indistinct, but discernible, and the polished metal skin made it relatively easy to see even at 400 kilometres. "Could be," she said. "I can't tell at this distance, but it's certainly one of the three *Warriors.*"

The three starships, *Warrior, Aspirant*, and *Exultant*, were all parked in the same orbit, spaced more or less equally around the planet. Externally, there was no way to tell one from the other unless you got close enough to see their names. They would all depart over the next week, setting out to explore different galactic quadrants, perhaps plant Barzakian colonies on suitable, uninhabited planets. A *Warrior* class starship carried a crew of 318, with room allotted for an additional 800 potential colonists.

Eventually, they expected to return and report what they had seen. Romiwero wondered if anyone would care. Thousands of years would have passed by the time they returned. Would anyone even speak their language? It was difficult enough understanding Old Gehunite, and there had only been a few centuries of linguistic evolution since that was spoken. Long enough, though, for "*grachzich*[1]," to turn into "*grosh*," and "*noravionish*[2]," into "*norish.*"

When they returned, they'd announce themselves using their radios. She was fairly sure no one would know what they were saying by then.

"Oh, well," she said, "the computers can handle it."

Her mother looked at her curiously. "Handle what?"

"Oh, sorry. I was just thinking out loud. When we get back, well, it's going to be so far in the future I don't imagine anyone will still speak the way we do."

"I suppose you're right."

Romiwero gazed up at the ship, then at her watch. I think that one's mine, she thought. If she'd remembered the orbits right it *should* be *Warrior* passing overhead about this time.

"The moons are nice tonight," Korasi said. Emthemlu, the

---

[1]   Yes
[2]   This

smaller of Barzak's two moons, was just rising. Nakli had been up for some time.

Romiwero nodded. She found Nakli, with its scarred surface always so suggestive of a human face, more aesthetically pleasing. It was much bigger, a pleasing white globe in the night sky. Emthemlu was only 60 kilometres at its widest point, shaped like a ragged, diseased kidney. It hadn't even begun to assume a globular shape.

"I suppose I should go back inside," Romiwero said.

"People want to see you," her mother said. "That's why they're all here."

◆   ◆   ◆

Sub-lieutenant Marina Fehmadaatin sat in the captain's chair on *Warrior*'s bridge. Looking at the view-screen, she could see the planet curving away above her. It always felt odd. If you were orbiting a planet, you expected the planet to be beneath you, not above you. It seemed more logical.

Logic had nothing to do with orbital mechanics. Ever since humanity had first ventured into space, inverted orbits had been standard. Originally, this had been to reduce solar heating through the open cargo bays of the early orbiters. These days, it was more custom than anything else. *Warrior*'s "up" and "down" were internally determined by the ship's artificial gravity system.

Custom, tradition, was important in the Imperial Navy. Over five hundred years of tradition regulated everything from the divisions of the day at sea — or in space — to what was served in the enlisted messes, wardroom, and chief petty officers' mess, to their uniforms, ranks, and the very design of the ship. There had even been talk of making the bridges on *Warrior* class starships outwardly look like those of old battleships.

Practicality had won out on that front. A battleship only had to steer in two directions; a starship had to manoeuvre in four direction. There was also a question of comfort. In seagoing warships, only the captain was afforded a place to sit down. On *Warrior*'s bridge, the captain, or the deck officer if the captain wasn't on the bridge, sat in a slightly elevated chair at the forward end of the bridge, where she would have a perfect view of the holographic view-screen. Flipping open the right armrest on the captain's chair revealed view-screen controls, and the left armrest concealed emergency controls.

Helm control was a curved console to port, and slightly abaft the captain's chair. The engineering officer sat at a similar console to starboard. The rest of the bridge crew occupied stations along the port and starboard bulkheads.

There was very little happening at the moment. Marina was bored. Glancing at her watch, she noticed she had another 82 minutes to go before her relief arrived on the bridge. Not quite an hour.[3] Most of the crew was planetside, saying good-bye to their families. This wasn't like a simple jaunt around the solar system, where the ship might be gone a few weeks, or even a few months.

So far as anyone they were leaving on Barzak was concerned, they were leaving forever. Depending upon what they found during their voyage, they could be gone a few hundred years, or a few thousand.

Marina had said good-bye to her husband earlier that day, before catching a shuttle in Callaahavn. Galnor had taken it well, she thought. Not that he had much choice in the matter. Or even cared that she was leaving. They'd only been married for six months, after dating the last two years at the Imperial Naval College in Salmik.

Once they were home, it hadn't taken long for them to realise that the main attraction had been nothing more significant than being among the small contingent of Callaaite midshipmen in the class of 524. When Marina was selected to go with *Warrior*, they took it in different ways.

Marina felt that it was in keeping with Callaaite tradition, going off adventuring. Galnor merely conceded that it was cheaper, and simpler, than getting a divorce. There was nothing secret about the ship's planned mission, nor about the 200 light year jump at the beginning of it. For legal purposes, everyone in the crew would be presumed dead from the moment they made the jump, as they could not return in the lifetime of anyone then alive. Galnor would be free to remarry.

So would Marina, though she suspected Galnor's opportunities would be greater. Her status, she decided, would be slightly different. Galnor would be a widower, but only administratively, as Marina would certainly still be alive somewhere out in space. Her

---

3   A Gehunite hour consisted of 100 minutes, divided into 100 seconds. A Gehunite day consisted of 30 hours, making all Gehunite horological components, except for the day itself, shorter than their modern equivalents.

widowhood, on the other hand, would be literal. They would make the jump in 525, and at the end of it, the universe would have advanced to 725.

Marina found she was looking forward to widowhood. She'd miss Galnor, but not that much. She'd miss her parents more. Mahthint[4], her dog, was coming with her. She didn't care about her husband, but she'd have missed the dog.

♦   ♦   ♦

Romiwero stood in the middle of her bedroom, looking around at the bare walls, and the indentations in the carpet where the furniture had been. The furniture, along with the pictures, weapons, and mementos that had been hanging on the walls, were aboard the ship now. The carpet would be there as well, were it not so worn. There was nothing here for her now.

She walked downstairs into the living room. Her parents were there, trying to look like they hadn't been waiting.

"Just about time to go," she said.

Her father stood up. He'd put on his uniform for the occasion, including his sword. She was wearing hers as well, the lovely antique blade that had been her great-grandfather's. The blade wasn't as shiny as the one she'd been issued when she graduated from the Naval College, but it was made of tempered, carbon steel in a time when it was assumed swords would be used in battle, and not just on the quarterdeck.

Her mobile buzzed softly in her pocket. She took it out, thumbed the switch, and pressed the message icon on the touch-screen. "The shuttle is out front," she said.

"We're proud of you, you know," her father said.

"I know."

She started for the door, her parents following. She picked up her cap from the hall table and opened the front door. Her father collected his own cap and followed her out.

The shuttle door opened. Romiwero hugged her mother. She faced her father, drew herself to attention, and saluted. He returned it formally, then embraced her. She kissed him on the cheek, turned, and trotted up the steps into the shuttle.

The pilot looked at her curiously for a moment, then concentrated on his controls. It wasn't every day you saw a captain hugging an admiral.

---

4   Pronounced MAHT-hint. Callaaish for "death dog."

The shuttle lifted off. It would take just over an hour to climb to his passenger's ship's orbit. The flight was timed carefully, so that the shuttle and the starship would be at the same place at the same time. He could understand the logic. The crew would naturally want to remain with their families until the last minute.

"We should rendezvous with your ship at 27:81," the pilot said.

"Thank you," Romiwero replied. She looked at him, then past him, through the windscreen. It was well past dark when they lifted off and now, as they gained altitude and the atmosphere diminished, more and more stars were winking into view. They were already high enough that the stars had stopped twinkling.

"I don't think I could do it," the pilot said, rather timidly.

"Do what?"

"Leave. Go the way you'll be doing. Leave everything behind."

"We're bringing most of it with us," Romiwero said. "The ship is enormous. There's plenty of room in the crew section to duplicate our houses or apartments. The interiors, at least. It'll be like flying off into the cosmos without leaving home."

"No, it's not that, Captain. It's the people. I know there are some married couples going, but I also know that much of your crew will be leaving everyone behind."

Romiwero nodded. Including herself, she thought.

She wasn't married. She hadn't been in any serious relationships in the past several years. The last five years had been dedicated to ensuring that *Warrior* was completed and fitted out. She was leaving her parents, her immediate family, behind, but no one else. The same thing had been happening in her family for generations, with the only real difference being that before the risk was dying in battle, and now it was outliving everyone and being light years away when they died.

How long will it be before we get back here? she wondered. How many years by the ship's chronometers? And how many years in planetary time? The first, obviously, would be much shorter than the second.

◆   ◆   ◆

Captain Kara Brynnazen, of His Imperial Majesty's Corps of Marines, was pacing her office in *Warrior*'s Marine Barracks. Her elder brother, Arik, was sitting behind her desk, looking far too complacent, in her opinion.

The office door was locked, which explained Arik's relaxed posture. If the door was open, elder brother or not, he'd have stood respectfully while talking to his kid sister. She was a Marine captain, equivalent to a Navy lieutenant. He was a chief petty officer, rated as a master at arms. His sister outranked him by a considerable degree. So it was only when they were alone that the family relationship trumped the military one, and they could just be big brother and little sister.

Or not so little sister. At 180 centimetres, she was nearly as tall as her brother.

"You worry too much, Kara," Arik said.

"You don't have to deal with a company of Marines."

Arik laughed. "Sure I do. Who do you think gets to arrest their drunken carcasses and drag them back to the barracks?"

"That's not the same, Arik. We're scheduled to be gone for years. And who knows what we'll find once we come home?"

Arik shook his head. "Not home," he said. "I think that's pretty clear. We won't be back for several hundred years at the earliest. Probably more like thousands, at least where people on Barzak are concerned. We'll just be these legendary people who vanished into deep space many centuries ago. Hell, most people likely won't even believe we ever really existed."

"You're not helping. I like to think they'll remember us."

"They will. I just don't think they'll remember us long enough for us to get back."

Kara looked at the clock on the bulkhead above the door. "Almost 30 hours," she said. "About time for me to get home and you to make your rounds, I think."

Arik stood and walked to the door. "Give my regards to Waldor," he said. Waldor was her dog.

Kara sat down at her desk, straightening the personnel folders in her in box. She had 140 Marines under her command. One Lieutenant, four Second Lieutenants, a First Sergeant, four Colour Sergeants, no Sergeants—headquarters had decided that each of the four platoons would have a colour sergeant instead—sixteen Corporals, an equal number of Lance Corporals, and ninety-eight Marines. The presumption was that, before the ship returned to Barzak, everyone would likely move up at least one grade.

The result would be a bit top-heavy as companies go, with a major commanding, a captain as executive officer, lieutenants as platoon commanders, and the first sergeant stepping up to sergeant major. The colour sergeants would likely remain as they were, but receive the pay of a first sergeant, the corporals end up as sergeants, the lance corporals as corporals, and the Marines as lance corporals.

Unless somebody screwed up. The Corps gave advancement to good Marines, but could be just as quick to demote the incompetent. Given the nature of the mission, it was also possible that some of her Marines would opt to become colonists, or transfer to the Navy. She thought the latter was a ridiculous idea, but it was allowed. And some sailors were decent enough people.

Her big brother, for example.

Anyway, she had to put up with the Navy. She was twenty-three, almost twenty-four. She might decide to get married sometime in the next few years. The most likely candidates would be naval officers.

Two

Romiwero settled into her chair in front of the main view-screen. She was wearing her dress uniform. It seemed appropriate for leaving orbit. For embarking on a mission that might see them travelling thousands of light years before coming home.

Home? Would Barzak still be home by the time they returned? A lot could happen in a few thousand years. Who really remembered what the world had been like even 10,000 years ago? Archaeologists had their opinions. Not everyone agreed with them. That culture had been literate, but they'd used an alphabet no one today could decipher. A long document might be a poem of epic beauty and significance. Or it could be an ancient law regulating the taxation of pack camels rented for a long journey. There was no way to tell.

It hadn't been that long since most people believed in magic. The founding of the Gehunite Empire was heavily laden with that sort of thing. Salmik was a demigod, born to a prominent Kaamite pirate's virgin daughter and a giant wolf that was actually L'Mik, come down to earth. He married an ancient widow who had shown kindness to an old beggar—also a disguised L'Mik—who had been restored to youth and beauty.

One story claimed that Callaa's Queen Alura IV, was said to have fought a battle against a group of Arzucaldan assassins with the goddess Onira fighting at her side.

Romiwero doubted all those stories. The people obviously existed. A youthful Alura and an elderly Salmik were contemporaries, and her own fifth great-grandfather had known both of them in those long-ago days. There were no doubt great battles fought. The Empire was new, just beginning its expansion. Legendary deeds were performed. Gehun and Arzucalda had begun their centuries long rivalry, as both sought to dominate the world.

Sub-lieutenant Fehmadaatin's sword dated from that period, and had been handed down by her ancestors for more than 500 years. Forged from Callaaite steel, it was still functional. Or would be, if there was any need to fight with a sword in the modern age.

She looked to her right. Commander (E) Greshvor was seated at the engineering panel. *Warrior*'s engines were controlled from the bridge. For safety reasons, no one went into the engine rooms except in an emergency.

"Everything ready in your department, Elir?" Romiwero asked.

The engineer swivelled and regarded his captain. "Top line, Captain," he said. "All systems show normal."

"Excellent. Ring down ready."

"Ring down ready, aye."

It was a formality. Greshvor was relaying the order to himself. It was a matter of custom to treat the bridge controls as if they were an old-fashioned engine-room telegraph. All services had their traditions, and the Navy had more than most.

She looked to her left now. Sub-lieutenant Fehmadaatin was at the helm, but looking over at her captain. Her normal function was navigator, but she was taking the helm herself this morning. "Ready, Marina?"

"Ready, Captain."

Romiwero nodded. She swivelled her chair around. Normally, only the deck officer, engineer, navigator, signals rating, and a yeoman were on the bridge. Normally. She counted eight officers and a dozen other ranks at the moment. Everyone wanted to be on the bridge when history was made.

She swung her chair back to its usual position. "Stand by to leave orbit," she said.

"Course for jump point calculated," Marina reported.

"Engines ready," Greshvor reported.

"Very well. Ahead slow. Break her out of orbit and set course for jump point."

The ship was orbiting at 400 kilometres, at a velocity of 7,670 metres per second. At that speed and altitude, the forward motion of the ship exactly balanced the force of gravity, so that the planet's surface, in effect, dropped away at the same speed the ship was moving forward. An orbit was nothing more than the ship falling to earth while moving fast enough to stay at the same altitude.

As the engines came on line, speed began to increase, slowly at first. Five minutes after the departure order was given, *Warrior* had increased speed to 34 kilometres per second and was accelerating at a rate of five kilometres per minute.

Inside the ship, this was noticeable only as a slight vibration in the fabric of the vessel. At these speeds, the vibration came from the engines. The needle-like, streamlined design made no appreciable difference at this point. It was only when they were approaching full speed that the presence of roughly one hydrogen atom for every cubic metre of space came into play. What was essentially a vacuum at 50 kilometres per second began to seem rather dense at 120,000 kilometres per second.

"Clear of Emthemlu's orbit, Captain," Marina reported. "Speed is steady at 200 kilometres per second. Course is two-five-eight by five-seven." *Warrior* was travelling a course of 258° while maintaining an angle of 0° in relation to the planetary rotational plane.

"Excellent. Maintain course and speed. Set steaming watch. Lieutenant Affiknur, you have the deck."

Affiknur walked up from where she had been standing. As Romiwero climbed down from her chair, Affiknur climbed into it. "I have the deck, Captain," he said, formally taking the conn. "Speed is 200 kilometres per second, course two-five-eight by naught."

They would maintain that course and speed until they were past Nakli's orbit, roughly 385,000 kilometres above Barzak. They would increase to one-quarter speed from there to Kinzor's orbit, then reduce to one-eighth speed while transiting the asteroid belt between Kinzor and Alizor.

Then the run-in would begin. Once they were past Alizor's orbit—the planet itself would be on the other side of the sun—*Warrior* would increase to full speed. The jump point was midway between the orbits of Reknar and Zardek. They would be travelling at a velocity of 127,000 kilometres per second when the jump drive was engaged.

From that point, everything behind them would be gone.

Three

REVEREND FRED GORDON LOOKED OUT OVER THE HOUSE CHAMBER from his seat in the visitors' gallery. Things seemed to be going well. He'd told his father that they would, despite the old man's doubts.

Willy Gordon was legendary. He'd done more to create modern evangelical Christianity than any other preacher in the last century. Oh, there'd been charismatic preachers before. Lots of them. But Gordon had thought it all out. He'd realised, early on, that no matter what God's plan might be, segregation was on the way out, so he'd insisted on integrated audiences at his revival meetings right from the start.

The local preachers hadn't cared for that, but Gordon had pointed out the obvious. Just because you said whites and blacks *could* sit together didn't mean they actually *would*. The blacks would be pacified, knowing they could sit anywhere they wanted, but for the most part they'd still self-segregate themselves, preferring to sit with their own kind. It made the elder Gordon come across as a champion of civil rights, which was good for business, so to speak.

He'd preached in favour of Israel, too. Said it was God's plan being fulfilled. That God wanted his Chosen People to return to their ancestral homeland. Okay, sure, Willy Gordon didn't actually *like* Jews. They were a stubborn, stiff-necked people who still failed to recognise Jesus as their promised Messiah. The thing was, for Jesus to return, quite a few scholars argued that the Jews had to return to Israel first. They had to be gathered there, where they would either finally recognise Jesus, or be consigned to hell on his Second Coming. The United States *needed* Israel, so there would be a place to ship all the Jews when it finally became possible to get rid of them.

Looking down from the gallery, Fred Gordon could see Senator Howard Jameson, the head of the Texas delegation, conferring with another delegate. There were 150 delegates, three from each state, gathered in the House chamber.

The delegates were here to make history. There was a public agenda, the reason that had been agreed upon by the various states. Then there was the real agenda.

Activists had been promoting a "Convention of the States" for quite a few years. The premise was that, because Congress wouldn't, or couldn't act, the states would call for a convention to propose some necessary amendments to the Constitution. Two were on the official agenda. The first would finally throw out Roe and make abortion illegal under all circumstances. Gordon wasn't that sure about that one, but it was a sop to the Catholics, whose medical ethics manuals made it clear that, if circumstances seemed to require abortion to save the mother's life, it still wasn't permitted, because it was God who made those choices and maybe He *wanted* the mother to die and the baby to live. Or the baby to die and the mother live. Or both to die, or both to live. That was up to God, not some physician who would potentially make a wrong choice and so thwart God's plan.

The second returned jurisdiction over marriage to the states, and established once and for all that only the states could decide what was, and wasn't, a valid marriage within their borders. The stated intent was to allow the states to outlaw same-sex marriages, and allow them to stop having to recognise those from other states. What they really planned to pass went a little farther. It would *not* return jurisdiction over the legality of same-sex marriages to the states. Those would be made illegal at the federal level. It *would* return jurisdiction over any *other* marriage qualifications, effectively throwing Loving under the bus. Any state that wanted to would now be able to ban racially or religiously mixed marriages. He hoped that his own home state of Alabama would strongly consider doing just that.

God didn't like race mixing. Gordon was sure of that. He wasn't so sure about either amendment. The fact that Roe existed, and gays could marry each other, were good for several million a year in donations from indignant evangelicals. Eliminate those two and he'd have to think of something else to stir people up and keep the money flowing.

Jameson had shown him the proposed new Constitution. There were some radical differences between it and the original. It shifted things around considerably.

From a legislative viewpoint, the most radical change was replacing the House and Senate with a unicameral Congress. Admittedly, there was a certain risk involved. It was just possible that the Democrats might eke out a majority. But that was balanced by the elimination of House/Senate deadlocks, reconciliation committees, duplicated effort, and having to go back and change perfectly good bills because the other house edited half a dozen words in their version.

The new, unified Congress would be set up like the Senate, with a third of the members elected every two years for six-year terms.

The Supreme Court would be left alone, but for a single, vitally-important change. The Court would lose the power to nullify a law, or to make new law, by declaring something unconstitutional. If Congress passed a law, and the president signed it, then *obviously* it passed constitutional muster, and it wouldn't be subjected to the whims of unelected judges.

The president would gain the power to make law. That sort of existed already, in the form of Executive Orders, but the new Constitution would give these greater force. If the president decreed a new law, then Congress would have only three months to override it.

Gordon presumed that would happen only rarely. An override required a 9/10 majority of Congress. Not of the members present, but of the entire Congress. Gordon doubted there'd be many sessions where that many members were even present.

Presidents would still run for four-year terms, and still do so on the first Tuesday in November of years divisible by four. The term limit was being removed. If the people wanted to keep a president around longer than eight years, they'd be able to do so.

He was particularly proud of the new preamble. "We, the people of the United States of America, under the protection and guidance of God Almighty, and of his Son, Jesus, do hereby proclaim and ordain this Constitution of the United States, to be the Supreme Law of the Land. Amen."

This time it acknowledged God, and made it damn clear this was the Christian God, not a Jewish, or Hindu, or Buddhist, or Muslim God. That idiotic "religious test" provision was gone, too. What the hell was wrong with limiting government service to Christians?" Gordon wondered. How could you trust anyone else?

There was a lot more, too. Freedom of religion was retained and strengthened, but only for Christians. Added was a ten-percent faith tax, based on net income, which would go to whichever church the taxpayer designated. Atheists, Jews, Muslims, and other heathens would still pay the tax, but the money would be shared equally by all the churches in their community.

A couple of Jewish delegates had made it into the Convention. They were arguing that the local synagogues should participate in the tax money. Jameson had assured Gordon that wasn't going to happen. If they wanted to go to *shul*, the Jews would have to continue to support the places without any government help. Their faith tax would support a church, the way God wanted.

His good friend Rabbi Mirsky informed him that rumours of what the Convention intended to do had some Jews talking about moving to Israel. That was fine with Gordon. Jews didn't belong in a Christian country. Not unless they were like Mirsky, keeping Jewish traditions and rituals, but integrating Jesus into them. The rest could leave.

There were already protests. Misguided Liberals taking to the streets to complain. Gordon thought that would help. It was easy enough to seed a few violent types into the protests. Burn a few cars, break some windows. The Liberals would get the blame, and that would make the right-wing public all the more eager to "fix" the problem. The Right had been doing that for a long time, intensifying the practice after the last election, and somehow no one ever seemed to catch on.

Some people never would. There were still people in Germany who believed the communists had set the Reichstag fire in 1933.

The prediction was that the new Constitution would be approved after no more than a month of debate. Then it would be up to the states to ratify it. Jameson had told Gordon that this was more or less assured. Republicans controlled the legislature in enough states to make sure it happened. With enough care taken to draw legislative boundaries, those majorities were unlikely to change. You kept state legislators in line by reminding them that there was always someone else wanting their job, and that someone was likely to be more conservative than they were. So they'd vote for the new Constitution just to keep that other candidate out of the primary.

Most of it would take effect on ratification. Converting Congress would be spread out over six years. Presidential term limits would be removed in 2025. Gordon didn't think there was much chance of the incumbent getting re-elected, but no one was willing to take that risk.

The Vice President entered the chamber and walked up to the rostrum. He would be President of the Convention.

Gordon patted his inside jacket pocket. In a minute or two, the VP would gavel the session to order. Then he'd recognise Gordon, and invite him to come down into the chamber and deliver the opening prayer.

Four

THE INTERCOM STATION NEXT TO ROMIWERO'S BED BUZZED insistently. She sat up and pressed the button. "Captain," she said.

"Jump coordinates in fifty minutes, Captain," the deck officer reported from the bridge.

"On my way."

Romiwero sat on the edge of the bed. Leaning over, she found her shoes and pulled them on. She stood and walked to the old wardrobe, which had been brought up from her bedroom at home, along with the rest of the furniture. She opened it and took out a work uniform top. Carrying this to the bed, she threaded her belt through the loops in the top.

She looked at herself in the dressing table mirror as she pulled the top on. She was 30-years-old, 170 centimetres tall, and likely in the best physical condition in her life. She quickly buttoned the top and buckled the belt. The belt loops extended 25 millimetres below the edge of the top, with snaps at the bottom that attached them to the trousers. It gave the work uniform the appearance of a jumpsuit, but eliminated the nuisance of having to take the whole damned thing off every time you needed to use the head.

Quickly, she ran a brush through her long, red hair, then gathered it in back and used an elastic band to fix it into a pony tail. This was followed by the black silk ribbon that had been customary in the Imperial Navy since the death of Salmik the Great. Originally, this had been worn by male officers, in the days when clubbed hair was still common. Men wore their hair much shorter now, so the ribbon had become the property of those female officers who wore pony tails.

Satisfied with her appearance, Romiwero walked out of her bedroom and downstairs. Her quarters aboard *Warrior* were an exact duplicate of her family home. With holographic views from the windows, it was enough to fool you, until you walked out the front door to find a corridor instead of a front garden.

Exiting her quarters, Romiwero turned right and quickly walked the twenty metres to the bridge. Being the captain had some advantages, proximity to the bridge being one of them.

"Captain on the bridge," the quartermaster of the watch announced.

Commander Oshrorehno, Romiwero's second in command, got up from the command chair as Romiwero entered. "Approaching 12.8 solar units, Captain," he reported. "Course zero-one-five by two-eight-five, speed 127,300 kilometres per second."

"Very good. Captain has the deck."

She sat in her chair and swivelled it around to starboard. Navigator, situation report?"

"On course, Captain," Fehmadaatin reported. "Jump is calculated and coordinates locked in."

"Time to jump?"

"Ten minutes, Captain."

"Very good."

Romiwero swivelled her chair back to its forward-facing position. The holographic view-screen was showing what was in front of the ship. The view was oddly calming. At the speed they were travelling, she thought, it always seemed like things should be happening much faster. Instead, she was presented with a stationary starfield.

It might be different if there were planets in view. Might. Distances were still so vast in the outer solar system that even the approach to a planet seemed rather leisurely until the ship was quite close. The stars were so far away that it simply wasn't possible to travel fast enough to give the illusion they were moving.

It was common in space movies, and on television, but those were special effects.

Most of the inner planets were behind them. Barzak, where they had come from, was nothing more than a bright, blue gleam far behind them. Yorik, speediest of the planets, and closest to the sun, was on the other side of the sun, and wouldn't be visible against their system's star even if it wasn't. The same could be said for Zalash, the second planet.

Zalash was nearly the same size as Barzak, but had a carbon dioxide atmosphere and dense cloud cover that invited the sun's heat to enter, but was reluctant to let it back out. The temperature at ground level was about 470°.

Their own planet, Barzak, was third from the sun. From space, it was mostly blue, and mostly water. Oh, there was plenty of land to support a population of some four-billion, but it was still three-quarters water.

Kinzor, the fourth planet, was a good bit smaller than Barzak, but after a few years of work it supported a thriving colony. The colonists lived underground. Surface construction was almost entirely restricted to vast blocks of glasshouses, where the plants could take advantage of the high carbon dioxide content of the atmosphere. It was easier to control the temperature underground, where the atmosphere was thicker thanks to positive-pressure ventilation systems. The colony remained largely dependent on Barzak for many things. Manufacturing facilities were being built there, and the planet had the resources needed to become self-sustaining. It just hadn't reached that point yet.

All that was behind them now. So was Alizor, the largest of the planets, with its flock of moons, and Reknur, with its prominent ring system. Zardek lay ahead, and then Moreck, but they wouldn't be passing those orbits in the usual sense. The jump point was 12.8 solar units from Barzak's orbit. When they reached it, in—she looked at the chronometer—three minutes, they would find themselves some two hundred light years away.

I wonder what we'll find there, she thought. Are there others out there? Other humans? Other space-faring beings? Friends? Enemies? People, or things, who just want to be left alone?

"Fifty seconds, Captain. Jump sequence on automatic."

As the countdown timer hit zero, the ship seemed to quiver slightly. And that was all there was to it, Romiwero thought. Most of the crew would barely notice anything had happened. Unless, as she was, they were looking at a view-screen. The stars were essentially the same, but not quite. At the moment the ship had jumped, the stars had taken a weird, jerky shift from their previous positions. Not far, but noticeable.

More clearly, in the near distance, a new star had appeared. Corvus, Gehunite astronomers had named it. It was a "yellow" dwarf star, similar to Barzak's. The suspicion was that it might have a similar system of planets.

"Distance to star?" Romiwero asked.

Fehmadaatin looked up from her calculations. "About 20 solar units, Captain." A solar unit was the distance from Barzak to the sun, roughly 150,000,000 kilometres.

"Slow to half speed," Romiwero ordered. "It's time to do some exploring."

Five

Colonel John Baring, United States Border Security Force, was having a problem with the fence systems. A few years back, a president had started to build a literal wall along the Mexican border. Baring had been in high school then, but even as a high school student it was obvious to him that the man was a nut. All you had to do was look at a topographical map—something Boy Scouts knew how to do—to see that the job wasn't practical.

There was a lot of crappy terrain along the Mexican border. There was also a shitload of water on either end of it and, anyway, most illegal immigrants back then came in legally and just never left when their visas expired.

In the end, about the time Baring was a rookie, sanity had prevailed and the wall became a fence. The original was eighteen feet high, made of reinforced chain link with razor wire at the top, and extended six feet into the ground anywhere the ground was soft enough to dig. If it was solid rock, obviously, that couldn't be done, so the bottom edge was simply secured to the rock with thick steel strapping and bolts set a foot deep in the rock.

Every mile, there was an opening, carefully monitored with closed circuit television cameras, intended to allow animals to cross the border. Baring doubted that anyone back then had really cared about migrating jaguars, but it earned the politicians points with the animal rights people, and helped mitigate the fallout when the administration was simultaneously working to protect the border and gutting the endangered species act to make things more convenient for their corporate sponsors.

There were junior agents who did nothing all day but monitor those cameras. If they saw a human being come through, a remotely-piloted drone was dispatched to herd the intruder back to where he came from. If he wouldn't cooperate, the drones were armed. No one cared if an illegal border crosser was shot and killed. At least, no one who mattered.

In a spirit of fairness, the same system was installed along the Canadian border. Mostly, it worked out okay, though there were some problems with towns that straddled the border up in Maine.

The single fence system had worked for a few years. Then two more fences were added, on the American side, installed twenty and forty yards from the original. These were simpler, six strands of electrified barbed wire on metal posts. The sort of thing you'd install around a pasture, but with less space between the strands.

Now they were working on the final touch. Every fifty yards along both borders, round concrete supports were being installed. A dome-shaped turret was fitted to the top of each support, designed to operate autonomously. Each dome held a six-barrelled minigun, firing 5.56-millimetre ammunition, the same rounds fired by the American military's standard issue Selwin rifle.[5]

The turrets used a combination of infrared, visual, and sonic sensors for targeting. If something was detected coming through the border fences, the turret would rotate to cover the target. Speaker systems would issue orders to halt in appropriate languages, English and Spanish along the Mexican border, English and French on the Canadian. If the target stopped, further orders would then be given to turn around and go back. If the target complied, that would be the end of it.

If the target didn't stop, or started to come further into US territory instead of going back, a six-round burst would be fired, aimed to strike the ground about ten yards in front of the target. If that didn't turn him back, the turret went on automatic and directed a three-second burst into the target.

---

5   The Selwin M-28 rifle was adopted as the official long-arm for the U.S. military in October 2028, as a replacement for the elderly M-16. The Selwin was 35″ long, with a removable box magazine holding 30 rounds. It fired the same 5.56-mm round used by the M-16, but was less sensitive to fouling and considerably more accurate at longer ranges.

Baring thought that was a little excessive, to be honest. In three seconds the minigun would fire between 100 and 130 rounds. It depended upon how quickly the motor spun up, how well lubricated the system was, and whether any rounds misfired. Baring thought a half-second burst should be sufficient. That would put about fifteen rounds into the target. More than enough to do the job, and a lot less mess to clean up.

But they were having a problem with the recognition system. It was targeting anything warm blooded, which meant they were killing a lot more animals than people. The system was supposed to be able to recognise animals and let them go. Illegal entry was punishable by death for people, but not for critters. Your average deer, peccary, mountain lion, wolf, or coyote, couldn't understand English, or any other language, and wasn't likely to be a criminal rapist, murderer, or drug smuggler anyway.

That just wasn't right, Baring felt. Obviously, no one cared if they killed some criminal trying to sneak into the country. That was standard policy within two miles of the border. Past that limit, they'd just arrest them and send them back where they came from.

It was less of a problem these days, in any case. Not that many Mexicans were trying to sneak into the United States. There was more of a future for them if they stayed home. A limited number of agricultural workers were allowed in every year. Once chipped, it was relatively easy to keep track of them, and they were sent back home at the end of the season.

True, the choice of warning languages sometimes proved problematic. Warnings to stop in English and Spanish didn't always help that much if the illegal only spoke Mandarin, but the warning burst was understandable in any language. Regardless, there was no good reason to be killing animals while trying to keep criminals out of the country. Baring didn't care that much about a few dead Mexicans, but it bothered the hell out of him to kill some innocent deer.

Thoroughly flayed by the miniguns, there wasn't even the potential side benefit of some fresh venison.

There had been some requests that the system be adjusted so that it would *intentionally* shoot any coyotes encountered east of the Mississippi, where they were an invasive species causing problems for the native wildlife. They tried, but no one could figure out a way for the system to tell the difference between one canid and another, and the last thing they wanted was for it to start shooting foxes and domestic dogs. The citizenry would tolerate killing illegal immigrants, but if you started shooting their pets, or the native predators you were trying to protect from the coyotes, you could end up with an armed uprising.

It was a software issue, he was sure. And it would have to be addressed. People were going to start getting upset if they found out the border defences were shooting fucking Bambi instead of criminals.

Once that was taken care of, Baring could get back to chasing down drug smugglers. They were more of a problem anyway. Smuggling was mostly a problem along the northern border now. The old Mexican cartels had been put out of business after the government reclassified most Schedule I drugs as legal and allowed them to be sold in any pharmacy. Prices dropped, quality was regulated—which eliminated 90% of the overdose issues—and there was now tax revenue to be had from the sales. A few addicts still died, but not as many as before, and making the drugs legal seemed to reduce the demand. Like anything else, once drugs were no longer forbidden, they didn't seem as tempting.

True, it wasn't as lucrative for the politicians as it had been when most drugs were illegal. Ethical pharmaceutical manufacturers made campaign contributions, but weren't nearly as ready to offer the sort of unreported, personal contributions the cartels had employed to make sure their product stayed illegal and overpriced.

Most of the smuggling these days was birth control pills, condoms, diaphragms, and other anti-pregnancy aids. The Department of Public Morality closely regulated access to birth control, making sure it was only used for medical purposes. His own wife had problems with irregular periods, so she was allowed a prescription. A lot of women found they had the same problem, provided they could find the right doctor, and a pharmacy that would fill the prescription. That was up to the pharmacists, and the Catholic ones were known to turn away anyone seeking birth control.

Six

ARIGOR VOSTEK ADJUSTED THE AIM OF HIS TELESCOPE until Barzak took up most of the image area. He had been watching his home planet every day, knowing what was going to happen, yet always hoping it wouldn't.

The whole matter had been settled five months earlier. A large asteroid had wandered into the inner solar system and smashed head-on into Emthemlu. In itself, this wasn't unusual. The small moon had been struck many times in the past. But it had been different this time. The errant asteroid was big, a rounded mass of nickel-iron some 4.7 kilometres in diameter, travelling through the inner solar system at 57.8 kilometres per second. This was extremely fast for an asteroid, but this was an unusual asteroid.

Normally, asteroids orbit the sun in the same direction as the planets. Thus, in approaching Barzak, it would be expected that the asteroid would be catching up with the planet, its relative speed consequently reduced. But this big chunk of metal had been wandering deep space for millions of years before being caught in the sun's gravity well and pulled into the inner solar system on a decaying retrograde orbit. It passed near Alizor, and the gas giant had nearly captured it. It would have been better had that happened.

But it didn't. The asteroid made nearly a complete orbit of Alizor, gaining speed as it did so from the huge planet's gravity, and was then ejected on an arc towards the sun. So it approached Barzak, and its moons, from the wrong direction, the planet adding its own velocity to the asteroid's, instead of subtracting it.

The last factor, the one Vostek believed most important, was that it struck Emthemlu at the point in its orbit where the trajectories of asteroid and moon were exactly 150° apart. The two collided head-on, with a combined impact great enough to slow the moon's forward velocity by 18 kilometres per hour. Not a very great loss of speed, but it was enough.

That slight speed reduction was enough for Barzak's gravity to pull the tiny moon a little closer. Had the original orbit been higher, perhaps it would have settled into a new, closer orbit. Instead, the orbit began to decay.

Three months after the impact, there was no longer any question of the outcome. At some time in the next year Emthemlu's forward velocity would no longer be able to balance the pull of Barzak's gravity and the ugly little moon would fall out of orbit and smash into the planet.

Vostek would be able to watch the end of the world from his observatory on Kinzor. The question was, would the destruction of Barzak mean the destruction of the Kinzor colony? They were still dependent on Barzak for far too much, he thought.

The two planets were currently in opposition, placing them roughly 56,000,000 kilometres from each other on the same side of the sun. Arzucalda was rotating into view. The planet was in darkness, except for the broad swath of light reflected from Nakli.

Kinzor, in contrast, would be one of the brightest objects in the sky when viewed from Barzak. The sun was shining on the face of Kinzor that faced Barzak, and on the face of Barzak that faced away from Kinzor.

There had been talk of evacuating the planet. But talk was meaningless without action following up. There were no starships anywhere near Barzak. The three *Warrior*s had been gone for nearly two hundred years. The even larger *Courageous* was still under construction. She wouldn't be completed for another eight years, rather longer than Barzak had left.

And how much difference would it make? *Courageous* was designed to carry a crew of 420, and an additional 2,300 colonists. The current population of Barzak was 6,972,400,000, more or less. Another 18,000 lived on Nakli, and 43,000 on Kinzor. The Nakli colony wouldn't last more than a few months if they lost contact with Barzak.

Living deep underground, the Nakli colonists could extract oxygen from subterranean ice, which also supplied drinking water.

But the larger moon had no atmosphere, and nothing much could be grown in the artificial caverns where everyone lived. Food had to be brought up from the planet, with freighters arriving daily.

Conditions were a little better on Kinzor, where crops did rather well under glass. The planet's natural atmosphere was mostly carbon dioxide. People couldn't breathe it, but plants loved it. Vast glasshouses on the surface provided both food and a source of oxygen for the subterranean colonies. Early on, there had been talk of planting vegetation everywhere, with the intention of raising the oxygen content of the thin atmosphere, and perhaps even making the surface a place where people could live without needing to wear spacesuits.

They'd given up on that idea. Kinzor was solid all the way to the core, so it lacked Barzak's magnetosphere, which served to deflect the solar winds that had long ago stripped most of Kinzor's original atmosphere and liquid water.

Vostek was looking at the telescope's display when Arzucalda disappeared. One moment it was there, the next there was a blinding flash, followed by an atmospheric shock wave strong enough to be visible through the telescope.

This was followed by a spreading cloud of darkness, the combined remains of Emthemlu and the once-powerful island. Hidden under the debris cloud, a massive tsunami would be spreading out from the centre of the Eastern Sea. Vostek doubted that any coastal cities would still be there in the morning.

After some time, the debris clouds started to glow. Ejecta from the impact had been blown well above the upper limits of the atmosphere, but as it had essentially gone straight up, instead of settling into orbit, it was starting to come back down. The planet's rotation assured that the rain of ejecta spread over a wide swath around the northern hemisphere.

Most of the ejecta itself burned up in the atmosphere, but with so much falling at the same time, the infra-red light generated was radiated down onto the surface strongly enough to ignite anything that would burn. From Kinzor, it appeared that most of the northern half of the planet was on fire, adding billions of cubic metres of thick, black smoke to the debris clouds that already hung over most of the planet.

This cloud of combined smoke and dust would blot out the sun for months over the entire planet. Crops would fail, temperatures would drop. Some 65,000,000 years ago, an asteroid, perhaps a sixth the mass of Emthemlu, had smashed into Barzak, bringing about the extinction of most of the planet's biota. Small mammals survived, eventually becoming the dominant species in the form of Barzak's two human subspecies. The old apex species, the dinosaurs, had been wiped out except for smaller types that evolved into birds, and some crocodilians and amphibians.

He thought that humanity would survive this disaster. Some would, at least. Most likely those living in the south. Everyone in the northern hemisphere was probably already dead, or trying desperately to find a way to escape the raging fires that would soon kill them. Civilisation was likely done for. Those who could leave the planet no doubt would. Those who couldn't would most likely find themselves reduced to a bare subsistence living, perhaps in small, self-contained bands of a few dozen individuals.

Was there a way of fitting existing passenger and cargo ships with jump drive? If there wasn't, it was all over. Most of the surviving ships could travel no faster than 40,000 kilometres per second. The nearest star was 4.25 light years away, so it would take a bit over 20 years to make the journey. And to what purpose? Neither of the two stars in that system possessed planets that would be habitable for humans.

They'd have to keep going. Probably for centuries before they'd find a place to settle.

Barzak, he thought, was most likely going to have to start over again once the effects of the disaster had passed. However long that took. Whether any technology would also survive, or the survivors would be forced to go back to doing things in a more primitive fashion, he could only guess.

Whichever it turned out to be, he doubted he'd be around to see. The people on Nakli would go first. They had roughly a two-week food supply stored away. After that, they'd begin to starve. With only the few long-range shuttles kept on Nakli to ferry them back to a Barzak that, for the next several years would be inhospitable at best, most would no doubt die on the remaining moon.

Kinzor could grow food, and they could produce their own water and breathable air. What they didn't have was fuel. There was uranium on the planet, but they lacked their own processing facilities. Large-scale solar farms on the surface might produce enough

power to sustain a civilisation but, again, they didn't have sufficient panels, and the facilities for manufacturing them were—had
been—down on Barzak.

And unlike what was left of Barzak, they couldn't switch over to
burning fossil fuels, as their ancestors had once done. There wasn't
enough oxygen available to sustain combustion on that level and
leave enough for everyone to breathe.

The colony would manage for a few years. In the end, they
would either have to return to Barzak or die on Kinzor.

Seven

WARRIOR WAS CRUISING AT A LEISURELY 60,000 KILOMETRES PER hour, well outside any solar system. In the sick bay, Chief Sick Berth Attendant Kos Rigakh pulled the sheet over his boss. Surgeon Commander Eldir was just about as dead as could be. This wasn't the first death Rigakh had seen in the last thirteen years, but it was the one that affected him the most.

Space exploration was dangerous work. They had lost crew members to various causes. The ship was stuffed full of complex machinery. Some of it had moving parts, and people weren't always careful enough.

Planetary exploration presented its own hazards. If there were cliffs, it seemed inevitable that someone would manage to fall off one from time to time. The natives weren't always friendly, though they made every effort to avoid making contact with any planet that hadn't at least started to venture into space. Logic suggested that any culture capable of space flight should also be scientifically advanced enough not to just start shooting the first time they ran into someone who had the same capabilities.

Most of the time, that worked. Sometimes it didn't.

Rigakh had been with the landing party on Karkosh. *Warrior* had spent three months in orbit around Karkosh, listening to their broadcasts, letting their computers work on the language until they had an efficient translation programme. It was only after they were sure they'd be able to communicate that they'd sent a shuttle down to the planet.

Karkosh met the basic criteria for contact. It hosted a technological species. The inhabitants were articulate, and could be talked to. There were satellites in orbit. And, most import of all, it had a mass fairly close to Barzak's, and a nitrogen-oxygen atmosphere that Barzakians could breathe without special equipment.

So far as anyone could tell, no one was fighting a war. That was always an important consideration. Imperial Gehunite regulations prohibited getting involved in local conflicts. Or in doing anything to interfere with local development. They could provide humanitarian aid, but that was about it.

The Karkoshians, it turned out, weren't very friendly. The first group they'd encountered had tried to take over the shuttle. Three members of the landing party were shot before they could get away.

Surgeon Commander Eldir, however, had simply died. The doctor had been eating his breakfast in the wardroom and suddenly bent forward and dropped onto his plate. The autopsy, its scope somewhat limited by the only actual doctor in the crew being the one on the table, had found an aortic aneurism. When that ruptured, Eldir had bled to death in less than a minute. Rigakh had suspected something like that as soon as he opened up the dead doctor's chest. It wasn't supposed to be full of blood.

Rigakh cleaned up in the sick bay's shower, then dressed in a clean working uniform. He collected the printout of his report and slipped it into a file folder. The captain liked things printed out. She said it made it easier for her to concentrate when she was reading.

He took the lift up twelve decks to the command level. Heading toward the bow, it was a five-minute walk to the bridge. The captain was standing by the navigator's station.

"What did you find, Chief?" Romiwero asked.

"His aorta burst," Rigakh said. "Nothing anyone could have done. Maybe if it had been diagnosed earlier it could have been repaired, but once it burst he was dead in seconds."

The captain nodded. "I see. Very well. Prepare him for burial. We'll have the funeral tomorrow at eighteen hours."

"Aye, aye, Captain."

Rigakh headed back to the sick bay. Eldir would be buried in the usual way, his body laid out in a sealed casket and ejected within the gravity field of a convenient star. Gravity would take care of the rest.

Romiwero leaned over the navigator's station. "Where's the closest place we can recruit a doctor?"

Fehmadaatin punched the query into the computer. After a moment, the answer appeared on her screen. "Looks like New Barzak," she said.

"How close are we?"

"Sixty-four light years. Shall I work out the parameters for the jump, Captain?"

"Tomorrow. After the funeral. For now, just get us close to the nearest star so we have someplace to consign Surgeon Commander Eldir's body."

"If we increase to full, we should be close enough by tomorrow afternoon."

"Fine. Do that."

"I'll lay in a course."

"It would be New Barzak," Romiwero commented, grumpily. "How long since the last time we were there?"

More work with the computer. "Seven months ship time," Fehmadaatin said. "Figuring in the jumps we've made since then, that works out to 4,327 years real time."

Romiwero shook her head. "I wonder if anyone still remembers we exist. We'll have to orbit for a while and put the computers to work on the language. I don't doubt it will have evolved into something we can't understand by now."

"Will we have to go down to the surface, Captain?"

"I'm hoping not. The colonists seem to like it, but I always feel like I'm carrying another person on my back when I'm down there."

New Barzak had a mass of 1.84 compared to Barzak. It truly was like carrying an extra person around trying to move on the planet's surface. Or like carrying 84-percent of another person, at least. She weighed 53.9 kilograms on Barzak, or on the ship. On New Barzak she weighed 99.17 kilograms.

It was particularly annoying that they knew how to build gravity generators into the soles of their boots that would normalise gravity on any planet with less than Barzak's normal mass, but there was no way to reverse that. They could negate gravity on something as large as a shuttle, but the field generators couldn't be made small enough for adaptation to individual use. There were a few New Barzakites aboard the ship, recruited on previous visits, who used their own gravity boots to *increase* the ship's artificial gravity, so that they wouldn't go bouncing down the corridors.

Warrior had dropped off the first colonists early in the mission. In real time, the colonists had had a bit over 48,000 years to evolve to fit their adopted planet's conditions. They were all uniformly short and stocky, powerfully built. Physically, on New Barzak, their strength and athletic ability was roughly the same as a Barzakite back home. In normal Barzakian gravity they became enormously strong.

◆   ◆   ◆

A system patrol ship met them a few hours after they emerged from jump space. The ship queried them in unintelligible gibberish, peppered here and there with a word they could almost understand. *Warrior* answered in clear, concise Gehunite, which was just as unintelligible to the New Barzakites, again bar the odd word or two.

The flags painted on the hulls were the same, though, which was reassuring.

It required a little over two days[6] for the language programmes to synch up, so that the Gehunites aboard *Warrior* could properly communicate with the New Barzakites on the planet. The colonists were comprehending faster than the crew, as they still had ancient texts in the Gehunite language spoken when they first arrived on the planet, as well as scholars who could read it.

Speaking it was another matter. The scholarly opinion of the correct pronunciation was a bit off the mark. Not too surprising, considering how long ago their ancestors had arrived on the planet, and how long it had been since *Warrior* last returned for a visit. Romiwero would have pronounced the name of the planet Barzakinu. The natives now pronounced it Borshkni.

New Barzak had had one advantage over most planets. The direct ancestors of the entire population had arrived there at the same time, and only spread slowly from the first settlements. They had enjoyed a technological civilisation for the whole time, so even settlements on different continents had remained in touch via electronic media. There were regional differences in accents and idioms, but everyone on the planet still spoke the same language.

---

6   A day on New Barzak was 45 Barzakian hours in length (36 hours in our present system), so by shipboard time two days on New Barzak would have been three days in earth time.

That hadn't been the case back home, Romiwero thought. As humanity had spread over the globe, isolated settlements had lost touch with their old lands. In the days before steam ships and radio, an ocean had been a genuine obstacle. Even a river could cut off communication from one side to the other.

The nearly four century expansion of the Gehunite Empire had united most of the planet. And while there was no insistence that everyone speak Gehunite, most conquered nations did, once they were admitted to full membership. That had been the vision of Salmik the Great, that each constituent country in his empire remain autonomous, yet at the same time a part of the Empire. The eighteen languages in old Rantos gradually dwindled until nearly everyone spoke Gehunite in daily life, and reserved their old native tongues for family and friends. Except in Callaa and Feria, which remained independent, a single language had effectively replaced the old ones.

Even Callaa and Feria taught their children the imperial tongue. Callaa remained independent for historic reasons — Emperor Felim I, Salmik's son and heir — had married a Callaaite princess, forever after joining the two royal houses. It also remained independent because no one was crazy enough to consider invading.

Romiwero glanced over at Fehmadaatin, who was seated at the navigation console. The lovely blond Callaaite was likely the most dangerous fighter in the crew. Except for a couple other Callaaites, trained in the same techniques, even the Marines were reluctant to get into the practice ring with her.

The Callaaite defence system was simple. There was only one overland invasion route, and only one fjord penetrated the iron-bound coast to the interior. If anyone invaded, these routes were sealed off, and the Reserve was mobilised. As the Reserve consisted of every citizen over the age of fifteen, that meant Callaa could have an Army of twelve-million in the field within a day of giving the mobilisation order.

Feria, nestled in the mountains of central Rantos, was more useful as a neutral than a victim. Besides, their Reserve was nearly as large and well-equipped as Callaa's.

A Leading Yeoman entered from the communications centre with a signal flimsy. She handed this off to the captain.

"Communications are established," she announced. "The planetary government will be sending up a delegation within the hour." She looked around the bridge. "So, Lieutenant Fehmadaatin, call

your relief and get into your dress uniform. Yeoman, my compliments to the Ambassador and inform her that her presence will be
required at the main entry port."

"Aye, aye," the yeoman replied, hurrying out.

Fehmadaatin looked up. "Swords?" she asked.

"Swords," Romiwero said. "I know no one likes the damned
things, but protocol is protocol."

Fehmadaatin nodded. She picked up an intercom handset and
punched in a number. "You're needed early," she said, when her
relief answered. "I have to dress up and act official."

She replaced the handset and looked up at the captain. "On
his way, Captain," she said.

"Good." She turned to Oshrorehno. "Commander, you have
the deck. I'm going to change."

♦   ♦   ♦

Captain Kimewe Romiwero looked at herself in the full-length mirror on the back of her bedroom door. Thirteen years, she thought,
and the uniform still fits. She studied the dark-blue jacket, with
its uncomfortable standing collar, looking for any stray specks of
lint. The four rings of gold lace, surmounted by the imperial crown
device, were somewhat darkened with age. But the gold buttons
were bright, as was the gold oval belt buckle, emblazoned with the
Imperial Navy's crown and crossed anchors device. The snug fitting
while trousers looked good, and her tall boots were nicely shined.
Her grandfather's old sword hung vertically at her side, the upper
ring slipped over the hook on her belt. It was more convenient to
wear it that way. Let down onto the leather straps, it could move
around more and present a tripping hazard.

"I guess you're ready," she said to her image.

The main entry port, which opened, via an airlock, onto Number 1 Shuttle Bay, was five decks down and nearly a kilometre aft.
Romiwero walked. Others in the passageway, either lazier or in a
greater hurry, used electric carts to get around the huge ship.

Romiwero was interested in seeing what sort of shuttle the
locals arrived in. Everything in *Warrior* was bang up to date for
when they left Barzak, but the colonies had had a very long time to
improve things, even if only thirteen years had passed aboard the
ship. Mostly, she expected a New Barzakian shuttle to be smaller,
though likely faster and longer ranged. Everything on that planet

was more squat, as the planets greater mass and stronger gravity had naturally caused the locals to become shorter and stronger.

Fehmadaatin was already in the entry port. The ambassador arrived a few minutes after the captain.

Princess Felia wore a diplomatic uniform, not a naval one. Though essentially the same, the diplomatic version omitted the rank lace around the sleeves, and had an elaborate, gold-wire embroidered facing on the jacket. She was a royal princess, but whether that was all, or she was now much more, was unknown. There was a presumption that either the royal line continued without her back home, or their home planet had evolved away from monarchy by now.

"They should be here shortly," Romiwero said.

"This sort of thing always makes me nervous," Felia said. "It's not very long for us, but it's an extremely long time for them."

"They know why we're here?"

"Yes. Once communications were established, we told them why we'd come back. It's a chance for some of the crew who joined on our last visit to spend some time at home. And, of course, we need a new doctor."

"I think we have room for another dozen or so to join the crew, too," Romiwero said.

"I'll see what we can do." Felia smiled. "They're bringing a prospective doctor with them."

"Good to know."

"Shuttle arriving, Captain," a rating said. "Bay doors are closed. Seven minutes to re-pressurise the bay."

"Thank you."

"It would be faster if we'd gone down," Felia said.

Romiwero nodded. "True. We'd also be exhausted after walking the first hundred metres. Much easier for them to adapt to our gravity than for us to adapt to theirs."

"Have you ever wondered what it must have been like for the first colonists? Back before enough generations had passed for them to really adapt to this place?"

"I suppose it was just like it was for us back then. Except they stayed and put up with it while we wandered off amongst the stars."

"Landing bay is pressurised, Captain," the rating announced. "They're debarking now."

It was a two-step process getting everyone into the entry port.

First the surface party crowded into the airlock, then, after the door was shut behind them, came through into the ship. The airlock was a precaution. No one ever entered the landing bay when it was depressurised. The airlock was just in case the space doors ever failed open, and it was necessary to get a repair party into the bay with it open to space. It also served as a decontamination chamber for personnel or objects being brought aboard from outside the ship.

The New Barzakian party were walking very carefully. It wasn't so much that their weight had diminished by almost half—an 80-kilogram New Barzakite weighed exactly the same as an 80-kilogram old Barzakite—as that they were so much stronger for a given weight. The amount of muscle force needed to walk normally on the planet was enough to lift one of them ten to twenty centimetres into the air with each step.

The New Barzakites in the crew fell into two groups. The first simply adjusted, generally losing a certain amount of muscle as they acclimated, and eventually losing enough that, should they return to their home planet, they'd suffer the same handicap as an old Barzakite. At least, they would until they re-adjusted and built up their strength again.

The others wore gravity boots, adjusted to increase the ship's artificial gravity by 84 percent. They retained their normal musculature, and could visit their home world without difficultly.

"Welcome aboard," Romiwero said, a digital translator clipped to her belt allowing her to be understood. An earpiece linked to the translator let her understand the visitors. "I am Captain Kimewe Romiwero, of His Imperial Majesty's Starship *Warrior*. And this," indicating Felia, "is our Ambassador-at-Large, Her Highness, Princess Felia."

The delegation's leader, a tall—for a New Barzakite—gentleman in what she supposed was some sort of uniform, stepped forward. "I am General Galwin Trednor," he said. "It's my great pleasure to welcome you back to our planet." He paused. "You *do* understand that we don't really consider ourselves to be a colonial possession anymore, I presume."

Felia laughed. "Have no fear on that account, General," she said. "When we left your ancestors here, the presumption was that it would likely be several thousand years of your time before we returned. If we returned at all."

"Besides," Romiwero said. "Given the choice, we'd prefer not to go down onto the planet if we can avoid it. I've been there, and it's exhausting trying to move around with your heavier gravity."

Trednor chuckled and flexed his feet. The action would have lifted him onto his toes at home. Here it bounced him nearly twenty centimetres off the deck. "Understandable, Captain," he said with a smile.

Romiwero gestured towards the corridor door. "If you and your party would care to come with us, General," she said, "we laid on some refreshments in the wardroom."

"Excellent." He gestured to a completely bald man, wearing a blue uniform. "Grekim," he said. "You may as well present yourself now."

The man put down the two bags he was carrying and came forward, putting his cap back on his head as he did so. The Gehunite officers were wearing swords, so they were covered despite being technically indoors. That changed the protocol slightly.

His right hand formed into a fist, which he slapped sharply against the upper left side of his chest. "Surgeon Commander Grekim Vordik," he introduced himself, "come aboard to join."

Romiwero returned the salute in the old Gehunite fashion, touching her right forefinger to the peak of her cap. "Welcome aboard, Doctor. Come along to the welcome party now." She turned to the landing bay rating. "Have someone take the medical officer's gear to his temporary quarters, will you, Malazen?"

"Aye, aye, Captain."

"Temporary?" Vordik asked.

"We tend to feel that, once joined, this ship is likely to be our permanent home. Probably for the rest of our lives. You'll be able to have your permanent quarters configured and decorated in whatever way seems most homelike to you. Most of the crew have duplicated their original homes. A few just set their quarters up the way they want them to look."

"Except the Marines," Fehmadaatin said.

Romiwero nodded. "Except the Marines. They seem to *like* living in a barracks. They don't have to, they just do." She looked him over carefully. "We'll get you new uniforms as well." She grinned. "I presume that *is* a uniform you're wearing?"

General Trednor answered. "That's what the Navy wears on the planet these days. My uniform is Army, in case you were wondering."

"No swords, sir?" Fehmadaatin inquired.

"Not for centuries. Hell, we haven't had an actual war in the last 300 years. Even when we had them, they didn't amount to much. Our military these days is strictly a planetary defence organisation. There are others out there who are *not* human, you know."

"Of course," Romiwero said. "We have a few crew members who aren't human. Most species, by the time they get into space, have learnt to behave themselves."

◆   ◆   ◆

Surgeon Commander Grekim Vordik lay back on his bunk, his hands behind his head. It had been an interesting day. After the reception, where he'd had the opportunity to meet the other officers, he'd spent several hours with the Warrant Officer Ship's Constructor, working out what would be done for his permanent quarters. Vordik wasn't fond of his apartment, which was quite small and boasted nothing to recommend it beyond proximity to the hospital, so together with the carpenter he'd instead designed what he thought of as his "dream home."

When the constructors were finished with it, he'd be moving into a three-bedroom, two level traditional 'house' with a view of the Krednar Sea. The view would be holographic, though he was forced to admit he hadn't been able to tell this short of sticking his hand through a sample window in the constructor's office and finding there was no more than ten centimetres of depth beyond the sash.

He'd never have been able to afford a house like that at home. That was something else that was different aboard *Warrior*. They didn't use money here. Everything he'd need, quarters, uniforms, food, recreation, were provided as needed. If they visited a planet where money was still used, ship's funds were available for the crew to spend as needed.

When he was finished with the constructor, he was shepherded to the ship's tailor shop to be measured for new uniforms. He would be issued service dress, dress, and full dress uniforms, as well as six sets of working uniforms, boots and shoes, and as many sets of surgical coveralls and lab coats as he needed.

The uniforms he came aboard with would go into the cupboard and probably stay there. The new ones would have old fashioned sleeve lace on the dress uniforms. Three 15-millimetre rings of gold lace, with a 5-millimetre strip of scarlet cloth between them, and the imperial crown device above the topmost ring. On the working uniforms, his rank would be indicated by two silver stars on the shoulder straps, with scarlet rims around the stars indicating a surgeon. Engineers, he learnt, wore green separators and rims, and the supply and pay corps types wore purple.

Civilians, and there were a fair number of them aboard, didn't wear uniforms. No one had retired yet, but when they did they would also switch to mufti.

He was bringing some new equipment with him. The diagnostic and treatment equipment aboard *Warrior* had no doubt been state of the art when the ship was built, but there had been significant advances since then. A factory that built diagnostic cots was building a half dozen units, scaled up for old Barzakite physiology. Vordik stood 150 centimetres, which was a bit on the tall side for a New Barzakite. The tallest member of *Warrior*'s crew was a gunner's mate who stood 203 centimetres. The new cots were being scaled up to allow someone his size to use them, though, obviously, it was rare to find anyone that tall.

The cots would do essentially the same job of monitoring vital signs as the present equipment, but wouldn't require attaching anything to the patient.

It was going to be quite an adventure, he thought. When the opportunity to serve in one of the old Imperial starships was offered, he'd jumped at. He was an only child, and his parents were dead. There wasn't anyone he was close to. The prospect of vanishing several hundred years into the future on the first jump wasn't that bothersome. There really wasn't anyone he'd be leaving behind.

Eight

MONDAY, 21ST JANUARY, 2097 DAWNED CRISP AND COOL in Washington, DC. At noon, Will Gordon would publicly take the oath of office as the fifty-fifth President of the United States. He'd already been privately sworn in at noon the previous day. The public ceremony was always put off until the following day when 20th January fell on a Sunday.

It promised to be a nice day. The temperature was expected to be in the upper sixties by noon. The skies were expected to be clear.

Everything was ready. The stands had been erected on the west front of the Capitol. President Collins was packed, and Gordon's things were ready to move into the White House. The move was also postponed from the previous day. It wouldn't do to have the movers working on a Sunday. The Episcopal Bishop of Washington was at the National Cathedral, ready to start the prayer service once Gordon and the outgoing president arrived with their families.

Gordon wasn't sure how he felt about the prayer service. He'd have preferred a proper Baptist preacher conduct it, not an Episcopalian. Their connection with the Anglican Communion always seemed problematic to Gordon. The Archbishop of Canterbury was a lesbian, for Christ's sake, so just how Christian could they possibly be?

Well, his brother Tom would preach the sermon. And the local bishop was on record as condemning the British Anglicans for the election of an obvious pervert as Archbishop. It was just that Gordon suspected the man wasn't entirely sincere. That he was just trying to stay on the good side of the government.

Things were going to be different in his administration, Gordon thought. Ed Collins was a good man, but there were things he'd let pass that should have been stopped. He'd seen reports that as many as 30-percent of the border gun turrets were out of commission, leaving gaps where illegals could slip through.

Just a few days ago, Collins had pardoned over 200 gay men, releasing them back into society, when the law said they should have been executed. It had also been some time since anyone seriously investigated women who'd gone on foreign vacations, apparently pregnant, and returned very clearly *not* pregnant. Gordon figured the released gays would get caught again soon enough, and this time there'd be no pardons or commutations. There wasn't anything he could do about the women, but he could make sure that in future there'd be proper investigations and, if evidence of an abortion was found, the murderous traitors to their divine destiny could be put on trial and executed.

It was what the electorate wanted. They wanted someone who would strictly enforce the law. Particularly, they wanted someone who would enforce morality. If that meant executing baby murderers and sodomites, then that was what needed to happen.

The one thing he was going to miss was his television show. He'd spent eighteen years building an audience. He'd enjoyed sitting in the studio almost every day—the Sunday shows were prerecorded—and advising his viewers on how to live their lives in a proper, Christian manner. Telling them what to do, who to care about, who to disparage, how to relate to God and Jesus.

He'd miss the money, too. Being president only paid $1,500,000 a year, with another half million for expenses. His television ministry had brought in that much every week.

It was funny. His grandfather had been part of the team that brought about the Second Constitutional Convention, way back in 2019. The intention had been to create a new form of government, where ordinary people would have a little more to say, and the various churches would finally get their due. Yet he would be the first president who literally came from a clerical background. He was a fifth-generation evangelist.

His great-great-grandfather, Albert Gordon, had started

things off back in the 1920s, travelling around the country in a small caravan of cars and trucks, stopping in various, mostly southern towns, setting up their tents, and spending however many days the locals kept coming in holding fiery revival meetings.

His great-grandfather, Willy Gordon, had taken things up a notch. After World War II, instead of carting around a tent, he'd started renting football stadiums. You could get a few hundred people into a tent. You could get thousands into a stadium.

One crusade, in Cleveland, had filled every seat in the old Municipal Stadium, all 80,000 of them, with another 30,000 on the field. Old Willy knew how to put on a show. He'd also been one of the first to realise that evangelical crusades made good television, and that people who watched the massive services on TV could be persuaded to send money to an address superimposed on the screen during the collections.

His grandfather, Fred, had continued the stadium crusades, but his main concentration became television and radio. He'd also continued his father's efforts to influence politics in favour of evangelical Christianity. People listened to him, despite the fact that, more often than not, he really didn't know what the hell he was talking about.

Fred had latched onto some important concepts. In the 1970s he'd started the American Ethics Foundation.[7] The original idea had come after Brown and other Supreme Court decisions ending segregated public schools. Christian academies had quickly sprung up, taking advantage of their church connected status to provide white-only schools as an alternative to the now integrated public schools.

It hadn't taken long for the IRS to come after the academies. You could have a private school attached to your church, they said, but if you didn't allow minority students you couldn't be tax exempt. The AEF was organised to fight that. They didn't exactly phrase it that way. They just talked about traditional American values, and Judeo-Christian traditions—by which they meant Christian traditions, and screw the damned Jews—but the main point was to get the IRS to back off.

After a few years of that, it had occurred to Fred that coming

---

7   So far as the author has been able to determine, there is no such organisation. Even if there was, one suspects it would bear no resemblance to the Gordon family's questionable charity.

out against abortion was an even better idea. People were getting used to the idea of integration, so it didn't bring in as much money as it used to. But *everyone* loved babies, even if most Protestants then thought of the whole anti-abortion idea as essentially Catholic. Protestant denominations had all originally supported Roe, until they caught on to the money-making power of being against it.

Putting the power of the AEF, and its multi-million name mailing lists behind the "anti" philosophy, and cleverly calling it "pro-life" rather than "anti-abortion," eventually got quite a number of national Protestant church governing bodies to reverse their pro-Roe stances. It also brought in a fortune in donations. Lots more than being anti-integration ever had.

The new president's dad, another Albert, had carried on from there. He still ran the occasional crusade, still counselled political leaders — much easier under the new Constitution than it had been under the old one, with its secular slant — and still spent a lot of time on television.

So now it was Will Gordon's turn, and after 19 years on television he was taking the next logical step. He'd run for president and won.

Nine

CAPTAIN KIMEWE ROMIWERO TOOK HER SEAT at the head of the conference table. Most of the senior staff was present. The junior officers were running the ship, except for Commander (E) Greshvor, who always considered his engines more important than the daily staff meeting, unless there happened to be an actual issue with the engines on the agenda. There never was.

"It's time," Romiwero announced. "We're in the right sector of the galaxy, and it's been fifteen years since we departed. It's time to go home."

"Is there a home to return to?" Oshrorehno asked. "By their reckoning, we've been gone for a ridiculously long time."

Romiwero shrugged. "We won't know until we get there, will we? But the colonies we founded are still thriving, and they still remember who we are, even if we usually have to get computers involved to communicate. There's no reason to suspect that some version of the Empire won't still hold sway."

"It's been our experience," Felia commented, "that languages continue to evolve, but once an advanced technological society is created, it will continue more or less indefinitely."

"Ours, too," Lieutenant Commander Zhvassish offered. "My contingent is all for the idea of visiting your home planet." He chuckled, one of the habits he'd picked up living with Barzakites for the last eight years. "We've never seen a whole planet dominated by mammals before. *Native* mammals, I mean. Obviously, the colonies don't count, as the population was imported."

Zhvassish was a Griknaite, a non-human, bipedal, tailless reptile. He was tall, 191 centimetres, and mostly green, with yellow, slit-pupiled eyes. When he spoke, his lipless mouth displayed a great many pointed teeth. He was, to be honest, a rather scary looking individual, for all that Griknaites were, in general, significantly less inclined to get into trouble than humans. Scary but peaceful, was the general opinion of the species.

"Do you suppose any of your line survives?" Fehmadaatin asked Felia. "If none do, you know what that means."

The princess nodded. "I don't think it will count for that much, though," she said. "I'm sure *somebody* is running the place."

Romiwero rapped her knuckles on the table. "Lieutenant Fehmadaatin, you're the navigator. What do you propose?"

"There's an acceptable jump point on our present course, at a distance of about 177.26 Solar Units. At full speed, that should require 58 hours. Figure about 63 hours, once you factor in accelerating to 127,000 kilometres per second from our present speed."

"How far is the jump?" Oshrorehno asked.

"Six hundred seventy-three light years."

Romiwero looked thoughtful. "Where will we emerge?"

"More or less where we started," Fehmadaatin replied. "Approximately 12.8 solar units from Barzak, between the orbits of Reknur and Zardek."

"Approximately?" Felia asked.

"It depends on where Barzak actually is in its orbit. That distance if we emerge in line with the planet and it's on our side of the sun. Farther, of course, if it happens to be on the other side when we get there."

"Ah."

"Lay in a course," Romiwero ordered. "Advise engineering to prepare for a full speed run, and run a full diagnostic on the jump drive."

The latter action was routine. No one was quite sure what would happen if the drive failed in the middle of a jump. Nor did anyone wish to be the person who found out.

◆   ◆   ◆

Six hundred seventy-three light years away, on a point of land between the Bosporus and the Sea of Marmara, a battle was raging.

The world was changing amid the clash of swords, and the screaming of defiance and triumph in Greek and Arabic.

Clutching his sword in one hand and his shield in the other, Constantine XI, now dressed as an ordinary soldier, slashed at an Ottoman horseman. The Turk's lower arm came off, spraying the embattled emperor with blood and momentarily blinding him.

A moment was all that was necessary. A janissary thrust a spear through the emperor's chest and he collapsed instantly. His body jerked reflexively for a moment and then lay still. Because he was not wearing his imperial garments, none of the attacking Turks paid him any attention. He was just another dead soldier, so far as they were concerned.

Neither the janissary, nor the dead emperor, had any idea that far out in space, a group of people they had no idea had ever existed, had just made the decision to return to earth after an absence of thousands of years. Had anyone told either of them, the only reaction would have been utter disbelief.

Ten

THE FIRST TO NOTICE THAT SOMETHING HAD HAPPENED was an astronomer at the Royal Observatory at Greenwich. Doctor Carla Tuttle was an astronomy professor at Queen's College, Oxford. At forty-five, she had written four books, but had never discovered anything significant. Not even a comet. There was nothing out in the cosmos with her name on it, and that was the goal of every astronomer, whether they admitted it or not. They wanted a comet, or a new star, or, well, something important.

Wouldn't it be fantastic, she thought, if she could be the first to identify an exoplanet supporting life? To be the first human being to prove that we were not, absolutely were not, alone in the universe?

After several years of trying, Tuttle had been assigned a three-hour block on the Hawking Stellar Array. That morning, Tuesday, 2nd April, 2126, from midnight universal time until 0300, the array was hers to control. She could point it where she wanted to look. Mostly empty space, at least in the visible spectrum, but that was fine with her. The Hawking had capabilities other than just what a human could see with her limited visual capacity.

The array, a set of seven big, multi-articulated mirrors was positioned above the equator in a meticulously calculated retrograde orbit. It required just over a year for the array to make a complete orbit, so at any given time the field of view would remain essentially stationary. That morning, the array was pointed at a star cluster which, Tuttle hoped, might do something interesting during her three hours of viewing time.

Like most professional astronomers, Tuttle wasn't viewing the stars through a lens. That sort of thing was for amateurs, limited to earthbound optical telescopes. The Hawking array used cameras—high density, digital sensors, really, but everyone still called them cameras—and the resulting images, reduced to compressed digital signals, were relayed to ground stations, spotted around the world. Infrared and x-ray imaging sensors added to the data stream.

For Tuttle's session, the data went first to a ground station on Diego Garcia, located on what had been an American naval base before the UK government decided to evict all American military units from British soil. From there, the data was relayed to Greenwich, where Tuttle could view the raw images on a high-resolution monitor in very nearly real time.

That was a convenience. It was fun to watch the images as they came in, but Tuttle recognised that she wasn't going to learn much that way. This was why everything was being recorded. Long-term analysis, with the help of a computer, would be where the real meat was to be found.

Tuttle would have two years for that. Once her session ended, a two-year clock would start. During that time, no one else would have access to the data unless she authorised it. There would be complaints from the amateurs. There always were. Why should data from a publicly-funded source be the exclusive property of only one person, even if only for a couple years?

Well, Tuttle thought, why should a professional astronomer spend several years planning a session, programming the parameters, and waiting for the observation time to be available and the array pointed in the right direction, and then give away the results? If she couldn't finish her work in two years, the others could look at it then.

At least, that was the usual practice.

It happened at 0147:18. A single black pixel in the upper left quadrant of the screen suddenly turned white. A second later, the white glare had expanded to a diameter of 30 pixels.

Tuttle was mesmerised as the glowing area continued to expand, until the white circle, after only three seconds, was over 300 pixels in diameter.

I have my own supernova, was her first thought. Then she was wondering just how big the cosmic explosion had to be. Nothing had ever been detected in that region of space before. It was absolutely empty in the visual spectrum, and barely registered in the infra-red or x-ray spectra. If this was a supernova, it had to be millions, perhaps even billions, of light years from earth.

Dinosaurs were walking this planet when this happened, she thought. It might even predate them. It could be so far away that there had been no planet here when that star exploded.

She felt suddenly frightened. If this was that far away, and expanding at that rate, something was wrong.

Supernovas always happened a very long way from earth. There were no stars close to earth capable of exploding. That meant that any supernova would be fun to look at, but harmless. Distance was a safety factor. Like the sun, the closer stars would ultimately expand as they used up their fuel, then collapse and die. It was the collapse that caused some stars to explode, but that end required far more mass than any nearby star contained.

Ultimately, the sun would expand past earth's orbit, destroying the planet, but it wasn't something anyone needed to worry about for a few billion more years.

Tuttle had read quite a few books, published early in the 21st century, predicting doom. One of her favourites, written by an astronomer, had listed various ways the planet could be destroyed. Strangely, not that many people had been worried about those scenarios, all of which were still quite capable of ending life on the planet.

It was the *other* doomsday predictions they'd obsessed over. In 2012, there was a brief panic in some circles when it was pointed out that the Mayan long cycle calendar would end on 21st December of that year. The surviving Mayans had *not* been among those panicking at this "predicted end of time." The Mayans had decided that, if the calendar ended after 5,000 years, the logical thing to do at that point was start over, just as you'd do with any other calendar.

Others had predicted ridiculous scenarios where the earth's crust would start sliding around, causing universal earthquakes and tidal waves. Others predicted plagues, or the arrival of a rogue planet that would smash into earth and destroy everything. A lot of fundamentalist Christians had predicted Jesus would return, and all the hallucinatory nonsense in Revelation would happen.

What actually happened was nothing, beyond a few scientifically ridiculous motion pictures, and a lot of books that abruptly stopped selling on 22nd December.

One of the scenarios from that manufactured panic was that Betelgeuse would go supernova and wipe out all earthly life. Could that star blow up? Certainly. It was a red giant, and reliably predicted to be close to the point where it would run out of fuel and collapse, triggering a supernova.

But it was also over 600 light years away, so even if it did go supernova it was too far away to do any damage on earth, with the possible exception of a gamma ray burst. The star's orientation precluded that happening. Gamma ray bursts emerged at a dying star's poles, and Betelgeuse's weren't pointing towards Earth.

Now it was 2126, and as far as anyone could say Betelgeuse was still there. You could never be sure, obviously, as what she saw when she looked at Betelgeuse was what the star looked like in 1512. It could have blown up at any time since and no one would know until the light reached the earth 614 years later. For that matter, the *sun* could suddenly go out and no one would know until eight minutes later. Light was astonishingly fast, but it still took time to cover astronomical distances.

Whatever Tuttle was seeing now, it obviously wasn't Betelgeuse. If the stellar explosion the Hawking was now observing was as far from earth as she thought it was, then the explosion had expanded more than a light year in less than a second. It made her wonder if this was a supernova at all. At even a million light years, this thing would have to be expanding faster than the speed of light to grow that large that quickly. Faster than Einstein's theories said was possible. Nothing could move faster than light.

With one exception. The conversion of a quantum singularity into energy and matter could do that, during its expansion phase. That wouldn't last long, less than a second, really, and at the end you'd have a new universe.

"No," Tuttle said aloud, "that's not possible."

It was the sort of thing every astronomer wanted to see—but only in a theoretical sort of way. The problem with actually observing the expansion phase of a new Big Bang was that there was already a universe here. The one she was living in. It would be like overwriting a file on a computer. You'd have all this new data recorded, but what was already there would be wiped out.

Then the glow started to fade. In less than a minute it had vanished completely. So, it appeared the universe wasn't about to be overwritten after all. This was even more mysterious. A supernova might have expanded that fast, presuming it was considerably closer than she'd thought, which would make the diameter of the explosion significantly smaller, but it wouldn't vanish. That would normally take months, and could be expected to leave a new nebula, or at least a considerable cosmic debris cloud, behind it.

So just what had she seen? Whatever it was, it was probably visible from earth using an ordinary optical telescope. Perhaps it wouldn't even require a telescope. If she wanted credit for the discovery, she'd have to work fast. She wasn't going to have two years to report this, she thought. More like two hours.

It was time to let the computer get to work on the thing. See what it could make of it.

Tuttle typed in a series of commands. Most computers worked with a voice interface, but astronomers and other scientists still preferred to use the keyboard. No matter how good voice recognition software had become, it still had problems with equations.

And here was the answer. Estimated distance to event, 12.8 astronomical units.

"What the fuck?"

"Doc?" Allan Grosvenor, the Oxford PhD candidate in astronomy who was assisting her, hadn't been looking at the screen and so had missed all the excitement. He'd been her assistant for four months now, and this was the first time he'd heard her even raise her voice.

"Nothing." Tuttle was keeping this to herself until she could check the calculations again. The computer had to be wrong. That distance was *inside* the solar system. Still a very long way from earth, out beyond the orbit of Saturn, but well inside that of Uranus. According to the computer, something had blown up — or, at least, created a gigantic energy surge manifesting as visible light — about 1,915,763,000 kilometres from earth.

She started checking the figures again, at the same time composing the news release in her head, just in case it all checked out. Something very interesting was going on in space.

♦   ♦   ♦

Curiously, the next person to notice anything was not an astronomer, professional or amateur. It was a fifteen-year-old girl from

Denver, working her Ham radio. There were still millions of Hams keeping amateur radio alive around the world. Only a handful, though, continued to use Morse code and analogue broadcast frequencies, instead of the more modern—and simpler—digital channels and voice. Sara Ellsworth's grandfather had been one of them, and he'd infected his granddaughter with the bug, teaching her code when she was still quite young.

Her grandfather was gone now, but Sara still had his equipment in her room, and his antennas mounted to a 75' tower attached to the back of the house.

It was slightly more than an hour after Doctor Tuttle had seen the energy surge out past Saturn. Sara, who knew nothing of that startling event, was working code on the 80-metre band. Had she been outside at 6:47 pm, it was just possible she might have seen the brilliant flash in the sky, though it had likely been too light outside to notice it. As it was, she was engaged in a discussion about fly fishing with a teenaged boy in Saskatoon. That was when she heard something strange coming from the speaker.

"That's not right," she muttered. "This frequency is CW only."

But someone was sending in voice, and apparently from a fairly powerful transmitter. She hadn't the slightest idea what the person was saying.

Thinking it very odd, and definitely wrong, if not actually illegal, Sara turned on her recorder to get a digital record of the words. Whatever they were.

"*Ekto naamutari Barzaknyu, Osha* Romiwero *zhe kukram.*"

The voice seemed to be female, and simply repeated the same words, over and over. The monotonous broadcast lasted for five minutes, after which it stopped. It would start again an hour later.

I wonder who I should report this to, Sara mused. The words obviously weren't English. Was it just some foreigner on the wrong frequency, an innocent mistake? Should she complain to the FCC?

No, she thought, probably not. Why remind them that she existed? It was enough that she sent them their $1875 every year for her licence, which allowed her to operate her station, and gave the government explicit permission to monitor everything transmitted over it. There was no need to do more. Sending and receiving Morse code messages on the merits of dry versus wet flies was fine. Calling a government office and saying, "Somebody's messing around" might be carrying things a bit too far.

About the time the voice started again, someone was knocking on the front door. A minute later her father stuck his head into her room. "Ellen's here," he said, ushering in her classmate and then heading back to the living room.

"Did you hear the news?" Ellen asked.

"I'm on the radio, working code."

"You're weird."

"It's fun. You should try it."

"No. Anyway, can you get a secure web connection here?"

Sara glanced over her shoulder at the closed door. Was she sure her father had gone back downstairs? "Yeah."

"Then do it. There's something you've got to see."

"What?"

"Just get logged in."

Sara turned on the computer and started FreeWeb, which was hidden as a subprogramme on her email utility. FreeWeb would reroute the connection through a virtual private network server in Mexico. Everything sent over that connection would be encrypted. The web browser looked normal, but was configured to save nothing, and automatically performed a military-grade wipe of the temp file on exit. Computers could be searched, but as everything was overwritten seven times with a random pattern of ones and noughts, even the best search software couldn't find anything.

"Now, what am I supposed to be looking at?" she asked.

"The BBC. Search their site under Royal Observatory."

"Okay." She typed in the search terms. "What's that going to tell me about that needs this much security?"

"An explosion in space."

"Really?"

"That's what they're saying."

She found two clips and a story.

"It wasn't an explosion, from what we can tell," a woman explained. A caption identified her as Carla Tuttle, PhD, of the Royal Observatory, Greenwich, and Queen's College, Oxford.

"What do you make of it?" the presenter asked.

"Too early to say. There was a very strong energy surge—and we can't even say what sort of energy—located 12.8 astronomical units from earth. Just what caused it is still unknown."

"What's an astronomical unit?" The presenter was himself an astronomer, and knew perfectly well what Tuttle was talking about. The same couldn't be said with any assurance of everyone watching.

"It's the mean average distance from the earth to the sun. About 150-million kilometres."

"What's that in miles?"

"They're apparently hoping some American stations will pick this up," Sara commented.

"More likely thinking of us poor goofs on the internet," Ellen said. "This doesn't sound like something GNN would put on the air."

Tuttle looked rather annoyed at the question. She recognised the reason behind it and thought it was pandering to the ignorant. Still, she thought, I suppose we have to be nice to the Yanks. One day they'll liberate themselves and return to the civilised world.

"About 93-million," she said.

"*Ekto naamutari Barzaknyu, Osha* Romiwero *zhe kukram.*"

"Here we go again," Sara said.

"What is that?" Ellen asked.

"Somebody on a CW frequency babbling gibberish. Listen."

Ellen concentrated for a couple repetitions, then found herself tuning out. Was it possible to be bored by something you didn't even understand?

"That doesn't sound like anything I've ever heard." She thought for a moment. "Well, maybe the lunatics in church, but that sounds like an actual language, so that leaves the 'tongue speakers' out."

"It started a couple hours ago. She'll repeat that, over and over, for about five minutes, then stop for a while."

"Any idea why?"

"It's more annoying that way?"

"Be nice if we had some idea what she's saying."

"Well, it's not any language I can recognise. Something Scandinavian, maybe?"

"Shouldn't that sound more Germanish?"

Sara thought about it. "I suppose. It's not German, though. I took that last year. Uh oh!"

Sara lived in an old house. The stairs squeaked where the century-old nails had worked loose in the risers. That provided Sara with a good warning system. She touched a key and her computer's screen switched to a word-processing programme, displaying part of a page of English homework.

Sara's father stuck his head into her room. He didn't bother to knock. "Turn on the TV," he said. "Something going on out in space."

"Really?"

"They're interviewing some Brit astronomer on the Science News channel."

"Thanks."

Sara switched on the television and tuned it to the Science News channel. Sara thought the channel misnamed. While it occasionally presented some news, there was almost no science involved. The channel's most heavily advertised offering in the last few weeks had been, *The Flood: The Search for the Historic Noah.* Unlike actual historians, the ones appearing on the programme seemed to be finding him without much trouble.

Tuttle was on screen, this time on a remote linkup with the channel's so-called cosmology reporter. The BBC interviewer could be trusted to ask intelligent questions. Sara had serious doubts about the SNC guy, who would obviously have to conform to the channel's philosophy. Or the government's, take your pick. Every time she watched one of these interviews, she couldn't help wondering what the interviewer was thinking. How many of these guys knew they were lying to the public, and how many honestly believed the nonsense they were spouting?

"Miss Tuttle," the interviewer asked, "do you think it's possible that God is using this phenomenon to communicate with us directly? An impossible energy surge in deep space could be his way of getting our attention, couldn't it?"

Tuttle glared at the interviewer. Sara wondered if she was annoyed at the question, or at not being addressed by her proper title? She suspected the latter. Reporters were always asking stupid questions. Particularly American reporters.

"Idiot," Ellen muttered.

"Shhh! My parents might hear you."

"It was an energy surge," Tuttle said.

The channel cut back to the studio.

The BBC posted the rest of the interview a few minutes later. What the British astronomer had actually said was, "It was an energy surge. I have no idea what caused it, and it would be a little foolish to speculate. I do think we can be fairly sure it wasn't a mythical being, though."

Which explained why it had been cut off. Speculating that God had *not* done something, or might not exist, was a clear violation of FCC rules.

The two girls disconnected from the FreeWeb, but left the television on, just in case Sara's father came back in. He was strict when it came to insuring his family followed the rules.

Sara was never sure if he really *believed* what the government put out, or if he was just going along to keep out of trouble. Whichever it was, she wasn't going to risk letting him know what she really believed. She attended church, like she was supposed to. She praised Jesus, let herself be baptised when she was fourteen, and didn't even complain when the preacher started groping her in the process. It wasn't that unexpected. When her 'science' teachers explained how the universe was created, and how humanity could be reliably traced to two individuals living only a few thousand years ago, she paid attention and made sure her test papers agreed with the bullshit.

That was just what a smart person did, after all. People who didn't go along, who insisted on such radical ideas as placing experimental results above simply accepting what Moses said, had a tendency to suddenly move away and never be heard from again. You could believe a family might move away. It was a little harder to believe the family would stay, but a free-thinking teenage son would suddenly go off on his own. In a government car.

"I see your blabbermouth has shut up again," Ellen said.

"Maybe she's waiting for someone to answer."

"If she is, she's waiting an awful long time."

Sara thought about that. It had been quite a while, hadn't it?

"Why so quiet," Ellen asked.

Sara shook her head. "I was just thinking about something. Why send for five minutes, then nothing for an hour or so, then start again. Maybe she really is waiting for an answer."

"What are you getting at?"

"That energy bloom was way out in space. How long does it take a radio signal to travel 12.8 AU and back again?"

Ellen started punching away on the calculator app on her phone. "Longer than your chatty friend is waiting. One hundred and six minutes."

"Maybe they're getting closer."

"Sara, please. You're my best friend. Try not to turn into some sort of UFO nut, okay?"

"Well, there has to be *some* reason for this."

"Yeah, someone is playing a joke on you hams. Maybe somebody else caught this story and decided to have a little fun."

"You think so?"

"That voice sounded pretty human to me. Not like an alien."

"What's an alien sound like?"

"Different, I'd think."

Sara looked at the old radio. Her grandfather had bought it new back in the mid-21st century. It was a nice marriage of old and new technology. The guts were all solid state, but the operating principles dated back to the early 20th century.

Maybe it really was a joke. Maybe, she thought, it was time to joke back. Even knowing she wasn't supposed to, she keyed her microphone. "Person talking on CW channel," she said, trying to sound authoritative, "voice traffic is prohibited on this channel. You stop that now, hear?"

Thirty-three minutes later, 598,548,000 kilometres out in space, her voice emerged, weakly, from a speaker grill on *Warrior*'s bridge. Those gathered around it looked at each other curiously.

Romiwero slowly shook her head. "*Dek varavu vik?*" she said. *What the hell does that mean?*

Eleven

PRIME MINISTER SIR CHARLES VICKERS, BART., was leaning one elbow on his desk, his chin resting on his fist. The thin-film display that covered the entire top of the desk was showing four news channels, a direct video feed from the Ministry of Defence, and an indirect feed—courtesy of the Secret Intelligence Service—from American Air Defence Headquarters. The Yanks were always in a state of heightened alert, even though the chances anyone was planning to attack them were virtually nil. Vickers supposed the threat, constantly repeated through their news media, made it easier to distract their citizens from how little freedom they really had.

There was also a call from his husband, who was visiting his family in Leeds.

The intercom buzzed politely.

"Yes, Margaret?"

"President Grigori is on line six, Sir Charles."

"Thank you, Margaret." Vickers touched the screen above an active phone icon. "Sorry, Rick," he said to his husband. "The Russian president is calling. I'm going to have to get back to you."

"Okay. But as soon as you can, eh? My Uncle Geoff is here, and he's sounding as stupid as a Republican."

"Bye." The prime minister tapped another icon. "President Grigori," he said.

"Prime Minister. Are your people telling you the same things that mine are?"

"I'm being told we're about to be visited by some sort of space aliens. Is that what yours are saying?"

"Mine are saying 'invaded,' but essentially, yes." Grigori's English was precise, and spoken with what sounded more an American than a Russian accent."

"My husband just called me from Leeds," Vickers said. "He wanted to know if my office was really a super-strong, reinforced steel cubicle, or was that just something from an old television programme?"

"What did you tell him?"

"I told him he's safer in Leeds. No reinforced office, no bunkers."

"I have a bunker here," Grigori said.

"Nothing at all here. Not at Downing Street, anyway."

"Well, mine is left over from World War II, so I doubt that it would be very comfortable now. I don't even know if the lift still works."

"So, what do you make of the warnings?"

"There does seem to be *something* out there."

"Yes, but what?"

"Your guess is as good as mine. But I don't think it's Captain Kirk."

"Who?"

"Old American television show."

"Oh. That. I haven't seen one of those since I was at school."

"I always liked the Russian fellow," Grigori said. "He reminded me of my great-grandfather. 'We did it first.' Sometimes we really did, but mostly it was the Americans. Or you."

"Well, I'm fairly sure it's not that lot, anyway."

"It's someone who sounds human."

"That's good, I suppose. But *sounds* human doesn't have to mean *is* human. It may not even be a real voice."

"It reacts."

"Yes."

"Some amateur radio operator scolded them for broadcasting a voice message on a code only frequency. The message changed after that."

Vickers nodded. "Yes, but we still have no idea what they're saying." He slid a virtual control to the right and linked in the MOD. "What *are* they saying now, Brigadier?"

"'*Qva arigna voh?*' At least, that's what it sounds like to us."

"Brigadier Fitch, President Grigori is also on this call. Do we have anything new to report?"

"Mr. President, Prime Minister, not much. It's getting closer. That's about all we really know."

"How close?" Grigori asked.

"Too close, in my opinion, sir. About as far out as Mars' orbit."

"Any chance it's visible from the colony?" Vickers asked.

"None, Sir Charles. Mars is on the other side of the sun just now."

"No chance of launching a probe, then?"

"No practical chance. The thing was first detected when it was about 12.8 AU from earth. Now it's barely half an AU. And it's covered the distance in only 14 hours. That works out to over 131,000,000 kilometres an hour. Nothing we have can manage even a significant fraction of that speed."

"How close can we get?"

"Our fastest exploration ship would take three weeks to cover the same distance, presuming it could carry enough fuel to keep accelerating most of the way. Which it couldn't."

"Are we sure the thing is coming here, Brigadier?"

"About as sure as we can be. I suppose it's possible it will simply zip right on by and ignore us, but what are the odds? They obviously know we're here. They've reacted to that American amateur operator. So, if they know we're here, they have to be at least a little curious."

"Do you suppose they're friendly?"

"I certainly hope so, sir."

"Prime Minister, I have just received something from my scientific people," Grigori said. "The thing is slowing down."

Vickers frowned. That answered that question. Whoever they were, they not only knew that earth was inhabited, but apparently intended to stop and take a look.

♦   ♦   ♦

Aboard *Warrior*, dozens of view-screens were displaying earth television programmes, without sound. The ship's computers were "watching" the shows and "listening" to the dialogue. The active screens around the ship were simply the ones displaying the most action. That didn't make them any more interesting to the computers, but it did give the crew something more interesting to look at than nervous looking people sitting behind desks.

The channel that was getting the most attention was showing something called *Galaxy Quest*. Someone had turned up the sound on that, presumably for the background noises, as they could only speculate as to what anyone was saying.

They could recognise a primitive view of space, and even though no one could understand the actors, and recognising even without understanding that it was obvious whoever made this wasn't exactly up to date on the physics involved, there was more than enough action to keep them interested. The reaction of the actors — unlike the fictional Thermians in the movie, *Warrior*'s crew had no trouble recognising fiction when they saw it — to the jelly-like travel pods was good for a great deal of amusement. So was the rock monster. The journey through the bowels of the ship brought a suggestion from the chief engineer that some of this seemed like an interesting idea.

Engineers, the captain had mused, were naturally strange, always wanting to do things the hard way.

Meanwhile, the ship was slowing down, preparing to enter orbit, and the computers were chewing on the uploaded content. It wouldn't be long now.

◆　　　　　◆　　　　　◆

Captain Charles Sebastian, RN — people mostly called him by his rank, or by his last name — was six weeks away from returning to earth for good. He had spent the last year in command of the Sagan Space Platform, which had replaced the old International Space Station in 2062. It was significantly larger than the old station, with a crew of 270, most of them scientists.

At the moment, Sebastian was looking through one of the windows, as were most of the crew who didn't have something more important to do. If the platform wasn't in orbit, Sebastian thought, the thing would be in danger of capsizing with so much of the crew crowded along one side. But it *was* in orbit, so that didn't matter. Not when everyone was "weightless."

Down on earth, the PM was receiving a live television feed from the Space Platform, so he was seeing the same thing they were. Sebastian presumed even the Americans were watching. The official ones, at least. He had his doubts they were broadcasting this to the general public.

The alien ship, for there was no longer any question of what the thing was, was parked 1,500 metres off the Space Platform's port side. It was like nothing anyone had ever seen. Or even imagined.

To begin with, it was huge. Sebastian had used the platform's lasers to measure the alien ship, and came up with a length of 5.2 kilometres. It looked like a giant needle, coming to a long tapering point at the bow, and tapering again at the stern, though not to a point. The stern appeared to be squared off, and he presumed that was where the propulsion system was located. At the widest point, the ship appeared to measure roughly 450 metres across.

There were no visible doors or windows. The only speck of colour—if you could call black a colour—was a black, swallowtail flag painted on the hull near the stem, and what he presumed to be lettering beneath. The vessel's name, perhaps, in whatever alien tongue was spoken aboard.

Except for that, the ship's skin was an even silver colour, which Sebastian presumed meant that it was made of metal. He wondered what kind. Old movies always made alien craft out of some strange metal that didn't exist on earth, but Sebastian doubted that was possible. He suspected the universe was a lot more alike than people sometimes wanted to think, and that the periodic table would be the same no matter where you happened to be.

Everything was made in stars, after all, so it just followed that the same elements would be found everywhere. Aliens might concoct a previously unknown *alloy*, but the metals it was created from would be known. Anyway, they'd explored several planets and moons throughout the solar system, and so far no one had found anything that couldn't be found on Earth.

Once the alien ship had settled into orbit next to the Space Platform everything became a sort of anti-climax. It just sat there, doing nothing, for the next two and half days.

There was a good deal of speculation as to what was going on over there. Generally, the lack of activity was taken as a *good* sign. If the aliens were hostile, they could have simply blasted the platform the moment they arrived.

A few cited old movies, where the aliens just sat there for a while, gathering their forces, before attacking simultaneously all over the world. But no additional ships had turned up, so possibly they were just doing surveys using sensors that earth's technology couldn't detect.

"Captain! Something's happening!"

Sebastian glanced across the compartment at Jenkins. "What's going on?" he asked, turning back to the window.

"It's opening up." Jenkins was a civilian scientist. She never called him sir.

Sure enough, the seamless silver of the ship was now marred by a dark, circular opening about a quarter of the way back from the bow. As Sebastian watched, three small pods emerged from the opening, which quickly closed behind them, seeming to vanish as it did.

The pods, flat sided, slightly triangular polygons with round domes at the top, floated in a leisurely way toward the Space Platform. "I think we're about to be checked out," Sebastian said.

"Some sort of probes?" Jenkins wondered aloud. "I mean, those can't be what they look like. Can they?"

"I certainly hope not. No, probes of some sort, I expect."

One of the pods approached Sebastian's window. As it did, the dome and a portion of the midsection opened, exposing a clear window and allowing him to see inside.

"Not a probe," Sebastian said. "Transport."

There was a face looking back at him through the clear section. A very human looking face, which he found more than a little surprising. Aliens in the cinema generally looked like humans because they were played by humans wearing prosthetic makeup, but the scientific consensus was that intelligent life on other planets was likely to be a lot more varied. This alien looked like an ordinary human woman. Vaguely exotic looking, but certainly human.

The occupant smiled and waved. Sebastian blinked several times and waved back, a little uncertainly. The woman then gestured toward the Space Platform, pointing at herself—she was clearly female—and then at the platform. The context was clear enough.

I'd like to come aboard.

Sebastian nodded and pointed towards his right. There was a cargo airlock over there with a door large enough for the pods to fit through. The woman nodded and drifted her pod in the indicated direction. The two others followed.

Sebastian pulled himself through the platform to the airlock controls. He soon had the outer door open, and watched through the viewport in the inner door as the three pods drifted neatly through the outer door and came to rest on the floor of the air-lock. He closed the outer door, and when the pressure had equalised, opened the inner door and floated into the airlock, with Jenkins following closely.

Twelve

THE THREE PODS RESTED SOLIDLY ON THE AIRLOCK DECK. Rather more solidly than made sense to Sebastian, as they weren't tied down. It would be more normal for them to simply float in place. Only the first had its viewport open, and from up close the woman inside looked to be quite attractive.

Sebastian watched as she did something just out of his sight below the viewport. After a moment she seemed satisfied and, reaching down, retrieved a small, transparent face mask, which she put on over her nose and mouth. Then the front of the pod opened and she stepped out.

Or tried to. In the weightless environment of the platform, her first step simply propelled her upwards.

She lifted her arms, got her hands on the overhead, and pushed herself back down. Grinning, she manipulated a small instrument packet on her belt, and there was a metallic click as she seemed to be abruptly pulled the last few centimetres and the soles of her boots slapped against the deck.

She looked, Sebastian decided, very human indeed. She was about 170 centimetres in height, with a very good figure. Her costume looked military. Her feet and calves were encased in highly polished black boots, very much like riding boots. Her legs were covered by snug, white trousers, looking rather like riding breeches, but without the patches. Above this she wore a deep blue military tunic, with a standing collar. The tunic was single breasted, fastening up the centre with gold buttons.

Her red hair was gathered at the back into a pony tail, and she wore a blue peaked cap, like a French 'kepi,' with a highly-polished leather peak surrounded by gold wire embroidery in a curious pattern. The gold emblem at the front of the cap consisted of two crossed anchors surmounted by a crown. The same insignia was on the oval, gold buckle of her black leather belt.

Four rings of gold lace, remarkably like those on his own dress uniform, but slightly wider, and without the executive curl, circled each sleeve near the cuff. Where the curl would have been on his own uniform, she wore an embroidered gold crown device. A sword was attached to her belt at the left side, with a straight, leather sheath with gold fittings, and gold quillons and pommel. Sebastian wondered if it was a practical weapon or, like his own sword, an unsharpened ceremonial weapon.

She said something he didn't understand, but a moment later he heard, "No gravity generators, I see."

It took Sebastian a few seconds to realise that he was standing there, holding himself down by hanging onto a handrail, with his mouth fallen open. The unintelligible words had obviously come, slightly muffled by the mask, from her mouth. The ones he understood came from the instrument packet on her belt.

"How did you do that?" he asked.

A pause, more gibberish as she tapped the instrument packet, then, "There's a translator built into this."

"Both ways?"

"I hear you through an earpiece," she replied.

"Not instantaneous, though."

"Faster from your language to mine, I think. Your grammar is very different from ours. More flexible. Ours is very formal, and the verb is always the last word in a sentence."

Which, Sebastian realised, would certainly make simultaneous translation rather difficult. The same problem existed with German and Japanese.

"So, you don't just stick a fish in your ear, then?" he said.

She looked at him curiously. "What?"

He shrugged. "An old story. Fiction. Sorry."

"What language are you actually speaking?" Jenkins asked.

"Gehunite. Well, that appears to be what you would most likely call it, at least. In our own language we would say '*Gehunkili.*'" She smiled. "The language of Gehun, that means."

"I see." Sebastian didn't, but he figured that was to be expected.

"In any event," she said, "my name is Kimewe Romiwero, and I am the captain of His Imperial Majesty's Starship *Warrior*, over there."

"Kind of a belligerent name, isn't it?" Jenkins commented. "The ship's name, I mean."

"There were twelve before her with the same name. We're very traditional about that sort of thing."

"Twelve starships?"

"No, just twelve ships. Eight were sailing vessels, one a heavy cruiser, the next two were submarines, and then a system patrol ship. Mine is the first starship to carry the name." She frowned suddenly. "Very likely she'll be the only one."

"Imperial majesty's starship? You have an emperor, then?"

"Don't you?"

"My country has a king, but he has no real power. Doctor Jenkins here is an American refugee, and her former country has a president."

"Or dictator," Jenkins muttered. "Take your pick."

"We had an emperor when the ship was commissioned," Romiwero said. That was a very long time ago, and a great deal has obviously changed, so I rather doubt the House of Salmik even exists today."

The other two pods had opened by now and disgorged their occupants. One was an extremely short man, no more than 150 centimetres in height, but built like a power lifter. Though his height certainly placed him within the dwarf range, there was nothing out of proportion. If you put him in an empty room, with nothing around him to indicate scale, you'd presume he was of normal stature until you got close.

His uniform was the same as Romiwero's, but without the sword and there was no gold-wire ornamentation around his cap peak. The three gold rings around his sleeves had scarlet bands between them, and Sebastian wondered if the significance was the same. Before he put his cap on, Sebastian had noticed that he either shaved his head, or was completely bald.

The other man was a good bit taller, perhaps 183 centimetres, and powerfully built. He was darker than the other two, but not black. More of a Mediterranean type, Sebastian thought. His hair was a very light brown, cut short, and he also wore a similar uniform. But his trousers were the same shade of dark blue as his jacket, and his boots were of a different style, more like Wellingtons than riding boots. His belt buckle was rectangular and appeared to be brass rather than gold. His cap device was smaller, also brass, and had a circular brass backing. Instead of cuff rings, he wore a rectangular patch of sky-blue velvet on either side of his collar. The patch was bordered by gold wire, and a gold disk was centred in the patch.

The strangest thing about the man was his face, for his forehead was strong and rather square, with a very pronounced brow, yet he had a rather weak chin.

Captain Romiwero did the introductions. The short fellow was introduced as Surgeon Commander Grekim Vordik, *Warrior*'s chief medical officer. Sebastian smiled at that, for it seemed to confirm his speculation about the man's rank insignia. The tall chap was Arik Brynnazen, *Warrior*'s master at arms, and by rank a Commissioned Warrant Officer.

"Do you do any medical research aboard this station?" Vordik asked.

"Some. Why?"

"Bacteria, Viruses. You'll notice we're wearing these masks?"

"Of course."

"They're for protection from microorganisms," he explained. "The atmosphere here is obviously breathable, but we don't want to breath in anything contagious. It's been a very long time since the last time this ship was here, and no doubt the germs have continued to evolve, so it's very likely we'd have limited or no immunity to a lot of diseases. If you have blood and tissue samples aboard, I can analyse them and come up with vaccines."

"I'm not sure if we do. I'd have to ask our doctor."

"I'd be very grateful if you would, Captain," the doctor said.

Sebastian floated over to an intercom panel and pressed a button. "Doctor to airlock echo," he said.

"Thank you," Vordik said. "If I can run proper samples through my equipment, I can create vaccines for just about anything your crew members are immune to." He smiled. "Of course, I also create vaccines to immunise you against anything *we* might be carrying, though your risk is likely lower than our own."

"I'm not sure I understand."

"Any germs we carry are likely to be less evolved forms of the ones you're normally exposed to. There's a fairly strong chance you'll already be immune to most of them."

An attractive, middle-aged blond woman floated into the airlock. "Are these the visitors?" she asked.

"This is our doctor," Sebastian said, "Joanna Phillips."

Phillips was staring at Brynnazen. "Wow," she said.

Brynnazen raised an eyebrow. Did this doctor see something Vordik had missed?

"Uh, sorry. It's just that you look…"

Sebastian broke in. He had a feeling he knew what she was going to say and this was no time for possible diplomatic kerfuffles. "Jo, Doctor Vordik wants to know if we have blood and tissue samples aboard. He wants to make vaccines for their crew. I guess he feels they might be vulnerable to human diseases."

Romiwero looked at him curiously. "Well, naturally…"

"Naturally?"

"The Yanks are going to hate this," Phillips said. "Our first real contact with space aliens and they look just like us. I suppose President Gordon will claim this is proof of Jesus or something."

"If he does, it will just confirm he's an idiot," Jenkins said, "but more likely he'll just say the whole thing is a hoax." She had no use for the people who ruled her home country now, which was why she'd escaped to the UK when the opportunity presented itself.

"Aliens?" This was Brynnazen.

"Well, you're not from here, are you?" Sebastian said.

He looked at him as if he were simple-minded. It had been a very long time, but still…

"The Doctor isn't," Romiwero said. "He was born on New Barzak, but Arik and I were both born on this planet. It's changed a lot since we've been gone, but this is where we're from."

"So, you're human?"

"Yes." She shook her head slightly and smiled. "There are billions of us, scattered around the cosmos."

"You three look very different, though," Phillips said. "From each other, I mean."

"I suppose we are," Vordik said. "I am what we call *Weehti magnim barzakinu.* That is, a member of the *Weehti*, you'd say human, species, the *magnim* subspecies, and further evolved to live comfortably on New Barzak, which has a greater mass, and so stronger gravity, than this planet. It favours a shorter, stronger human type.

The captain is of the *magnim* subspecies, as, I rather suspect, are you. Arik is *Weehti gornim*, a different human subspecies, also native to this planet."

"Holy shit," Phillips said. "So he actually *is* Neanderthal. I guess the archaeologists were wrong."

"Wrong about what?" Brynnazen asked.

"They claimed you couldn't talk."

What an odd idea, he thought. "I most certainly can. When I have something to say."

"I can see that. But there's still one problem."

"What's that?" Romiwero asked.

"Neanderthals have been extinct for something like 35,000 years. So how could you have come from a future where *he* wouldn't exist?"

Romiwero looked at the other two, then at Phillips. "Future?"

"That ship of yours," Sebastian said, "is far, far beyond our technological capabilities. The fact that you've obvious got something built into your boots that allows you to stand on the deck instead of floating is beyond our capabilities. It'll likely be many years before we can do that sort of thing, and as we are the most advanced civilisation that's existed on this planet so far, it follows that you have to be from the future."

"We don't come from the future," Romiwero said. "Time travel isn't possible, except in the usual direction. By ship's time, we've been in space for fifteen years. Much of that was spent in jumpspace, though, and jumpspace is, well, a very odd place. According to our calendar, we left in our year 525." She smiled wryly. "That's dated from the foundation of the Gehunite Empire, of course, which was 1817 on the previous calendar, or roughly four and half billion something on a planetary scale. Going by stellar positions, we would have left here 86,985 years ago."

"I'm much younger than they are," Vordik offered. "I joined the ship at New Barzak two years ago by ship time, so I've only been hopping about in space for roughly 12,000 earth years."

"I'm having a hard time with this," Sebastian said. "A civilisation advanced enough to build a ship like yours should have been advanced enough to still be around. How could it have disappeared? As far as we know, at the time you say you left here, the only people who existed were living in caves, or hiding in trees. They wouldn't even start growing crops for another 75,000 years or so."

"No," Romiwero said, "we were mostly living in cities. And we'd been raising crops and animals for a very long time by then. But I think I can guess what happened."

"What?"

"Emthemlu is missing. And so is Arzucalda."

Sebastian looked at Phillips and Jenkins, who both shook their heads. "No idea what either of those would be," he said.

"Emthemlu was the other moon. Arzucalda was a large island, more or less in the middle of the ocean below us right now. If they're both missing, it does rather suggest how an entire civilisation could have vanished and humans regressed to earlier stages of development."

"How big was this other moon?"

"Relatively small. About 60 kilometres at the widest point. It wasn't even massive enough to have started to become round. It orbited much closer than Nakli, too."

"Nakli?" Jenkins asked.

"The moon that's still there."

"Ah."

"We just call it the moon," Sebastian said. "Because it's the only one, so it doesn't really need a name."

"There used to be two, so it did back then."

"If a 60-kilometre moon deorbited," Sebastian said, "it would certainly be enough to destroy a civilisation. It would probably be enough to cause the extinction of nearly everything. The asteroid that killed off the dinosaurs was only about 10 kilometres. It's surprising anything at all survived that large an impact."

"Emthemlu was larger," Romiwero suggested, "but it wouldn't have been travelling nearly as fast. It orbited at about 130,000 kilometres. The impact certainly would have been devastating, but the effect might not have been much greater than the other, which, coming from deep space, would have been travelling much, much faster."

"There's been an ice age since then, too," Jenkins mentioned.

"Which would have scoured away any evidence of an old civilisation at least as far south as the glaciers made it," Sebastian admitted.

"What do you plan to do here?" Phillips asked.

Romiwero smiled. "We've been away for fifteen years. My crew could do with a bit of leave. Even if their homes are long gone, this is still where most of us came from."

"How many of you are there?"

"Three hundred twenty-six," Romiwero replied.

"May we presume," Sebastian asked, "that you have no plans on trying to take over?"

"Take over what?"

"This planet."

"We have a very strict non-interference policy," the captain replied. "Our entire civilisation is gone, and an unrelated one has replaced it. So far as we're concerned, this planet now falls into the same category as any inhabited alien world. You've developed your own civilisation and culture, and we're required to respect that. Unless you're doing something horrible, like eating each other. We do try to discourage that sort of thing if we happen to run across it."

"No," Jenkins said, "we don't do that anymore."

Vordik looked at her curiously. "Did you? Recently?"

"I think it was completely stopped by about 150 years ago," Sebastian said. "Except for a few religious holdouts." He saw that his visitors were looking at him curiously. "There were a couple of remote cultures that believed honouring the dead meant eating them. These were relatives who died naturally," he added, "not people they killed."

Vordik shook his head. "That sounds remarkably stupid."

"It was," Phillips said. "Caused some very strange diseases."

"I'd imagine it would."

"Are there any other inhabited planets out there?" Jenkins asked. "Ones where the inhabitants are *not* human?"

"Lots of them," Vordik said. "Besides the human colonies, there are a great many planets where intelligent life evolved, and most of it doesn't resemble us very much."

"Such as?"

"Grikna," Brynnazen suggested. "That's another space-faring culture, and they're reptiles."

"Scary," Phillips said.

"Why? They're nice enough."

"Reptiles are, well, cold blooded, and we've always presumed they lack emotions, so they'd also lack compassion. And there's that whole eating your food while it's still alive factor."

"Barzakite reptiles are like that, to be sure," Vordik said. "But on Grikna they've evolved a bit more. They're bipedal, for one thing, and they no longer have their tails. With intelligence came a more evolved brain, with a more developed frontal cortex. And by the time you've developed enough to build tools, and certainly by the time you're ready to start exploring space, you've generally developed the ability to cooperate and stopped killing each other."

Sebastian and Phillips looked at each other. Earthlings had been going into space since the 1960s, but there were still far too many people down there who thought killing their fellows was a grand way to get their ideas across.

"What's Barzakite?" Sebastian asked.

"From Barzak," Brynnazen said. "It's what the planet was called when we lived here."

"Morshivnites," Romiwero suggested. "Now they are *very* different from us."

"Not outside their conception, though," Brynnazen said. "You remember that entertainment the crew enjoyed so much?"

"Yes, very much like Morshivnites."

The platform crew were becoming confused again. "Entertainment?" Sebastian asked.

Romiwero nodded. "That's how we programmed our language modules. While we were waiting to make contact, our ship's computers were uploading every bit of electronic communication we could. That included a lot of your entertainment offerings. Motion pictures, television shows, and so forth. Early on, the crew particularly liked one called *Galaxy Quest*, because there was enough action that they could enjoy it without understanding exactly what was being said. The friendly aliens in that looked very much like Morshivnites when their disguises were turned off."

"They're cephalopods?" Phillips asked. As old as that movie was, she still watched it herself from time to time.

"They are. Brilliant technicians, too. I'm surprised you've never encountered them. They've been exploring space a lot longer than we have, and they certainly know where this planet is."

"Most likely decided this place wasn't ready yet," Brynnazen said. "Just as we would have, had we not been from here in the first place. Anyone monitoring electronic emissions from here would no doubt have decided this planet wasn't civilised enough to contact based on what they saw. After all, how long did it take *us* to eliminate war?"

"You'd stopped having wars?" Sebastian asked.

"The last was the War of 382. At least, the last before we left."

Phillips looked pointedly at Romiwero. "If you don't have wars any more, why are you wearing a sword?"

"It's a part of the uniform. This visit to your space station is an official contact between governments, so the protocol is to wear dress uniform." She smiled. "The working uniform, I'm happy to say, does *not* include a sword. They tend to get in the way."

"True enough," Sebastian said. "The few times I've had to wear mine, I always thought it was a damned nuisance." He laughed, thinking of more than one wedding when he'd have preferred mufti. "After all, it's not as if there was much need to repel boarders at the MOD. Yours is rather nicer than mine, I must say."

"It was originally my great-grandfather's. The design was a little different by the time I graduated the Academy in 512, but regulations allow the wearing of family swords. You *could* fight with this one, if you ever needed to. Most of the ones the new officers were being issued by then weren't strong enough for combat. They just looked good."

"Same now," Sebastian said. "Mine has a stainless-steel blade. Fine for tableware, but too brittle for a proper sword blade."

"Master Byrnnazen's is actually the most impressive," Romiwero said. "But he rarely wears it. Warrant officers aren't required to."

"It belonged to one of my ancestors," he said. "She used it back at the very beginning of the Empire, more than 500-years-old. Beautifully made, and very well balanced, but it's not really a proper warrant officer's sword. It's not really a *naval* sword, for that matter."

"You're Navy?" He'd more or less presumed that, based almost entirely on the resemblance of their uniforms to contemporary naval fashion, but hadn't thought to confirm it.

"The Navy was the logical choice as the operating force once we moved into space," Romiwero said. "We've always been the explorers. Spaceships are a lot like the old naval vessels, with big crews and obviously very self-contained. The Air Force tried to muscle in during the early days of space exploration, but Air Force officers simply didn't have the experience they needed to run big ships. Even the biggest aeroplanes never had more than a handful of crew members."

"This is all very interesting," Vordik said, "but getting those samples is probably more important just now. I have an entire crew that needs immunising, unless you want them to spend their whole leave aboard ship."

Sebastian nodded. "Jo, why don't we move this to the sick bay."

"This way."

Used to the zero-gravity environment as he was, and able to move quite rapidly around the platform, Sebastian was a bit envious of the Barzakites' ability to walk around normally. Even after Romiwero had explained the technology, he still didn't understand it. He'd been thinking magnetic boots, but apparently that wasn't it. Some mechanism in the soles of their boots was capable of manipulating gravity.

At Sebastian's suggestion, Romiwero had left her sword in her travel pod. That meant they could also leave their caps, saving them the trouble of carrying them. Fine with her. She almost never wore the sword, and had clipped it to her belt today only because protocol required it.

Romiwero found the impromptu tour fascinating. It was a little hard to believe they hadn't come up with some sort of artificial gravity, though. The technology wasn't that complicated, or so it seemed to her. Technology is rarely complicated once you've figured out how to do something. It's figuring it out in the first place that's difficult. Internal combustion engines and electric motors were both ridiculously simple devices, working on very basic principles, and both had developed at an astonishing rate once the first example was demonstrated. But getting to that first example had taken centuries, and during most of those centuries it had simply not occurred to anyone that such things were even possible.

You can't invent an electric motor if you have no idea what electricity is, or how to create or transport it.

"This is our sick bay," Phillips announced. It was a small, carefully organised space. Along one bulkhead were arranged four berths, stacked much higher than would have been practical on earth. In the weightless environment of the platform medical personnel didn't have to stand on the deck to treat their patients.

Another bulkhead was devoted to lab equipment. Storage compartments, cold, hot, and ambient, were arranged along another. Some test equipment was fastened to the inner surface of a circular recess in one bulkhead. While there was no effective artificial gravity on the platform, the inner ring of the recess could be rotated like a low-speed centrifuge to create a virtual "down" necessary for certain tests.

Phillips opened a refrigerated cabinet and removed a number of sealed test tubes. She also collected a number of phials from the refrigerator, and more from an ambient cabinet.

"These are your samples," Phillips said. "None of these come from anyone who's actually sick, by the way. We take samples monthly, as a part of the general medical protocol. The phials contain vaccines. I presume there's no need to develop new versions if they already exist, right?"

Vordik nodded. "I'll want to study them, perhaps modify them slightly, but that should be a great time saver."

Phillips put everything into a travel container. She went to close it, but Vordik stopped her. "Before you close that, if I may…"

He removed a small, oblong device from a pouch on his belt and held it over the open container. The device looked like a single piece of smooth plastic, but Vordik pressed his thumb on the upper surface and a blue glow was emitted from one end. He moved the device over the container for a few seconds, until it emitted a low tone.

"You may seal it now," he said, replacing the device in his pouch.

"What is that?" Phillips asked, though she was sure she knew the answer.

"A disinfection device. It kills any surface bacteria and viruses. The emissions are non-penetrating, so it doesn't affect the samples. It just insures there are no pathogens on the containers. We'll go through the same process, on a larger scale, when we return to the ship."

"Which we should do," Romiwero said. "The doctor needs to get to work on the immunisations. And we'll need to make contact with your various governments about leave."

"I hope you're carrying a few diplomats," Sebastian said. "It's going to be interesting dealing with all of those countries."

"How many are there now?"

"I'm not sure. Several hundred?"

"Nothing ever gets easier, does it?" Brynnazen said.

"How many countries were there when you left?"

"Four," Romiwero replied. "Gehun, Kaam, Callaa, and Feria."

"That's all?"

"The Gehunite Empire accounted for most of the planet," Romiwero explained. "The War of 382 ended the consolidation period, when Arzucalda was brought into the Empire. Arzucalda had been the only serious rival for power, and if they'd been less ambitious there'd have been no war and probably no consolidation."

"Kinmon[8] wanted a war," Brynnazen said. "He wanted a war, and he wanted to expand Arzucalda's own empire. But he was foolish. He thought if he staged coordinated attacks against our Navy, put it out of action first, his own forces would be able to do whatever they liked. He made a couple of mistakes, though."

Sebastian was interested. It reminded him of more recent history, when Imperial Japan had tried the same thing. "Such as?"

"He launched coordinated attacks against the main naval bases, and these proved to be as devastating as he'd hoped. But his pilots went after the big ships, and didn't pay that much attention to the submarines. That was a major error." He gestured at Romiwero. "Her great-great-grandmother was weapons officer in an earlier *Warrior*, under Commander Maniah, when that boat penetrated Talim Bay a few weeks after the attacks and destroyed half a dozen Arzucaldan warships, including the battleship *Arzucalda*. Now, the *Arzucalda* wasn't a new ship, to be sure, and wasn't even seaworthy at the time, with her reactors being refuelled, but the psychological effect was huge.

"They made an even bigger mistake when they attacked Suimehreon Harbour with a carrier task force. It's still a well-known story."

"It was taught at the Naval College," Romiwero said. "A reminder to never get too confident that you know everything."

"Not part of our history," Sebastian said.

"The Arzucaldan admiral assumed his task force was alone and sent all of his planes off on the attack. He was wrong. One of our battleships was on a training cruise about thirty miles away. By the time any of the planes returned, with their bomb racks empty, all but one of the carriers had been sunk and the last was running away as fast as she could. The pilots had to ditch, and the surviving carrier found a submarine waiting for her a few hours later."

---

8   Alver Kinmon (332–386), Arzucaldan dictator 372–385, executed by hanging 7th Ninemonth 386. Elected Arzucaldan Chief Minister in 372 on a platform of eliminating L'Mikist influence in Arzucalda, which he blamed for the country's defeat in the War of 361. Held responsible for the murder of 874,000 Arzucaldan L'Mikists.

"A battleship destroyed a carrier task force?" The very idea sounded vaguely blasphemous to Sebastian. It was accepted as naval gospel that air power would always prevail over gunnery.

"Pure luck. If he'd known the battleship was there, he'd have kept some planes back to deal with her[9]."

♦   ♦   ♦

The outer door opened, and the three pods emerged. Romiwero found herself wondering how well this was going to go. Sebastian had been friendly enough, but he wasn't a politician. Even as a naval officer, he was more of a scientist than a fighter. From what he'd said, there hadn't been a real war in decades. The military's primary job now seemed to be making sure things stayed that way. That apparently meant research, with very little in the way of force projection.

There was a new colony on Kinzor—or Mars, as it was now called—and she couldn't help feeling a little sorry for the colonists. Human beings were highly adaptable, but adaptations favoured environmental conditions. Vordik was short and powerful because his family had lived on New Barzak for millennia, and New Barzak had a mass of 1.84 compared to old Barzak. The stronger gravity favoured people who were shorter, more compact, and much stronger. The Martian colonists would undoubtedly evolve in precisely the opposite way, growing taller and less muscular in the lower gravity, and likely losing bone density as well. It had looked to be happening even in the relatively brief life of the old colony.

The old Martian colony was unknown to earth's present population, and doubtless had vanished shortly after Emthemlu destroyed Arzucalda. The platform's crew had also been unaware there had ever been a colony on Nakli.

A time would no doubt come when the Martian settlers could no longer comfortably visit their original home planet. Romiwero always felt that way when they called at New Barzak. Getting around felt like she was carrying an extra person. That was why she'd generally preferred to deal with the colonists by inviting them aboard the ship. It was much easier for someone to function in a weaker gravity than a stronger one.

Then there was Barzak—Earth now—itself. Diplomacy would be the key. This was no longer their planet. The Empire was long

---

9   See "Element of Surprise" in *Blackout & Other Stories*, © 2015, J.T. McDaniel, Riverdale Books, Dublin, Ohio

gone, so long gone that no one had even known it ever existed. New countries had sprung up, along with many more languages. Technology could handle the languages, of course. There was no point in trying to learn any of them. They wouldn't be there that long, and if they ever came back again it was unlikely that any current tongues would still be spoken.

She went into her suite, closing the door behind her. It was the one place she could always retreat to. Crew accommodations aboard *Warrior* were designed for comfort. The ship was so big, and the crew so small relative to her size, that even the lowliest apprentice stoker had private quarters that would have earned the envy of a fleet admiral a hundred years earlier.

Not that there were any apprentice stokers aboard now. After fifteen years' ship's time, the lowest rank was leading seaman, and the majority of the enlisted crew were either petty officers or chief petty officers. The only reason there were still leading seamen was that five of them were born trouble makers and kept being disrated as soon as they were promoted.

It was even worse for the officers. Romiwero would remain forever a captain. That was fine, but it also meant no one else was getting promoted unless she happened to suddenly drop dead. There were five commanders under her, all of them department heads, as well as Commander Oshrorehno, *The* Commander, her second in command. There were also fourteen lieutenant commanders. The rest were all lieutenants.

The last sub-lieutenant had been promoted eight years ago. Or perhaps it was 40,000 years ago? Relative time in jumpspace was confusing, no matter how carefully you considered it.

She could, to be sure, take a promotion to commodore, which would allow Oshrorehno to step up to captain. But it would mean becoming a *retired* commodore, and she wasn't ready for that just yet. Retirement meant becoming a passenger. Not yet.

Her suite consisted of eight rooms, on two decks, and internally was an exact duplicate of the old stone house, overlooking Tufaria Bay, where she had grown up. The house where generations of Romiweros had first seen salt water from the balcony off the master bedroom. It had been a beautiful view, and aboard ship there was still a balcony and still the same gorgeous view. Even after all these years aboard, she still found it nearly impossible to tell that the view was a hologram and not real. It was always night in deep space, but the view from the balcony, or through the windows, or from the flagstone terrace off the living room, reflected the variations in a normal 30-hour day.

A lot of the furniture was *from* the house. Some pieces, like the big wardrobe in her bedroom, dated back to the earliest days of the Empire. Some of it was newer. The bed had been purchased just before they left. The mattress was even newer, manufactured aboard ship only two years ago to replace the worn-out original.

Everyone had known *Warrior* wouldn't return within the lifetime of anyone they left behind. Or within the lifetime of any of their descendants, for that matter. At least, no descendants who would remember them, or have any knowledge that they had ever existed. She presumed she had living relatives even now. She also presumed she'd never know who they were. Because of this, the builders had done their best to duplicate places where each crew member was most comfortable. The ship's corridors and work spaces were utilitarian. The living quarters were anything but.

Going into her bedroom, Romiwero stripped down to her underwear and pulled a working uniform from the wardrobe.

She hung up her dress uniform. She presumed she'd wear it several more times during this visit. The highly-polished dress boots also went into the wardrobe, inverted on custom trees. Low quarter shoes, with non-slip soles and heels, were worn with working dress by everyone except the doctor and several other New Barzakites in the crew. They wore gravity boots adjusted to duplicate the heavier gravity of their home world, except in their quarters, where the gravity setting was always higher.

When she had changed, she left her suite and walked the short distance to the bridge.

"Captain on the bridge!"

"Carry on." Romiwero walked to her chair and sat down. The view-screen was displaying an oblique view of the planet as it rotated beneath them. They were orbiting west to east, and just now passing over the terminator into the daylight hemisphere.

At the moment, they were over water. What was now called the Atlantic Ocean, according to Captain Sebastian. The Eastern Sea, as it once was.

The new name came from the vanished Arzucalda, renamed Atlantis by Greek historians, and apparently until today generally written off as a myth.

Being blasted into oblivion by a falling moon wasn't quite the same thing as being destroyed by a pack of angry gods, of course, but no doubt any difference was lost on the inhabitants, who were just as abruptly slaughtered either way. Their story had been preserved, coming down to what modern-day earthlings called "classical" times as a legend. The why and how of it hadn't.

Lieutenant Marina Fehmadaatin came out of the lift, carrying a message form she had snagged from a signals yeoman on her way to the bridge. "Communication from the surface," she reported, handing over the form.

The signal had been received in English and translated by the ship's computer.

"The King of England and his Prime Minister would like to meet us," the captain said. "Someone find out where that is."

Fehmadaatin moved to her navigation console and worked on the terminal for a moment. A map was thrown up on the view-screen. "Here, the navigator reported. "Off the coast of Rantos."

"Right. Staff meeting in my ready room in ten minutes," Romiwero ordered. "All senior staff. And, Lieutenant Fehmadaatin…"

"Captain?"

"Give my compliments to the ambassador, and ask her to join us for this. Tell her that what we presumed has been confirmed. She is, indeed, the last, and we will henceforth take her new station into account."

Fehmadaatin smiled. "She won't care, Captain."

Romiwero nodded. "Nevertheless. We have to observe the protocol, don't we? I'll see the both of you in ten minutes."

Thirteen

THE REPORTERS SHOWED UP ON THE SECOND MORNING. After scolding the unknown broadcaster, Sara had naturally reported the exchange to the FCC. Her original intention of saying nothing to the government had given way to the natural instinct to stay out of trouble. Once she started talking, they'd know anyway, so at that point filing a report was the safest thing to do. She didn't expect anything to come of it. Someone was on the wrong frequency, she had told them to stop, here's the report. She'd had a suspicion who it might have been, but she left that out of the report. She wasn't sure if believing in space aliens was allowed.

The reporters were annoying, but it wasn't that hard to discourage them. After she said, "I don't know anything else" a few times they got bored and went away to bother someone else.

Even so, she had a brief day or two of fame. "The Girl Who Talked to the Aliens!" It was nonsense, she thought. Even if that was what she'd done, there had been no conversation. She'd just told them to shut up.

The FBI rang the doorbell just after noon on Friday, 5th April. There were two of them. They presented their credentials, identified themselves as Special Agents Sylvia Carruthers and George Morris, from FBI Headquarters in Washington, and asked to speak to Sara.

Joanne Ellsworth led them into the living room, pointed them to the couch, and went upstairs to get her daughter. What in the world had Sara done now? she wondered. Reporters were one thing, but now the FBI?

"What?" Sara called, from inside her room, when her mother knocked.

"The FBI is here. They want to talk to you."

The door opened. "The who?"

"The FBI. From Washington."

Sara blinked. This was a little scary. There was an FBI office in Denver. Why bring in agents from the other side of the country?

"Why are they here?"

"They didn't say." Joanne frowned. Too bad Art was at work, she thought. He'd have a better idea what to do.

"Come on," she said. "You'd better go talk to them."

Sara looked over her shoulder at her room. Was there anything incriminating in there? Her computer was logged into the Internet, through an approved provider, and connected to the high school server that hosted her assigned class work. Nothing to worry about there. All the books on her shelves were on the approved list. The questionable ones were in the attic, tucked away in an old steamer trunk that didn't appear to have been opened in years. There was an art to removing dust, and there was a slightly more difficult art to adding it.

Her Ham radio was turned off. If anyone wanted to turn it on, it was tuned to the same 80-metre CW band she normally worked. Shouldn't be any problems with that, either.

Was it because I talked on that channel? she wondered. Then she shook her head. No, the FCC would follow up on that, not the FBI. She'd reported it, and the reason. The inspector who'd taken the report hadn't indicated there'd be a problem. The other guy, the one who started sending voice on a code-only channel, was the one who'd get in trouble. The inspector was sure of that.

Closing the door behind her, she followed her mother down the stairs.

Special Agent Carruthers, Sara quickly decided, was putting far too much effort into making herself look plain. The woman had her blond hair pulled back into a tight bun. She wore no makeup, and an ill-fitting olive-green suit.

Her partner did most of the talking.

"You were on the radio this past Monday evening. Is that right?"

Sara nodded. "Most nights."

"Who were you talking to?"

"I wasn't talking."

"You just said you were on the radio."

"That's right."

"Then how is it you weren't talking. What were you doing, just listening?"

"We don't talk on that channel. Voice isn't allowed. We used Morse code."

"Okay, fine. But you *were* connecting with someone, right?"

"That's right."

"What were you, uh, Morse coding about?"

"Fly fishing."

"Fly fishing?" Morris said.

"I like fishing. We were discussing fly tying. He kept trying to convince me that wet flies would be more effective than the dry flies I usually make."

"Who's he?"

"I'd have to check the log. We don't always give our names, just our call signs. He had a VA5 call sign, and those are assigned to Hams in Saskatchewan."

Morris nodded. He knew this already. The National Security Agency kept track of all amateur radio operations. What he was interested in was whether this girl was going to report everything she'd done.

"What happened just after 10 o'clock that evening?"

"Someone had been using voice on that channel. That's not allowed. After a couple times, I got annoyed and told them to stop."

"Did they?"

"For a while. Then they started again, saying something else."

"What?"

"What?

"What did they say?" Morris asked.

"Oh." Sara shrugged. "I don't know. It wasn't in English."

"What did you say?"

"I told them to stop it."

"Anything since then?"

"After that, they started saying something else I couldn't understand."

"Did you know they were space aliens? Or someone pretending to be?"

"I just figured it was somebody trying to play a practical joke. I didn't really connect it to anything until after the TV started reporting on that explosion out in space."

"What do you know about that?" Morris asked.

"Not much. Just what I saw on TV, or heard on the radio. That there was a giant explosion way out beyond Saturn, and that it didn't pose any threat."

"What are your thoughts on that?"

"I'm not sure I have any. I mean, isn't it just some elaborate practical joke? That's what they've been saying on the news. I suppose the woman on the radio could be part of that, right?"

"How do you figure?" Apparently, Carruthers actually *could* talk.

"It stands to reason, doesn't it? If you're going to fake the arrival of space aliens, you'd want to fake communications from them, too, wouldn't you?"

Carruthers nodded. "I suppose you would," she said.

The two Federal agents stayed for another twenty minutes. They just kept asking the same questions over and over. They'd change the wording slightly, but the same questions kept coming up. What do you think? Who was on the radio? Why did you call the FCC? Why *didn't* you call us?"

Eventually, they seemed satisfied, if not exactly happy, with the answers and went on their way.

Fourteen

PRIME MINISTER SIR CHARLES VICKERS had never been this nervous in his life. Not even on that day, 22 years ago, when he'd asked Rick Morgan to marry him. He was then a newly elected MP from a minor district in Lincolnshire. Rick was a recently qualified barrister, with chambers in Gray's Inn.

It had all worked out rather well, bar the occasional annoyance of Rick's Uncle Geoff, who liked to pop in from time to time to tell them they were going to hell with all the other poofters.

That had been scary. The proposal, not Uncle Geoff, who was obviously a bit of a nutter. Rather like Will Gordon, the American president, who had been on television a few hours earlier reassuring his country's citizens that there really was no alien spaceship in orbit, and the whole thing was just an elaborate hoax being perpetrated by the liberal-socialist atheists who were continuing their conspiracy to destroy Christian America. A strange assertion, considering the ship could be seen from the ground.

Normally, fundamentalist idiots like Gordon didn't bother him, except this was a fundamentalist idiot who controlled a huge military and an arsenal of nuclear weapons. Fortunately, Vickers rarely had to deal directly with the man. When he did, it was most often electronically.

He liked Americans, generally, and there were a lot of them living in the UK these days. Mostly refugees, gays, atheists, Jews who didn't care to be second-class citizens, but also didn't feel like moving to Israel, and people who just couldn't keep their mouths shut and took the constitutional guarantee of free speech a bit more seriously than their government.

A lot of scientists, too. Once the government had started dictating the expected results of research, much of the scientific community had decided they wanted to live somewhere else. His housekeeper was an American, a bright young lady who had come to the UK for an abortion after being raped by her step-father and decided to stay in England, rather than risk execution at home if the wrong people found out what she'd done.

The spaceship scared him. Vickers had dealt with heads of state, lots of them, including his own king, but never with the representatives of a worldwide government that hadn't existed in over 86,000 years. How was that supposed to work? They could make the technical argument that they were the rightful rulers, after all.

He didn't think they would, to be sure. The Gehunites had made it quite clear that all they were interested in was a chance to visit their home planet for a while, a few months at most, and then they'd be off to deep space again for a few thousand more years. They'd also said they planned to do some recruiting, if anyone wanted to join their crew, but that hadn't been generally announced yet. Vickers presumed they'd have no shortage of applicants once it was.

But keeping earth's recent history in mind, the Gehunites had also made sure that governmental leaders were aware of just how much firepower *Warrior* was packing.

"Take everything you've fired or blown up in the last 400 years of fighting," was the analogy, "and then multiply that by a hundred." That sort of thing really did make him worry about Gordon. One of the earliest official communications had been to warn the Gehunites that the Americans, at least the ones running the country, were religious fanatics whose most fervent wish was to see the end of the world, believing it would lead to the Second Coming.

The Gehunite captain had assured Vickers that, if anything was launched at them from the United States, they'd simply blow up the missile and send a firmly worded diplomatic note. "They really can't do any damage to us," she told him on the video link. "You should be more worried about them damaging your own space platform, considering we're parked right next to it."

Warrior wouldn't be landing in London this afternoon, of course, and not just because their fanatical television watching had included the old *Star Trek* prequel series *Enterprise*, with its episode featuring a treacherous alternative Cochrane as a contrast to the friendly one in *First Contact*. Not much point in pulling a surprise takeover bid if the ship remained in orbit and out of reach.

From what the Gehunites had told them, *Warrior* had been built in orbit, and had never been intended to land on any planet. Vickers got the distinct impression that she wasn't even capable of it. The ship was just too damn big, for one thing. They would send some sort of shuttle with the captain and other dignitaries. It made things simpler; the shuttle dimensions they'd given meant it would be small enough to land in the palace quadrangle.

Warrior had been in orbit for a week now, and Downing Street was beginning to resemble an international hotel. Grigori was staying there, as he was a friend, and not just the President of Russia. Logically, he should have stayed at the embassy, but he liked Vickers a lot more than he liked his own ambassador. On one occasion, he had suggested that the reason the man had held the post for over a decade was that, in addition to being a skilled diplomat, it kept the arrogant bastard away from Moscow.

"Stalin would have just liquidated him," Grigori had said. "Unfortunately, we haven't been able to do that sort of thing since that lunatic in the early 21st century. And *he* couldn't do it openly. So we give him a nice job that keeps him away as much as possible. Besides, we have telephones now. Ambassadors are just messenger boys handing over official letters. If I really need anything, I'll call you directly."

London was presently full of heads of state. The King naturally took precedence, not only because the Gehunite shuttle was scheduled to land in the courtyard of Buckingham Palace, but also because, having come to the throne twenty years ago, he was the most senior. The King was now standing beside the Prime Minister, wearing the uniform of an admiral of the fleet, with his Queen standing quietly beside him.

Vickers suspected the Queen was looking forward to this rather more eagerly than her husband. She had a degree in astrophysics from Cambridge, and had been working for the UK Space Agency when her future husband, then a newly-commissioned sub-lieutenant in the Royal Navy assigned to the Sagan Space Platform for a six-month tour, found himself under her tutelage for the first three weeks.

Those three weeks of instruction had, thus far, resulted in a twenty-eight-year marriage and four children. The throne was quite secure for another generation, though there was some question as to whether the dynastic name would remain Windsor when the Princess of Wales ascended the throne as Victoria II. For the first time since the 1920s, the first-born of the then future king had been a girl. It was also the first time this had happened since the 1689 Bill of Rights and the 1701 Settlement Act were amended in 2015, changing succession from oldest male child of the monarch to the oldest child, regardless of sex.

Vickers dismissed the thought. The king was a very healthy 50, and would likely remain on the throne for another thirty to forty years. Poor Victoria was likely to be old enough to collect a pension before she came to the throne.

The Emperor of Japan was also in the group waiting just inside the palace vestibule. Technically, an emperor outranked a king, but Morihito had only ascended the throne two years ago. The emperor was wearing a morning suit, which wasn't nearly as impressive as the king's naval uniform. Japanese emperors hadn't worn any sort of military uniform since the end of World War II, and that was 181 years ago. The only exception had been Morihito's father, who had never expected to become emperor and opted for a naval career. But his elder brother had died childless, and so the throne had passed to him by default.

"Just about time," an aide said.

"Thank you," the king replied. As head of state, he would make the official greeting, once the Prime Minister introduced him. It was a ceremonial job, and that was why the UK still had a king, wasn't it?

The politicians, five presidents, three kings, one prince, four prime ministers, and one emperor, walked out onto a long Axminster runner just outside the palace door. This was placed close to the building, and ran along the wall. The idea was to leave as much room as possible in the enclosed quadrangle open. They knew how big the shuttle would be, but not how close to the landing spot it was safe to stand.

It was highly unusual to arrange an arrival in this way. Normally, the king would greet important visitors, including heads of state, in the audience room, inside the palace. This outdoor arrival ceremony was partly because of the large number of foreign dignitaries involved. To an even greater degree, it was also prompted by curiosity. Everyone wanted to see the shuttle touch down.

A huge crowd had gathered along the Mall, which had taken on a rather festive look with all the national flags hoisted on the poles lining the street. Gehun's, a solid black swallowtail, seemed to add a sombre note to the display. According to the Gehunites, Salmik the Great, the founder of their empire, had originally been, of all things, a pirate, and the national flag was the same one he'd flown aboard his ships.

Precisely on time, the shuttle craft flew slowly over the Mall, to the delight of the crowd, and descended vertically into the palace quadrangle. It was an elongated rectangle, with a wedge-shaped nose, and a squared off fuselage, only slightly bigger than a large military helicopter. Vickers couldn't see what it landed on, whether it had wheels or some sort of stubby legs. For that matter, he wasn't entirely sure it had landed at all. He had the sense that it might be hovering a few centimetres above the paving.

A door opened in the side, steps were deployed, and the Gehunites stepped out.

The first was Romiwero, whom Vickers recognised from photographs Sebastian had sent from the platform, and from speaking to her via video link. She was wearing her dress uniform, and had added several medals.

Just behind her was a slender blond woman, with two gold rings around her cuffs. Vickers noticed that her sword was of a different pattern, with a wider scabbard, cross hilt and a heavy, round pommel. It looked vaguely medieval. Hadn't Sebastian said something about some of the Gehunites carrying family swords?

Behind the two women, six tall male officers exited the shuttle, forming up in two lines at the door. They wore the regulation dress uniform, but over their tunics they wore highly polished laminar armour, reminiscent of some of the old Roman designs, and steel helmets instead of caps.

"*Horik-TAHL!*" one of them snapped, and they all came to attention, including Romiwero and the other officer. "*Gii-naak!*" The Gehunites all drew their swords and brought them up to the salute, using the same form as the British military.

"Sorry to spring this on you," the king said to Vickers. "I was asked, as a personal favour, not to mention who was going to be aboard. Didn't want to feed the Fleet Street vultures, you know."

"I thought the redhead was the captain," Grigori whispered.

"She is," Vickers replied. He looked at the king and queen, both of them smiling benignly, as if they hadn't just pulled something on their head of government. "But apparently there's someone else aboard with a higher rank."

A youthful-looking woman stepped from the shuttle. She was quite tall, slender, and had very blond hair, worn long. Her uniform trousers had a gold stripe down the outer seam, and there was gold piping around the edges of her uniform blouse. The pattern was the same as the other officers, but the front of the jacket was covered with gold embroidery. She wore several jewelled badges on her breast, and a medal of some sort was suspended from a pale blue ribbon worn around her neck. Instead of the usual crown and crossed anchor device, her belt buckle displayed only the crown.

Her sword was a cross hilted type, the scabbard intricately worked with gold wire. The cuffs of her uniform jacket were adorned with elaborate gold wire embroidery instead of rank insignia. The standing collar was also intricately embroidered, outlining black collar tabs in the centre of which were gold-embroidered crowns. Instead of a cap, an intertwined band of three heavy gold wires, adorned with a single, oval-cut emerald, rested on her head.

She held a flat, narrow wooden box in her left hand as she walked slowly up to the group waiting on the thick carpet runner, followed by Romiwero and the other officer. The honour guard remained by the shuttle, their swords now sheathed.

The Prime Minister stepped forward. "Good afternoon," he said. "I am Sir Charles Vickers, Prime Minister of the United Kingdom. May I present his Most Gracious Majesty, William VI, of the United Kingdom of Great Britain and Northern Ireland and of his other Realms and Territories King, Head of the Commonwealth, Defender of the Faith, and her Majesty Queen Martha."

Captain Romiwero stepped forward now. "Your Majesties, Sir Charles, I am Kimewe Romiwero, Captain of Her Imperial Majesty's Starship *Warrior*. May I present to your Majesties Her Imperial Majesty, Felia VII, of Gehun, New Barzak, and Iridalazhik, Empress, Protector of Kaam, beloved of L'Mik."

The king now stepped forward. "Good afternoon," he said. "It is my great pleasure to welcome you, and your people, to the United Kingdom."

The woman nodded slightly, and the king smiled coolly, feeling oddly uncomfortable. He wondered if this was how 19th century Britons had felt when meeting that chubby, formidable ancestor of his who had given her name to an entire age.

Felia held out the flat wooden box. "This is a gift for you and your people, your Majesty," she said.

He took the box, hesitating over the latch. "May I?"

"I should be very disappointed if you did not."

He opened the latch and hinged back the lid. The inside was lined with blue velvet, and contained an exquisitely crafted miniature sword. It appeared to be a miniature version of the one she wore.

"Beautiful," the king said. It would end up in the public collection at the Tower, he decided. He wasn't a politician, and could keep state gifts if he wanted to, but he preferred to follow the same rules. In any case, the contents of the Tower were technically his personal property, so even if he put the sword on display it was still his.

"This is an exact miniature replica of the sword carried by my ancestor, Salmik the Great, at the foundation of the Empire. A gift from my country that once was, to your country that now is."

The actual sword had undoubtedly been destroyed, along with everything else, when Emthemlu crashed to earth all those thousands of years ago. A full-size duplicate was in her suite aboard *Warrior*. The one she wore was identical except in length. Salmik had been an unusually tall man. His sword was 30 centimetres longer than hers.

"Now," Vickers said, "we are expected to say a few words."

"Naturally."

The Prime Minister moved to the microphone. This, he decided, would be the most unusual speech in his career.

"It is my privilege today, as Prime Minister of the United Kingdom and delegated representative of the other countries of this planet, to welcome these visitors from, well, as I understand it, from our own ancient past..."

♦   ♦   ♦

Sir Andrew MacNaughton, chief protocol officer at Buckingham Palace, had been in a quandary from the moment the state visit was announced. First, there was the issue of precedence. The status of the visiting heads of state was easily dealt with, precedence normally going to those with the longest time in office. He was rather grateful that the American president had decided not to attend. It bothered his sense of propriety to give the position of honour to that man, though his now twenty-nine years in office would have demanded it. The man gave him the creeps.

There was an obvious question of just where the Gehunites themselves fitted into the picture. Originally, it had seemed straightforward. The ship's captain was a military officer, holding the rank of captain, but could also be viewed as a sort of ex-officio ambassador. Now, quite unexpectedly, it seemed they'd added an empress to the mix. The automatic translators the Gehunites wore had styled her 'imperial majesty,' which at least solved the question of what to call her.

Now he had to rearrange the seating. Who had reigned longer, he wondered, Felia or Morihito? As the only two of imperial rank, the longer reigning would be seated closest to the king. He thought this might be the empress, as one could argue her reign had begun when the last of her line had died on earth, thousands of years ago. On the other hand, the Gehunites might take a different view of such things and consider her reign to be shorter. Hadn't Captain Sebastian referred to *Warrior* as "His" Imperial Majesty's Starship, and Captain Romiwero just said "Her" Imperial Majesty's Starship. Unless Sebastian had simply got the pronoun wrong, it could be the change in style indicated a very recent change of monarch.

There was also the question of what to feed these people. Did Gehunites have dietary restrictions? Did their religion forbid eating something, or perhaps *require* eating something else? He wasn't even sure what sort of religion they had. If he served the wrong thing, would they be offended? Someone should have checked on that. Probably, he thought, *he* should have checked on that.

But calling up a starship wasn't like calling the chancellery in Berlin and asking for the protocol office.

Sir Andrew decided to approach the Gehunite captain. Normally, he would have first talked to the other female officer, a lieutenant, he presumed, and most likely an aide of some sort, but to be brutally honest with himself she actually frightened him. There was just something about her, beautiful though she might be, that suggested this wasn't someone you bothered if you could avoid it. She reminded him a bit of a female DCI on the Prime Minister's protective detail, and that woman scared the hell out of him, despite his having spent ten years in the Coldstream Guards before taking up his current position

He walked over to Romiwero, and introduced himself. "I hope everything is going well for you so far," he said.

She nodded. "Quite pleasant. It's nice to be walking around down here after being away so long."

"There are one or two things I need to know, Captain, in order to ensure a pleasant visit to the palace. There are things we simply don't know about you, you see."

"Understandable."

"What was the significance of the miniature sword?"

"It's a replica of the Sword of State, one of the symbols of the Gehunite Empire. The original was carried by Salmik the Great, the founder of the Empire."

"And the lady is your empress, I believe?"

"Yes, Her Imperial Majesty Felia VII," Romiwero said. "As of our return, and confirmation of the extinction of the imperial line here, Empress of Gehun." She shrugged. "For whatever that means. For all practical purposes, that Empire no longer exists, so I suppose the title is more symbolic than anything."

"So you consider her reign to have just begun, then?"

"Officially."

"Excellent. To be honest, Captain, I wasn't quite sure where to seat her. If the Emperor of Japan wasn't here, of course, her title would make her the most senior 'foreign' leader. However, as he has officially reigned longer, Japan is most senior, and your empress follows him in precedence order."

"She's spent most of her career as an ambassador. I suspect she'd really be more comfortable if she still were."

"Ah." And wouldn't that be so much simpler a solution, he thought, before dismissing it. Protocol was what mattered, not preferences. "Now, there is something else we need to know, and apparently no one has thought to ask in planning this little gathering. We really don't know what you eat. Or, I guess more to the point, we don't know what you *don't* eat."

"What we *don't* eat?"

"Well, some of our own people have particular religious traditions that prohibit them from eating certain things. Some don't eat pork, or shellfish, or some of them don't eat any sort of meat. To be honest, we have no idea of what your religion might be, what you believe, or how it restricts what you do."

Romiwero nodded. "Most of us," she said, "come from a L'Mikist background. Lieutenant Fehmadaatin's family were Oniraites, being from Callaa. For the most part, those old religious traditions are just that, traditions. We observe the various holidays, mostly by getting the family together and eating too much, but no one really believes in supernatural beings anymore. Our putative religions don't have much of an effect on our daily lives, and even if they did, none of our old religions had any real influence on what we eat."

Sir Andrew nodded, feeling rather relieved. "Good. We can turn out some wonderful food here, and now that we know you'll be able to eat it all, we shall."

"It's going to be wonderful to eat real food again," she said. "Just about everything we eat aboard ship is cloned, so there's no real variety. I've been eating the same steak—from a genetic stand-point, literally the same steak—a couple times a week for the last fifteen years. We don't even clone the whole steer, just the steak. It's the same with vegetables, fruits, what have you."

"Thank you, Captain," he said, thinking that some of the more militant vegans might be intrigued by the idea of having steak without killing a cow. "I shall inform the kitchen."

MacNaughton hurried away, only to be instantly replaced by Vickers. It made Romiwero wonder about the hierarchy. The chief of protocol first, *then* the Prime Minister.

"I hope everything is going well," Vickers said.

"I believe it is. We were just discussing the menu. It's going to be quite a treat being able to eat natural foods for a while."

"Your empress is a charming young lady," Vickers commented.

"I've always found her to be."

"How much power does she actually have?"

"What do you mean?"

"Well, my king, for example, has very little in the way of real power. He is officially the head of state of the United Kingdom and the Commonwealth countries, but that doesn't involve being able to order anyone to do anything. Other than opening or dissolving Parliament, or calling for new elections, his job is mostly ceremonial. He makes an annual address to Parliament, but I write it for him, so it expresses the government's position much more than his own. He can confer knighthoods, or peerages at his own discretion, but, again, the government normally decides who goes on the honours list. I believe the last king to personally select a candidate for knighthood was his grandfather."

"Then the situation is very similar, I should think. When our government was still intact, the emperor's function was expressed as 'reign, but not rule.' Originally, the emperor had all the power. Ultimately, by the time we left, his only real power was to veto legislation, but, like your king, his primary function was mostly to be head of state. Now that my ship, and her two sisters, are possibly all that remains of Imperial Gehun, Felia's function is still mostly what it was when she embarked, that of an ambassador. She's empress simply because she's the last surviving member of the imperial family and we do like our ceremonial."

"Some people," Vickers said, "are a bit nervous about you being here."

"Why?"

"They're afraid you'll decide to take over again. You certainly have the firepower to do it if you want to."

She laughed. "Someone actually thinks a few hundred people aboard a starship could take over a world of ten-billion? Sorry, but that's just a little ridiculous. Besides, you're not ready for the sort of government we had. Too many little countries. You don't develop the sort of space programme we had if you can't get along with each other. No, so far as we're concerned, this is now just another technological civilisation that's not quite ready to venture far from its home world. The rules say we leave those alone. Normally, we'd just observe you from high orbit, without any physical interaction."

"And yet, you're here."

"Only because we're *from* here. Otherwise we'd have stayed beyond the your detection range and used our sensors to study you. We've learnt from other cultures how dangerous it can be to interfere. There was one planet where a Griknaite ship's doctor decided to stop an epidemic. The locals were pre-industrial, and when the same ship returned about 200 years later they found that the people not only hadn't progressed very much, but had reconfigured their society around the worship of lizards. All good things, they were now saying, were granted by Yahkish, the supreme lizard god."

"Really?"

"Yahkish was the doctor's name."

Vickers seemed suddenly puzzled. "The doctor was a lizard?"

"Griknaites are reptiles. A bit intimidating in appearance, but very pleasant, really."

"I don't think we've ever encountered them."

Romiwero smiled. "You might have. If they'd ever come here, they have stayed in orbit where you couldn't see them. There are several aboard my ship, if you'd care to meet them."

Vickers glanced across the room at the king. "These Griknaites," he mused, "they can't change their physical appearance, can they?"

Romiwero laughed. "No. We've encountered quite a number of species during our travels, and we've yet to find any shape-shifters. That ability remains the realm of fantasy stories."

"Well," Vickers sighed, "there *are* people here who believe it's possible."

◆   ◆   ◆

Empress Felia was a bit overwhelmed by the attention. It was all new to her. There had always been the presumption that she was now empress, but until their return to Barzak, and confirmation that her culture was not only extinct, but literally unknown and forgotten, it had been nothing more than a presumption. She hadn't really been that close to the throne.

In the ordinary course of events she would have remained a princess and nothing more. Her grandfather, Emperor Kalmik X, had eight children, of whom her father had been sixth. She was, herself, the third of five children. Both of her elder siblings had children, as did all her father's elder siblings. At the time *Warrior* set off on her mission, Felia had been twenty-eighth in the line of succession. Had she stayed behind, there wouldn't have been even an *un*reasonable chance she'd ever ascend the throne.

Now, that entire line was extinct, along with, presumably, all their descendants. That meant the job was now hers. By default. The two other *Warrior* class starships carried no imperial family members, so she was the only one left. Other than the odd state occasion, such as this one, it didn't mean very much. A ship with a crew of just over three hundred hardly constituted an empire. The colonial worlds had long since become entirely self-governing and were, in any case, so distant from each other that there was no reasonable way for them to even coordinate anything. Not when it could take a century or more to send a message and receive a reply. Their names were a part of her official title, but if she ever showed up on one of them and tried to assert authority she suspected her 'loyal subjects' would consider it all a great joke.

Aboard ship, she had two jobs, neither of which had much to do with running anything. Her primary role was as an exobiologist, cataloguing and categorising alien plants and animals. Over the last fifteen years she'd encountered hundreds of both, and had written three books. This visit, she realised, would give her the opportunity to publish them, once they were translated into modern languages.

Her other job was diplomatic. As a member of the imperial family she held the appointment of Imperial Ambassador at Large. When *Warrior* encountered another space faring civilisation, it was Felia's job to ensure the encounter remained peaceful. It almost always did. The problems, if there were any, came with cultures who were just starting to venture into space, and hadn't got around to solving all their issues at home first.

Like this one, when she thought about it.

The hostile, imperialistic space conquerors so common in earth's science fiction were a reflexion of the planet's current state of affairs. They didn't bear on reality.

The majority of space faring cultures were, like earth, still system bound. Without jump drive technology, the habitable planets were simply too far apart to visit.

"Developing a jump drive," she explained, "takes so much effort that it really isn't possible on a planet where they're still fighting each other."

"You don't give away the technology, then?" the king said.

"No. We don't interfere with development. At least, not with technological development. If they're still killing each other over trivial matters, well, we might suggest they think about other methods of settling their disputes. *Moral* persuasion is permitted— within limits."

"We really don't have wars anymore," Emperor Morihito offered. "Not between countries. There are sometimes problems with individuals, or with groups, who object to the idea that anyone would ever disagree with them. Sometimes they try to force others to comply. And I'm afraid we're all forced to maintain substantial military and naval forces, just in case the United States decides to become aggressive. They claim to still be a democratic republic, but for all practical purposes they've become a theocratic autocracy.

Unfortunately, sometimes countries like that decide the quickest solution to internal problems is to create an external enemy."

"There were a lot of problems with some religions wanting to force everyone else to adopt their beliefs in the 21st century," the king told her. "Not any more, though."

"It was mostly a matter of education," the French president said. "When a person's only source of information is a religious text, it's very easy to get him to act irrationally. Getting their children out of religious schools and into schools where they could learn how the world *really* works did wonders. It wasn't popular—many objected to teaching science if it conflicted with their mythology; the Americans still do—but the abolition of religious schools as an alternative to secular education *did* eventually solve the problem for everyone else."

"Some of those people caused a lot of trouble," Emperor Mori-hito said. "Particularly when they were attacking people who either couldn't, or wouldn't, fight back. It was a different story once confronted by modern armies determined to stop them."

Japan said this with a slightly deferential tone, remembering when his own country had been on an expansionist track. That was long before he was born, even before his grandfather was born, but he was a practical as well as a patriotic historian. He admitted his country's faults, if only to himself.

He also remembered the long period, after World War II, when Japan had constitutionally limited itself to "self-defence forces." That had lasted until the early 21st century, when the threat of Chinese expansion had made it necessary to amend the constitution and the Maritime Self Defence Force had once again been allowed to build capital ships and restyle itself as the Imperial Navy.

It still operated under that name, and still generally kept itself out of other people's business, but now it once again possessed aircraft carriers and other ships that could be used for power projection should the need ever arise. Beyond joint operations with the Americans and, ironically, the Chinese to suppress piracy, the need never had. The evolution of China's communist government into a capitalist-socialist one had blunted the country's ambitions. The Americans were more of a threat now.

"People don't like fighting that much," Japan continued. "Governments sometimes do, but the people *running* the government aren't the people who have to do the fighting. Over the last few decades, the people have been telling their leaders to find a different solution."

"There are people here," the king said, "who were extremely nervous when you arrived. There's rather a presumption that anyone coming from space is going to be unfriendly."

"I suppose some might be," Felia said. "But we're *from* here, even if our own civilisation is long gone."

"I do hope you will tell us that history."

Felia nodded. "Our ship's computers are hard at work on translating our history books into your modern languages."

"Definitely something I will read," King William said. "I suppose the publishers will assign editors to fix grammatical errors. Computers are often a bit too literal."

"If it works as well as the personal translators you've given us," Japan said, "there may not be much need for editing."

The Japanese Emperor was fluent in English, which he spoke with an accent acquired during four years at Oxford. It wasn't really that the Japanese had trouble with the sounds of some English letters—most people could wrap their tongues around *any* language with a bit of practice—so much as that most English teachers in Japan weren't native speakers, and learnt from others who weren't native speakers, so the pronunciation errors became ingrained.

He was speaking English now, but an earpiece allowed him to hear Felia's words in Japanese. He was also hearing the English translation via the speaker on her own translator. He found it interesting to note that the Japanese translation was more literal than the English, perhaps because the grammar was similar.

Fifteen

PRESIDENT WILL GORDON WAS UNHAPPY. The television networks were running their regular programming. They didn't have much of a choice on that, if they wanted to keep their licences. But it was harder to control the Internet, despite over a century of strict government supervision.

The Federal government had filters installed to prevent anyone from watching inappropriate material. It was a start, and worked for the casual user. Lots of others knew how to get around the filters. It was like the old submarine/sonar race, all the way back in the 1940s. The quieter the subs got, the more sensitive the sonar was made. No matter how good a filter the government came up with, someone was always finding a way around it.

If someone was watching network news, or what was on GNN, they'd get a little reporting on what was happening in London, presented with the proper perspective. It simply wasn't that important a story. That was the official position of the United States. Nothing important, and more than likely just an elaborate hoax. How could people come from before the planet existed? No, if these people believed they came from earth, they were simply mistaken. Possibly they came from some other planet that *looked* like earth, and just screwed up their navigation?

Gordon's younger brother, Tom, who was still in the family business, had presented the only logical explanation. The visitors *could* be from earth's distant past, but as the earth itself was barely 6,000 years old, they were obviously from an earlier creation.

The Gordons had never agreed with those who liked to claim that people and dinosaurs had once lived together, and the dinosaurs all died in the Flood. Will was more of the opinion that fossils were Satan's handiwork, intended to undermine faith by providing false evidence that the world was older than it really was. Tom allowed that there might be some merit to the consecutive creations theory, which argued that God had created the universe and the solar system, and then tried several times to populate the planet before finally getting it right with humanity. The previous efforts were simply wiped away, leaving that incongruous evidence behind. Other than the Creator himself, all those previous creations had nothing to do with the current one.

Gordon was upstairs at the White House, in the living room of the residence, watching the BBC reports of the visit. That feed wasn't available to most Americans—not legally, anyway—but he knew that a good number would have found a way to watch it. His religious beliefs dictated that the whole thing was impossible, which meant it had to be an elaborate scam. His common sense told him it was real. He wasn't stupid, after all. Like most professional evangelists, he didn't actually believe the nonsense he preached. He just knew what was best for people, which was obviously doing what they were told.

The situation was certainly dangerous. No one really knew anything about these people. He doubted they were Christians. He wasn't sure of that, but it seemed unlikely they would be. Yet God and the Trinity were eternal, weren't they? If there had been a previous advanced civilisation, didn't it stand to reason that God would have revealed himself to them as well?

No, he thought, it didn't. God had waited several thousand years before sending Jesus, which must have been hard on poor Abraham and the other patriarchs, who'd had to suffer in hell until after the crucifixion, when Jesus descended to Satan's realm to save them from further torment. He'd made a lot of money with that story, before he got into politics, and he was sticking to it.

Perhaps this was an opportunity for evangelism. If the Gehunites were *not* Christians, it stood to reason they would need saving. The danger was that they'd brought with them some weird religion that might, on the surface, seem more attractive than what was already here. If they couldn't be converted, he damn sure didn't want to risk them converting anyone else.

Still, they kept talking about non-interference, so perhaps that wouldn't be a problem. And they weren't planning to stay very long.

Nor would any of them be allowed to come to the United States. Immigration and tourism rules would be strictly enforced.

Gordon didn't want anyone getting between Americans and their faith. When people lost faith, they often started to question things. Even worse, at least from his brother's viewpoint, they often stopped giving to the church. Faith was important. No one could *prove* God was real, so it was important that people simply believed.

He looked back at his 29 years in office. A lot of things had happened since Inauguration Day, 2097. He'd got older. The United States had become more isolated—insulated, Tom would say—from the rest of the world. The population had grown to 342,000,000, after decades of negative growth.

But he'd inherited a good system. The Constitution guaranteed that power would remain where it belonged. The historian in him still wondered how that had ever happened. The Founding Fathers had gifted the United States with a workable Constitution in the late 18th century. It had functioned for over 200 years, but it was lacking in some areas. There was no protection of religion, for one thing, and the Constitution itself never once even mentioned God. An obvious oversight, Gordon presumed.

Fortunately, in 2019, enough of the states agreed to what had been promoted as a "convention of the states." That name was a stroke of genius. The promoters claimed the purpose was to propose amendments. Well, that had been the purpose of the original Constitutional Convention as well, to amend the Articles of Confederation. Once the delegates met they simply threw out the old Constitution and wrote a new one. So long as you could get enough state legislatures to go along, "amending" could just as easily mean rewriting the whole thing. Despite Liberal outcries, by late 2022 enough had and the new Constitution was law.

The people had thought the delegates were just going to take care of some basic problems, banning abortion under any circumstances, and imposing a Federal definition of marriage that wouldn't include same-sex couples.

They got the abortion ban, to be sure. Along with a Federal death penalty for anyone who had one, or for any doctor who performed one. The Supreme Court had its powers curtailed, and could no longer declare a law unconstitutional. Sovereign immunity was more firmly enshrined in the new Constitution, permanently eliminating any silly ideas about ordinary people having a right to sue the government.

Most importantly, the president gained the power to create law by executive order if Congress failed to act on an issue. True, a supermajority in Congress could overrule him, but how often could you get 90-percent of the members to agree on anything?

It was hard enough to get 90-percent of Congress into their chamber at the same time, and overriding an executive order required the vote of 90-percent of the *membership*, not just of the members present.

The new Constitution had done more than outlaw same-sex marriage. It had made homosexual congress a capital offence for men. Lesbians were subject to mandatory conversion therapy. Lesbians were women, after all, and more subject to their emotions than men, so it stood to reason they'd be more likely to fall prey to sexual predators and perverts. Anyway, once you hooked them up with a *real* man, they'd soon see the light.

From Gordon's point of view, the most important provision in the new Constitution had been the requirement that anyone holding any federal office, from the lowliest clerk to the highest elective offices, be a practicing Christian. It wasn't that important they believed, really, but they did have to attend church regularly, and pay their faith tax. That was distributed to the churches, the way God intended.

The main benefit, over the long run, had been that most of the perverts had moved somewhere else. It had also seen the elimination of heretical religious groups. The Jews had always been problematic, but as it was now possible to place reasonable restrictions on them, most of them had moved to Israel or, at least, to some other country. The same happened with most of the Muslims. A surprisingly large percentage of Catholics had left, too, once they figured out that the Protestant majority—the part of it that ran the Republican Party, at least—had never actually considered them "real" Christians.

Gordon's ideal had always been something along the lines of Cromwell's England, or Calvin's Geneva, but without the burning of heretics. Injecting them with Soporal did the trick just as effectively, if the heresy was blatant enough to warrant death, and it was a lot neater. People still had freedom of religion, after all. As long as it was Christian. They even tolerated atheists, provided they kept their damned mouths shut and paid their faith tax. If they tried to spread their nonsense, well, they could leave the country, or spend the rest of their lives in prison for violation of the blasphemy laws.

He didn't really care if space aliens started turning up. At least, he didn't care as long as they were reasonably friendly. People from earth's past, from before earth *existed*, dammit, were another thing entirely. The Bible said it wasn't possible, so it had to be some sort of hoax.

Had it been a mistake, closing down most of NASA's astronautics department? Just leaving a relatively small section to maintain the satellites, or put up new ones as needed?

"What am I supposed to do about this?" he wondered aloud.

"Not much you can do," his wife said, from the couch.

"That's the problem. Well, that, and I don't have any idea how to deal with this."

"Pray. That's what you'd tell anyone else, isn't it?"

The president frowned. Like that would really help. That was what you told people when they had problems, and you couldn't figure out an easy way to profit from their misery. "And what sort of answer would I get?"

His wife shrugged.

"Seems like I always get the same answer. I like to think God is saying, 'No.' 'No' just seems like a better answer than, 'No one is listening.'"

There were times that the First Lady thought her husband could benefit from long term analysis, but that was obviously impossible. He was the product of five generations of evangelists, and his younger brother still ran the ministry. He was, himself, ordained, could go back to preaching if he really wanted to. People expected his faith to be rock solid. They had to.

"What would your father do? Or your grandfather?"

"My father would have just gone to the president and told him to deal with it." He smiled weakly. "Well, strongly suggested, anyway. Him and Gramps were both pretty good at getting politicians to do whatever they wanted. I suppose Dad might have started a new crusade as well. Got the war chest filled."

"You can put Tom to work on that."

"True."

It wasn't a bad idea, really. His brother could rent a few big stadiums and take the show back on the road. His great-great-grandfather had done just that back in the early 21st century, when the brutal, but short-lived, Islamic State was causing problems, and the Religious Right was hammering away at a president they loudly proclaimed was a secret Muslim, and very possibly the anti-Christ.

True, the man had really just been a Rockefeller Republican who called himself a Democrat, and the Islamic State, while claiming to dispatch operatives to cause problems around the world, had already gained just about as much territory as it ever would, and would soon go into decline as the surrounding countries finally pulled themselves together and started to fight back. Most of their "agents" causing trouble in the United States, and other non-Arab majority countries, murdering people, setting off bombs, or what have you, had come up with the idea on their own and just *claimed* the Islamic State put them up to it.

People would believe anything, Gordon thought, as long as it agreed with their prejudices. If it was something they could be afraid of, they'd believe it even quicker. Americans had always been more concerned with perceptions than realities, and Christians still retained their perverse feeling that the stronger they grew, the more they were being persecuted by their victims. Give them an eloquent evangelist in a football stadium and they'd eat up every word and gladly throw their millions into the collection baskets.

Gramps had put on a fourteen-city crusade, netting almost sixty-seven million tax free dollars in the process. Tom could probably do the same thing, citing the Gehunites as the current threat, and raise three or four times that much. It was the perfect scam. Gramps had charged the faithful a nominal $40 to attend these giant rallies, then taken three collections during the service. Most people would throw a twenty into the collection bucket each time it was passed, so, even accounting for a few cheapskates, he'd averaged around $70 a head. Not a bad take when the average stadium held 80,000 or more people once you added on-field seating, and very few seats went unfilled.

Tom could probably net closer to $300 a head, taking inflation into account.

"The Prime Minister seems to be very friendly with these people," his wife said. "Do you suppose they know he's a pervert?"

Gordon shrugged. "Maybe they do. They may not care. I don't imagine they're Christians, after all. They may think sexual perversion is just fine and dandy."

"You should probably find out."

"Ambassador Miller will be attending the state dinner. He can have a little talk with them, find out what they're thinking."

On the television, everyone was milling around in a big reception room. Shortly they'd all move to the ballroom, which as the largest room in the palace was used for state dinners and other major events.

"I actually feel a little sorry for their empress," Gordon said. "I've had to sit through a few dinners with Miller. The man's an idiot."

"He likes you."

"He's a useful idiot. But he's still an idiot."

"I like the king," his wife said. "Handsome fellow."

"Well, his parents were both quite attractive. So were his grandparents and great-grandparents, for that matter. His great-grandmother looked like a fashion model when she was young."

They settled in to watch. It was going to be a long day.

♦   ♦   ♦

Sara Ellsworth was in her room, watching the state dinner on the FreeWeb with her friend Ellen. There had been reporters outside her house a few days earlier, when it was realised that she had unintentionally become the first person to communicate with *Warrior*—even if the communication had been nothing more than scolding them about being on the wrong frequency.

Fortunately, the notoriety had passed quickly. She hadn't known who she was scolding, she'd declared. That's what she'd told the FBI when they came nosing around. So far as she knew, it had just been someone who'd got their hands on a ham transceiver and didn't know what they were doing. A problem for the FCC, really, she suggested.

The FBI had bought it. Or seemed to buy it. At least, they'd gone away and, so far, hadn't come back. You couldn't be sure, though. It was becoming clear enough that the government considered giving any real credence to *Warrior*'s arrival to be a denial of the Genesis creation story. *Warrior*'s people claimed they departed more than 80,000 years before the universe existed, which, if it were true, meant the Bible was lying. Such a claim was blasphemy, punishable by a fine on the first offence, but by up to life in prison if repeated often enough.

Then, yesterday, a very pleasant middle-aged man had shown up at her front door, selling "family heirloom Bibles." It said so on the doors of his ancient sedan. He brought in his sample case, then spent several minutes making a rambling sales pitch while wandering around the living room, looking at the bric-a-brac and continually glancing at the screen of his mobile phone.

"You haven't memorised your pitch?" Sara asked him.

"I have, actually," he eventually said. "But I understand the FBI was here recently. I wanted to see if they'd left any souvenirs."

"What are you talking about?" her father asked.

The salesman touched the pocket where he'd put his mobile. "This has a bug detector," he said. "And it doesn't appear they left any."

"Huh?"

"Sorry, but I'm afraid I've mislead you," the salesman said, his vaguely southern American accent now replaced by something distinctly British. Had the Ellsworths been more familiar with Britain, they would have placed the man's origins somewhere around Edinburgh.

He produced a leather identity folder and handed it to Sara's father. "I'm actually Charles Colquhoun," he said. "I am a major in His Majesty's Highland Regiment, currently seconded as military attaché at our consulate in Denver."

Sara's mother looked at him curiously. First the FBI shows up, and now the British Army? She was also a little curious about how the man managed to get "keh-hoon" out of "Colquhoun." That would never have occurred to her.

"What's this about?" Sara's father asked.

"I've been asked to convey an invitation to your daughter, sir," Colquhoun said.

"What sort of invitation?"

"It comes from the captain of the Gehunite starship, sir. As your daughter was the first person to make contact, the captain is inviting her to visit the ship."

"Is that possible?" Sara asked.

"No," her father said. "Obviously it isn't. The whole thing is just a trick the British are pulling."

"Oh, it's quite real, sir," Colquhoun said.

"Well, she obviously can't go," Sara's mother said.

"My job," Colquhoun said, "is merely to convey the invitation.

Whether or not to accept is, naturally, your daughter's decision."

"No," Sara's father said, "it's ours. She's only 15. And she won't be going."

"Then I'll return to the consulate and convey your decision." He solemnly shook hands with each of them and walked back to his car. He left the big sample Bible on the coffee table.

"He also slipped this into my hand," Sara told Ellen, as they watched the dinner. She held out a slip of paper with a URL printed on it, along with the legend "FreeWeb only."

"What's that?" Ellen asked.

"I tried it last night, after everyone had gone to sleep. It connects to a web page at the British Consulate in Denver. The gist of it is, 'We know your parents don't want you to go, but if you really want to, fill out this form."

"What are you going to do?"

"I'm not sure. I've got a few days, apparently."

"Are you going?" Ellen wanted to know.

"I'd like to. How many chances do you think I'll get to go into space? Even just into orbit?"

"So go."

"My parents won't let me. Neither will the government, which I think is what my parents are afraid of anyway."

"Do you have to tell them?"

"I think they'd probably notice when one of those shuttles landed in our back yard. They'd certainly notice I was missing."

Sara was a science geek. That had scared the hell out of her when the FBI showed up. She had a lot of prohibited books tucked away in the attic. Evolution, geology, old American history books that seemed to suggest the Founding Fathers hadn't exactly been the fundamentalist Christians she learnt about in school.

"I wish I was older," she said. "There are stories on some British sites that the Gehunites are going to take a few people with them."

"I'd go," Ellen said.

"So would I. Even knowing it meant never seeing anyone I knew again, I'd go in a heartbeat. It would be the only chance I'd ever get to see deep space."

"Do you think they do?"

"Do what?"

"See deep space. From what I've been able to find out, with this jump drive of theirs, you're just in one place and then, more or less instantly, you're somewhere else several light years away and thirty or forty years later. I'm not sure they ever see what's in between."

"It would still be cool."

"Sara Supergeek strikes again."

"Absolutely."

Sixteen

LIEUTENANT MARINA FEHMADAATIN WAS ENJOYING HERSELF more than she'd expected. Shortly after they arrived, the palace staff had presented the visiting crew with menus and allowed them to pick their own food. They must have a very large kitchen, she thought. In addition to the names of the various food items, which obviously didn't mean very much to people who didn't speak the local language, and had to rely on translation software to read them, there were pictures, which helped a great deal. They depicted not only the finished dish, but also what went into it.

She'd guessed right with the *Wiener Schnitzel* and sauerkraut, which proved to be very much like the Callaaite *kufsnit* and *gresser-pik* she'd grown up with. The beer seemed a little weak, more like Gehunite beer than Callaaite, which contained more alcohol.

Warrior's crew contained fifty-four Callaaites. Another thirty-five were Kaamites or, like the doctor, native to a colonial or alien world. The rest were Gehunite. To listen to earth's news sources, *everyone* was Gehunite, but no doubt they were simplifying things. Or just couldn't tell the difference. Apparently their hosts had the same problem, with people referring to England as if it were the whole nation, and not merely the largest part of it.

Sometimes you couldn't tell anyway. Brynnazen, the master at arms, had a Callaaite name, and if you went back a few generations that's where his family came from. Brynnazen was born in Gehun, and didn't speak a word of his ancestors' language. Brynnazen was nothing more than a family surname to him, to be passed down, in the Gehunite fashion, from father to child.

That was fine for the boys, she thought, but it sounded more than a little odd when applied to his sister, who was also in the crew. Colonel Kara Brynnazen didn't look like anyone's son.

There were no surnames in Callaa. They had given names and matronymics. Convenient for establishing relationships within a generation, though it made for a very confusing phone directory. Her own name identified her as Marina, Fehma's daughter. Her mother was Fehma Geriadaatin. Her father was Adnor Marinazen. Marina was named after her paternal grandmother.

The empress' given name was Callaaite, though she was herself thoroughly Gehunite. She was named after a first century Callaaite queen who'd married Emperor Felim I, Salmik's eldest son. She didn't have an actual surname—none of the royal family did—but Salmikonmitiim served the purpose. It meant "of the house of Salmik," and was shared by all his descendants in the line of succession.

"Are you enjoying your meal?" It was the young Royal Air Force flight lieutenant seated next to her. Each of the *Warrior* crew members had been matched up with a military officer or scientist. Hers was a Scottish fighter pilot, which had initially made for some confusion until her translation software worked out his accent and compensated.

"It's quite good," she said. "Very much like what we used to have in my country while I was growing up."

"Was your mother a good cook?"

Marina laughed. "I have no idea. My father did all the cooking. My mother was too busy with regimental duties to pay any attention to domestic affairs."

"Your mother was military?"

"Colonel commanding, 7th Light Cavalry Regiment. They were a ceremonial unit, attached to the palace in Callaahavn. Horses haven't been used in combat in a very long time, but they do make a wonderful picture in ceremonial formations. Particularly with the troopers in traditional armour.

"Sounds a bit like our Household Cavalry. They're very impressive troops. We pick the soldiers for Guards units at least partly based on height. They have to be quite tall, very smartly turned out, and exemplary soldiers in every respect."

"Our system was similar. My mother was taller than I am. Minimum height requirement was 170 centimetres."

MacDowell raised an eyebrow. "Doesn't seem that tall. Guards have to be 183 centimetres or taller."

"Men weren't allowed in ceremonial units. There was a lot of controversy over allowing them into the military at all, but by the time I left we'd started allowing them in combat units. Not that there was anyone left to fight."

"Oh, well, we had the same thing a bit over a century ago. Except it was whether to allow women to serve in combat. There are still almost no women in our ceremonial units, but that's mostly because of the height requirement. Not that many women are tall enough to qualify. It's all about appearance with the guards."

"Callaa was a very small country. Our importance in world affairs originally came from the fighting abilities of our women. Mercenaries, for the most part. We didn't need that big a force for defence. An iron bound coast and steep mountains blocking the only overland access made invasion impractical."

"The women did the fighting?"

"Naturally."

"Against men?"

"Mostly."

"Wasn't that something of a disadvantage. Particularly before firearms came into the picture. Men are usually bigger, after all."

"We had steel swords and armour. At the time, no one else did. So our blades were something like half the weight of the other armies' iron weapons, and at the same time stronger and sharper. As for firearms, well, once they were introduced strength hardly mattered."

"Is that why your sword looks different from most of the others?"

"Yes. Mine is quite old, handed down in the family from before Salmik founded the Empire." She smiled. "Old enough to have a name, as it happens, which newer blades generally don't. In my language, it's called *Kafzecher*."

"What's that mean?" The British officer found this whole discussion fascinating. And a bit disturbing. He'd never met an actual Amazon before, and that certainly sounded like what this strikingly beautiful woman was.

"Head splitter."

"Ouch."

"Family tradition is that it was given that name the first time it was used in battle, when it split open the head of an enemy officer, helmet and all."

"Strong weapon."

Marina shrugged. "Probably an old leather helmet. It's a very good sword, but hacking away at iron armour is never a good idea, no matter how strong the blade."

"I suppose not."

He was quite good looking, Marina decided. Perhaps there was a chance for a bit of recreation on this visit.

"Are you married?" she asked.

"Yes. And two sons."

Too bad, Marina thought.

"What about you."

"I was when I left. That's nearly 87,000 years ago, so I suppose I'm a widow by now."

♦   ♦   ♦

Surgeon Commander Grekim Vordik sat on a metal stool in front of a lab table, reading a lengthy report. Forty-three matches so far. Not bad, considering how many thousands of years had passed. And that was just in the UK.

It was easier there, as the country had a universal DNA database. Once they started checking other countries it would be harder. Many only had records of criminals in their DNA registries, along with the relatively small number of people who had added their DNA voluntarily for identification purposes, or who had served in the military and had it collected for the same reason.

They were checking mitochondrial DNA. That stayed the same over many generations, though it only indicated descent in the female line. Forty-three of *Warrior*'s crew members had living relatives in the United Kingdom. He would have liked to have been able to say descendants, but knew that wasn't the right word. The crew member and the modern civilian shared a common female ancestor, but there was no way to prove that the line of descent went *through* the crew member. They could just as easily be 18th cousins, 23,000 time removed. There was no way to tell.

The curious thing was that several hundred modern Scots turned out to be related to the Brynnazens, and the result was causing quite a stir. There was a good bit of humour about Scots naturally favouring Neanderthals, who apparently were looked upon as crude and primitive by modern humans. It seemed there had also previously been a good bit of debate in scientific circles as to whether Magnim and Gornim could mate and produce fertile offspring. Vordik knew perfectly well that they could, but he had the advantage of knowing both subspecies as friends and colleagues, and contemporary scientists didn't.

The immunization programme had gone well. It turned out that there were several new diseases since *Warrior* had initially departed. Mostly evolved forms of old ones. Some of the old maladies had weakened and ceased to present much of problem. Some others had gone the other way, evolving from a minor complaint into something deadly. A rhinovirus that used to kill thousands of children every year now did little more than bring on a runny nose. Conversely, the old "running itch," once notable only for a minor rash and terrible itching, had at some point evolved into what English speakers called "smallpox," turning deadly before finally being eradicated in the late 20th century.

The crew was certainly excited. The ones born on earth, at least. Vordik hadn't been, so the idea of visiting was interesting, but had no deeper meaning. His family had lived on New Barzak for thousands of years before he signed on. He was curious about the planet, but it wasn't home.

He was seriously considering leaving his gravity boots on the ship, just for the novelty of gaining some slightly ridiculous athletic abilities on the smaller planet. In earth's gravity, he could easily manage a three to four metre vertical jump, and generally seemed to bounce more than walk. He could also lift outrageous weights. Where he came from, everything, including himself, weighed almost twice what it did on earth.

♦   ♦   ♦

Romiwero had very quickly concluded that the American ambassador was an idiot. It was rather sad, she thought. The man's questions and comments made it clear he thought her ship's return was nothing more than some elaborate hoax. This was something her background had never prepared her for. Gehunite culture was strongly scientific. The idea that someone could be presented with undeniable evidence, and then reject that evidence because it disagreed with an ancient, pre-scientific myth, was outside her experience.

It was also annoying, because he made it clear none of the crew would be allowed to visit his country. Romiwero wasn't the only person in the crew who was born in what was now the United States. The ancient nation of Gehun, after all, had occupied a peninsula that, while larger, roughly corresponded to modern Florida, before it entered its imperial phase under Salmik the Great. Her actual birthplace was now about 30 kilometres east of Miami, so there'd be no visiting that without some sort of submersible.

Still, it was annoying. Ambassador Miller didn't elucidate, but Romiwero had learnt that the United States had essentially been a dictatorship for decades, where theocratic concerns outweighed any other factors in setting policy. She supposed she'd have to read this Bible, though the translated text of the opening chapters didn't give her much reason to expect anything very sensible.

There might still be some slight questions about the first few milliseconds, but there was really no doubt that magic had nothing to do with the origins of the universe.

♦   ♦   ♦

Major Charles Colquhoun sat quietly at his desk, watching the live BBC feed on the screen mounted above the fireplace. The Consulate was open, so he was wearing his uniform, on this day with trousers, which were more convenient than the kilt. Both had to be pressed, but trousers didn't come with what always seemed like several thousand pleats.

On the screen, an elderly admiral had just proposed the loyal toast. Being a sailor, he remained seated, though just about everyone else instantly got to their feet. The king, who had risen to the rank of commander in the Royal Navy before his grandfather's death had brought his father to the throne and made him Prince of Wales, acknowledging the toast, also remained seated.

Colquhoun's computer monitor beeped, and he glanced over at the screen. The message indicator was blinking. He clicked on this. He was rather pleased to see that it was from the Ellsworth girl, and as it included the requested full face photograph with a plain background he already knew what it would say. She was taking them up on the offer.

Reading it over quickly confirmed this.

Colquhoun pressed a button on his phone. "Ostrum, will you ask Mr Johnson to come to my office, please?"

"Right away, sir," a voice said.

Johnson had two jobs at the consulate. Officially, he was the passport officer. Unofficially, he represented the Secret Intelligence Service. What he would do for the Ellsworth girl would touch on both.

"Something you need, Charlie?" Johnson asked, entering the office and closing the door behind him.

"It's on, John."

Colquhoun passed over a printout of the message.

"Lucky kid. Nobody's invited me up there."

"Oh, I'm sure they'd welcome your lot aboard."

Johnson chuckled. "Not if they had any sense, they wouldn't. That's the trouble with being a spy, Charlie. People don't really trust you."

"Well, I'll forward the message and photograph to your terminal."

"What are we calling her?"

"Her real name is Sara Elaine Ellsworth. I'd suggest we keep the Sara, but spell it with an 'h' on the end."

"Always a good idea to keep the given name," Johnson agreed. "That way people react to it naturally. What about the surname?"

"Something simple. Smith, maybe?"

"Sarah Smith. Should work. Give me a couple hours, the girl will have a completely valid UK passport."

"She sounds American. Her accent, I mean."

"I don't expect that will be a problem, Charlie. With any luck, she can fake a British accent sufficiently to fool an American."

"True. They're pretty easy to fool. Or we can simply have her passport show she was born in the UK, and add a lot of fake visa stamps to indicate she grew up in the US. Getting her to London will be your job, of course," Colquhoun said. "Best I don't go anywhere near that neighbourhood now. Her parents know what I look like."

"No problem. I'll have a passport with the same surname for myself. Just to insure against problems, we'll make them diplomatic."

"What's the plan?"

"I'll pick her up wherever she thinks best, then drive to Cullison Field. I keep my personal aeroplane there, and we'll fly in that to Seattle. My counterpart in Seattle will meet us there and drive us to Vancouver in a consulate vehicle. Between the diplomatic plates and passports, getting over the border won't be a problem. After that, she can be Sara Ellsworth again. I'll issue the proper documents to allow her to travel to the UK without an American passport."

"What about coming back?"

"That's up to her, isn't it? She may not want to. There'd be the question of explaining where she'd been, wouldn't there?"

Colquhoun nodded. "She'll likely want to return home, though."

"Then she'll be allowed to do so, obviously. If she does decide to stay in the UK, I have no doubt refugee status will be forthcoming."

Seventeen

STANDING A FEW YARDS FROM THE PARK ENTRANCE, Sara Ellsworth wondered if she was doing the right thing. She'd kept secrets from her parents before. What teenaged girl didn't? But never anything like this. Never anything so potentially life changing.

She glanced at her watch. It was 3:45. School had let out a quarter hour ago, but her parents didn't expect her home until 5:30. She'd told them she was auditioning for the TheArts musical.

They wouldn't have any trouble with that. The drama group really did have auditions scheduled for that afternoon, and she'd done school plays since first grade. The school was doing *Two by Two*. It was ancient, hence in the public domain and free to perform, which was considered a plus at the cash-strapped public school. It was also biblical, another plus. Their drama teacher had gone over the script, not changing much. Presumably the costumes would be a bit less revealing than they had been on Broadway, way back in the mid-20th century.

Her parents wouldn't be concerned until she failed to return home at the expected time. She wasn't even sure where she'd be by then. Maybe in an aeroplane. The Brits had said they'd fly her out of Denver.

A black car, with dark, tinted windows, pulled up and the front passenger's window rolled down. The man inside held up a manila file folder with a huge letter "G" printed on it in marker. The "G" was the expected signal. Sara was a pretty girl. The signal was her assurance that this was the right car, and not some random predator.

Sara nodded and approached the car. The lock button popped up, she opened the door, and climbed in. As she closed the door the window was rising.

"Safety belt," the man said, in a British accent.

She fastened her belt and the car began to move. "I'm John," the man said. "For now, John Smith. And you are now Sarah Smith. Your passport is in the glove box."

Sara opened it and took out the passport. The cover was scuffed, and there were several pages of entry and exit stamps. "I'm from London now?"

"According to that. And that's a *real* passport, by the way. Well, technically, it's forged in that that's obviously not your real name and all the information is false. But if anyone decided to run the passport number, they'd find it properly documented for the person described, and issued just over a year ago. A gift from his Majesty's government, you see, as a courtesy to the Gehunites."

Sara laughed involuntarily. "I can't believe I'm going to actually get to meet people who live in space. To *be* in space."

"I wish I could go with you. I'll accompany you as far as Vancouver. After that, you'll travel to London on your own."

"What do we do now? My parents won't miss me until around 5:30, but once they do they'll call Mrs Montague and she'll tell them I wasn't at the audition."

"We should be well on our way before then. They'll no doubt call the police, but they'll start looking in Denver, and we should be nearly in Seattle by then. If anyone there tries to stop you, show them your new passport. You're Sarah Smith, a resident of London, and any resemblance to this missing girl is obviously nothing more than a coincidence."

"Will the police buy that?"

"Take a closer look at that passport. The great big letters on the bottom of the front cover. 'Diplomatic Passport.' They could question that, to be sure, but when they check with our embassy the information on your passport will be confirmed. Officially, you're my daughter."

Sara nodded.

"You're not the first American we've slipped out of the country," 'Smith' added.

"Good to know," Sara said.

'Smith' touched the navigation display. "Cullison Field," he said, "general aviation terminal."

"Cullison Field, General Aviation Terminal," the unit repeated. "Estimated travel time is 27 minutes. Enjoy the trip."

"Start now," 'Smith ordered. He looked over at Sara as the car pulled away from the kerb. "Now, first stop is Cullison Field. I keep my personal aeroplane there. You'll find British made clothing in your sizes aboard, so by the time we land in Seattle what you're wearing will no longer match what your parents last saw you in."

"I don't sound very British."

"Have you tried."

"You mean something like this?"

'Smith' grimaced. "Good heavens, the ghost of Dick Van Dyke!"

"Who?"

"You've never seen *Mary Poppins?*"

"Sure. My high school did it last year."

"No, Sara, I mean the original motion picture. The one with Julie Andrews singing so beautifully, and speaking so perfectly, and Dick Van Dyke doing the most gawdawful Cockney accent ever heard."

"Mine sucks, huh?"

"Unfortunately." He grinned. "No worries. According to your passport, and what the embassy will tell anyone who asks, you've been in this country since you were three, so it stands to reason you might have developed an American accent.

◆   ◆   ◆

Captain Corallia Maniah, of her Imperial Majesty's Corps of Marines, was relaxing in a little pub, not too far from the Imperial War Museum, where she had spent most of the afternoon. She was in uniform, but had left her sword at the embassy. The British government had made that request, and no one from *Warrior* really objected. They didn't wear the things that often, and generally considered them a damned nuisance under most circumstances.

"Number 92 was the best," someone argued in a nearby booth.

"You're bloody insane," his companion retorted. "Eighty-seven was definitely better. The best ever."

"What, that old man? Couldn't hold a candle to 92."

"That's because you're a kid," the other said. I can remember all of them, as far back as 73 in first run. Even further in reruns."

"Those two girls are always the same, though, aren't they."

"Of course they're the same. One of them's bloody immortal, so she can't change, and the other one always comes back looking the same if anything happens to her. Anyway, they've been played by a computer programme just about forever, so why would they change?"

"One thing never made much sense, though," the first said. "I mean, it's 95 now, and they keep saying there can't be more than a dozen. They've been saying that for, what, 160-odd years now."

"Oh, you ignorant twat, they fixed that years ago. Think about it. If you're essential to keeping the universe going, it just figures they'd keep giving you more turns, doesn't it?"

"It's not like he's the only one. There's a whole bloody planet full of them, isn't there?"

Maniah decided this would be more interesting if she had any idea what the two men were talking about. Who in blazes was essential to keeping the universe going?

◆   ◆   ◆

Crossing into Canada was something of an anti-climax after all the worrying. A consulate limousine had met them at the airport in Seattle, and a little over two and a half hours later the driver had shown their passports to the American immigration officer and they'd crossed the border without the slightest delay. The officer hadn't even looked into the back of the car.

Looking out through the tinted windows, Sara couldn't help noticing the heavy concrete construction of the "welcome" centre. As they'd approached, she could also see the border defences. A triple row of fencing ran off into the distance on either side of the building. Bar the odd entry point, and the unavoidable interruption of the Great Lakes, that triple fence ran all the way to the Atlantic Ocean. Had done for a very long time.

Perhaps 50 yards past the building she'd noticed the squat concrete pillar of an automated exclusion station, with its round, dome-topped gun turret pointing its minigun towards Canada. She couldn't help wondering if anyone was ever foolish enough to try to sneak across that way. Or did the automated gun mount just waste ammunition shooting errant deer?

"I told you," 'Smith' said.

"I just can't believe I'm in Canada," Sara said, getting her mind back on what was happening. "The world is so much older here."

"One way to look at it, I suppose."

"I managed to get a look at a Canadian high school science textbook online once," she explained. "It said that the world was about four and half billion years old. The ones in my high school say somewhere between six and ten thousand years old."

"I see what you mean."

"Is it true unmarried people here can have sex without having to worry about going to jail?"

"I suppose so." 'Smith' was finding this a bit uncomfortable. Not the sort of conversation one should be having with an underage girl, he thought.

"How long to the airport?" he asked the driver.

"Time to destination?" the driver asked the car.

"Arrival at destination in 34 minutes with present traffic," the car answered. "Forty minutes if you drive."

"This car is a bit of a wise arse," the driver said.

"You could let it drive," Smith said. "I rarely take the wheel myself. I always have this fear something untoward will happen and I'll find my instincts have me on the wrong side of the road."

"I'll keep control myself, if you don't mind, sir. And I think I can manage in the same time as a bloody computer." He grinned. "Anyway, the girl will meet her new escort at the airport."

Smith looked at him curiously. "New escort? I thought we were just putting her on the plane and she'd fly on alone."

"There's a Gehunite officer who was playing tourist in Vancouver meeting her at the airport. They decided to take advantage of the situation and provide some extra security. She'll fly to London with her."

Sara grinned. "Great," she said. "This will be a whole big day of firsts. First time out of the country. First time hanging around with a spy."

"I'm not a spy," 'Smith' said.

"First time meeting someone who's been in space." She looked at 'Smith.' "Aren't you?"

"No. I'm the passport officer at the consulate."

"Uh huh."

He decided there was no real point in arguing. He was not a spy, but that was a semantic point. To his way of thinking, a spy was one of those cloak and dagger types. A modern-day James Bond.

He was an intelligence officer, which was an altogether more boring occupation.

♦   ♦   ♦

Lieutenant Marina Fehmadaatin relaxed in the British Airways First Class Lounge, enjoying the view of the runways at Vancouver International Airport. She had flown in five days ago, lured by the scenery, and then stayed on when it turned out the American girl would take them up on the invitation to visit the ship.

She had quickly discovered that, once changed into contemporary civilian clothes, no one paid the least attention to her unless she needed to talk. Her translator would then instantly identify her as someone from *Warrior*. The few words of English she'd managed to pick up so far weren't enough to get by, so she was reliant on the translator. Otherwise, the only attention she got was from men. No matter where she was from, she was a damned attractive woman.

Now she was back in uniform, the service dress version, which combined the navy tunic of the full-dress uniform with sky blue trousers, which were easier to keep clean than the spotless white worn with full dress. The trousers were snug fitting, with a narrow gold stripe down the outer seam. The belt and boots were the same as full dress, as was the cap. Her sword was left aboard the ship. It would have been impractical to travel with it in any case.

She opened her small travel case and removed a reading pad, which came on automatically when she opened the cover. It had amused her on the flight from London, when the elderly woman in the next seat had seemed thoroughly alarmed after glancing at the pad. Apparently there was something disturbing about the Callaaish alphabet, though Marina was never able to find out just what that might be. It certainly wasn't the book she was reading, which the woman obviously couldn't decipher. Unless she could, and was somehow disturbed by all the sex in the novel.

It was an earth novel, a British one, translated by the ship's computer. That was one of the problems with space travel, she thought. Even with *Warrior*'s nearly unlimited data storage capacity, the production of new reading material was somewhat limited. There were nearly two dozen authors in the crew, but only one of them wrote fiction, and he wasn't very good. Planetary visits were a good source of new books. Barzakian colonial worlds, at least.

Literature wasn't uniquely human, but other species' fiction tended to be less interesting. Griknaites were somewhat obsessed with reproduction, but being reptilian, the sex scenes in their novels usually seemed inordinately concerned with egg colour and building incubators. Morshivnite fiction was even stranger. They rarely mentioned sex. Marina had the distinct impression that they considered reproduction something of a nuisance. Their sole passion seemed to be writing about food. Food was more important in Morshivnite society than just about anything, including their offspring.

You could hardly blame them for parental indifference, Marina thought. A newborn Morshivnite was essentially a miniature adult. They had to be educated, taught maths, technology, and so forth. But they were more or less capable of fending for themselves from birth, could carry on an intelligent conversation by the time they were a couple weeks old, and absorbed information at a rate that would make a supercomputer jealous.

Gehunites started their children in school at three, but didn't start teaching writing until they were five. Most kids lacked the fine motor skills needed for writing until around that age. Reading was easier and could be taught much sooner. Primary school, the first six forms, was followed by another six years of secondary school. That was generally completed at age 15.

After secondary school, Gehunites had several options. Some continued to university for another four to eight years. Others entered apprenticeship programmes and learnt a skilled trade. The military was another option, with other ranks eligible for enlistment immediately after secondary school graduation. Officers were required to complete a four-year service college programme before commissioning.

Not that there had been much left of the military at the time *Warrior* had departed. There was a small Army and Air Force, just in case anyone decided to get rowdy. But there was really no one to fight. The ceremonial units were far more useful than those waiting around for combat. Marina didn't know anyone back home who had ever been in a battle.

The Navy, which also incorporated the Imperial Corps of Marines, had been larger, but most of the Navy was involved in space exploration. For the most part, within the solar system. *Warrior* was one of only three starships with jump drive capability. She had no idea where the other two might be now.

She smiled. Wouldn't it be wonderful if everyone had the same idea and decided to come home at the same time?

No, she thought, probably not. Contemporary society seemed nervous enough with just one ship visiting. How would they react to three? The current version of humanity seemed far more paranoid than their situation warranted. *Warrior* wasn't a threat, despite her massive firepower. She knew that. A lot of people on the ground apparently weren't convinced. The religious fanatics in the United States, in particular.

Gehunite society had learnt the dangers of that type thousands of years ago. They all knew the old myths, including the Callaaite legend of Onira herself literally materialising and fighting at the side of Alura IV. Marina had always liked that story. What must it be like, she wondered, to do battle with a goddess helping?

She didn't believe it, though. If there ever were gods and goddesses, they seemed to have passed from the scene long ago. It was better that way. When people believed, common sense fled. What was the purpose of religion, after all, except to provide an excuse for one group of people to hate another? Or to feel superior to them?

She felt an odd tingling at her waist. After a moment, she realised it was the mobile telephone the British had provided. She removed it from the belt pouch and slid the "call" icon to the right.

"*Grosh.*" *Warrior*'s technical people had installed a translation system into the phone. Whoever was calling would hear a slightly stilted version of her voice saying "Yes" in English.

"We have arrived at the airport," a male voice said.

"Good. I'll meet you at the security check point." She checked the watch she'd purchased for wear while visiting the planet. Modern time didn't readily translate to the 30-hour Gehunite day. It was simpler to just use a modern watch. "We leave in just over three hours."

"Only the girl will be coming through. Will you recognise her?"

"I'm the only person in this airport wearing an Imperial Navy uniform," Marina said. "I imagine it will be simpler for her to find me."

"Fair enough."

The man rang off. Marina replaced the mobile in its pouch, closed her reading pad, and stood up, automatically adjusting her uniform as she did so.

She walked quickly out of the lounge and headed for the security checkpoint.

◆   ◆   ◆

"I'm a little nervous," Sara said.

"Nothing to be nervous about," 'Smith' assured her. "One of *Warrior*'s officers will meet you after you've gone through security."

Sara frowned. "I hate that."

"What?"

"Airport security. Take your shoes off. Stand in the scanner. Lots of silly questions about your beliefs."

"That's in the US," 'Smith' said. "You're in Canada now. No one gives a damn about your religion. And you're carrying a diplomatic passport, so you won't so much be going *through* security as around it. You'll see."

"Really?"

"Really. Now, go on."

Sara hugged him impulsively. 'Smith' smiled uncomfortably. He tended to be extremely reserved in public.

I wish I could go with her, he thought. I always wanted to be an astronaut.

She got in line. There wouldn't be much for anyone to check, she thought. She just had the one small bag, and all it contained were her school clothes and homework. Her escort had told her she'd be provided with new clothes once she reached the UK.

It took about five minutes to reach the desk where the CATSA officer was checking identification documents. Sara took out her new passport and handed it to the officer.

"You go through there," the officer said, pointing to a lane to the right of the scanners marked "Aircrew."

'Smith' had been right, she thought. She kept her shoes on, and her bag wasn't scanned, though she noticed that a pilot's bag was. Hers was apparently being treated as privileged. I could like being a diplomat, she thought.

She frowned suddenly. That career was out of the question. She wasn't even sure she'd be able to return home after this adventure.

She glanced at her watch, still set to Denver time. Her parents would know she was missing by now. I should call them, she thought. I'm safely on my way now, in another country, and no one can stop me, so I can at least stop them worrying.

Coming out of security, she immediately noticed the Gehunite officer standing close to the wall. Do these guys shake hands? she wondered.

She walked over to her, feeling a bit scared.

Eighteen

THERE WERE FIVE MEMBERS OF THE DENVER DIVISION, American Homeland Police Agency, in the Ellsworths' living room, three uniformed patrolmen, and a pair of detectives. The FBI was expected momentarily. All police agencies in the United States had been nationalised in 2037, but the individual divisions still corresponded to the old local forces, recruited locally, and rarely crossed jurisdictions.

"You're sure your daughter hasn't just run away?" the older detective asked. "Girls her age sometimes do."

"No," Joanne Ellsworth said. "Sara told us she was auditioning for the school musical, and that she'd be home no later than 5:30."

It was now 8:45 pm. Joanne had called the police at 6:00 o'clock. The first patrol car had arrived 20 minutes later.

"I talked to the drama teacher," Art Ellsworth said. "She told me that Sara wasn't at the audition."

"Can you think of anyone who'd want to take her?"

"She's a pretty girl," Art said.

"And you're sure she didn't just stop off to see a friend?"

"Not without telling us. She wouldn't do that."

The phone rang.

"You know what to do," the detective said. "We're set up to trace the call."

Joanne Ellsworth looked at the phone. "It says 'international call,'" she said.

"Go ahead and answer it. We'll be listening in."

"International?" Art said. "Probably some scam artist."

"Answer it anyway. It could be the kidnappers, spoofing the caller ID."

Joanne picked up the receiver and pressed the 'talk' button. They had decided she should do the talking. Art was too shaken up.

"Hello," she said.

She listened for a few seconds. "You're *where?* What the hell are you doing in Vancouver?" She looked at the detective. "It's Sara," she said.

"Find out what's going on."

"You're going where? London? Sara, we told you that you couldn't do that. No, I don't care. Get yourself back here!"

Joanne put down the phone. "She hung up."

"She's in Vancouver?" the detective asked.

"On her way to London."

"What's going on?" Art asked.

"Sara is going to London," Joanne said.

"But we told her she couldn't. We told that damned Brit, too! What's the matter with her?"

The detective looked at them curiously. "You want to explain this?" he said.

"A British guy showed up here a few days ago. Pretended to be a bible salesman, but he wasn't."

"He was a spy," Joanne said. "Told us those space people wanted Sara to visit their ship. We told her she couldn't go and he left."

"At least," Art said, "we thought he did. He must have found some other way to get in touch with her and convinced her to go."

The detective nodded. "So," he said, "it's not a kidnapping."

"It's not? Why not?"

"Because, Mr Ellsworth, it sounds like your daughter left on her own. We can go after the British guy, though. I don't suppose there's any chance he gave you his name, is there?"

"He left his card," Joanne said. "It's in that big bible he left."

The detective opened the book, which was still on the coffee table. He found the card and glanced at it, then shook his head. "Nothing we can do, I'm afraid," he said.

Art and Joanne looked at him as if he were crazy. "Why not?" Joanne asked.

"According to this, he's the military attaché at the consulate in Denver. That means he has diplomatic immunity. We can't arrest him. We can't even ask him questions if doesn't want us to. The most we can do is ask the State Department to kick him out of the country."

"Will they?"

"Hard to say."

"What can we do about getting our daughter back?" Art had a feeling this wasn't going to work out very well.

Someone rang the doorbell, saving the detective from having to come up with an answer. He motioned for one of the uniformed officers to get the door.

"She wasn't kidnapped," he said, after the officer let in three FBI special agents.

"Oh?"

"She's in Canada, on her way to England."

"You don't say? What's that about?"

Joanne shrugged. "Are you the FBI?" These were different people from before.

"Yes, Ma'am," the FBI man said. "I'm Supervisory Special Agent Tom Bennett. These are my colleagues, Special Agent Jerry Kowalski and Special Agent Karl Topper."

"Detective Sergeant Earl FitzGerald," the lead detective said, "Denver AHPA."

"What's going on?" Bennett asked.

"Looks like the girl has run off to look at the space ship."

"What space ship?"

"The one the Brits have been talking about."

"That's a fake," Bennett said.

"Well, that still seems to be where she's gone. With some help from at least one guy at the British Consulate. Or so it seems."

Bennett nodded. He already knew who Sara Ellsworth was. The girl who'd talked to the aliens. Or whatever they really were. A potential troublemaker.

"Anything you need to pass on?" he asked. "We can take over from here."

FitzGerald shook his head. "I'll send you copies of the paperwork, but if the girl left voluntarily, this really isn't anything for us."

"Okay. We have to ask a few questions, but you guys can take off and go do something more useful."

The Denver cops didn't hang around any longer than it took them to pack up their equipment.

Bennett ran Art and Joanne through their story again. He agreed with FitzGerald about the British attaché likely being immune from any official action, other than a *personna non grata* notice.

He wasn't too happy with this part of his job. Officially, *Warrior* didn't exist. The whole thing was some sort of British conspiracy. Unofficially, he was perfectly aware that the official story was bullshit. For one thing, the damned ship was so big you could see it orbiting without a telescope.

The president's brother seemed to be going with a multiple creations explanation. The Gehunites' earth had been wiped clean, presumably in punishment for collective sin, and about 6,000 years ago God had started over.

It would have been a lot less trouble, Bennett thought, if the ship had just come from another planet millions of miles out in space. Aliens didn't conflict with the Bible; pre-creation humans did.

And if some British spy had contacted these people, how was it they hadn't told his office? How much did the girl's parents *really* know?

Nineteen

CAPTAIN CHARLES SEBASTIAN FOLLOWED ROMIWERO onto the bridge. It felt very odd to find himself walking normally while the giant ship orbited near his own platform. He realised he was rather tired out by the walk from the entry port to the bridge. Nearly a year of weightlessness had taken a greater toll on his leg muscles than he'd imagined it would.

It hadn't been that much of a surprise when Captain Romiwero invited him aboard. After all, he'd given her a tour of his own platform first. When she extended the invitation, the day after the Gehunites' reception by his Majesty and the other earth leaders, he'd happily accepted.

She'd sent a travel pod for him. Those still disturbed him in a strange way. It was their shape, he supposed. Tall, triangular polygons with a rounded top. A perfectly logical shape for a one-man transport, when you thought about it. It was just cultural conditioning that made him half expect the pods to suddenly start pursuing him en mass, metallically screaming, "Exterminate!"

The bridge design surprised him. Cinematic starship bridges had mostly followed the same pattern for well over a century. A captain's chair at the rear centre, helm and navigation stations between the captain and a big view-screen, and everything else around the outside, generally on a slightly higher level.

Here, everyone sat *behind* the captain, helm to port, engineering to starboard.

"This isn't what I expected," he said.

Romiwero nodded. "When the ship was designed, a major criterion was to keep things as familiar as possible. Living quarters were designed to resemble each crew member's home. The bridge design is based on old transport aircraft, though a good bit roomier."

"Your engineer is up here with you, then?" Sebastian said. "We always figured they'd be back with the engines."

"Not a good place to be on a ship like this one. There's a lot of shielding around the engines, but quite a bit of radiation still makes it into the engine spaces. It won't kill you, but after a couple weeks you won't be having any children, either."

"And you steer from here?"

"Right. That knob in the centre is the wheel, and controls yaw. The stick to the left controls pitch. Redundant instruments. Normally, the helmsman uses the display panel, but there are analogue instruments as a backup." She pointed. "Compass, horizon display, speed readout, course display, and so on."

"Wait," Sebastian said. "Compass? There's no north or south in space."

"No. The compass uses an arbitrary baseline. Within the solar system, it's a line from the centre of the sun through wherever Barzak—Earth—was at the time of departure. Horizon line is the base planetary orbital plane. Outside the solar system it's mostly a matter of calculating the vector between where we are and where we want to end up."

Sebastian looked up at the view-screen. The ones on his platform were state of the art, but you never really doubted you were looking at a digital display. These were far beyond that. It was like looking out through a perfectly-cleaned window. "I'd love to be sitting here when you're running at full speed, watching the stars zip past."

Romiwero laughed. "You've been watching too many of your own motion pictures," she said. "Most stars are light years apart. Even at near light speed they hardly seem to move at all. And when we're in jump space you don't see anything. You're just in one place and the next moment you're somewhere else and to the universe outside the ship years have passed."

"How far have you actually ventured from earth?"

"A little over eight thousand light years. Relative to the universe itself, travel in jump space is essentially at the speed of light. Relative to the ship, of course, it's a great deal faster."

Sebastian shrugged. He'd naturally studied physics in preparation for his career. Basic courses at Dartmouth, and more in depth study at Balliol College, Oxford. He was familiar with Newton, Einstein, Hawking, and Carruthers.[10] The basic concepts of wormholes and space warping had been part of what he studied, but it was all hypothesis. Not even a fully-fledged theory. Mostly because, while it seemed possible and didn't appear to violate any physical laws, the consensus was that the energy requirements were still well beyond present capabilities.

Beyond *any* capabilities, his professors had suggested.

"You're not going to explain how you do this, are you?" he asked. "This jump space concept."

Romiwero smiled. "No. You have to figure that out for yourselves."

"I can understand the physics," Sebastian said. "I just can't figure out how you manage to power it."

"From what I've seen in your literature," Romiwero said, "you're getting closer. Given some time, you'll get there."

"How much time?"

"Who can say. A few years. A few centuries."

"The Americans could probably manage it," he said. "If they wanted to. Used to be, that country produced some genuinely brilliant scientists. My command is named after one of them." He frowned. "Not now, though. Their government has spent the last century in a concerted effort to make their people more ignorant about science. They're thoroughly under the fundamentalist Christian thumb."

Romiwero nodded. "I wish I could go there," she said. "Visit my original home. Or as close to it as I can get, anyway. The place where I was born is well offshore now. As close as I can determine, about 30 kilometres east of someplace called Miami."

"That's far enough offshore," Sebastian said, "that I suppose it's possible you could ask the Royal Navy to put you aboard a ship and cruise over the site. I suspect they'd do that, if you asked."

10 Sir James Carruthers (1998–2067), theoretical physicist, Lucasian Professor of Mathematics, University of Cambridge, 2052–64. Nobel Prize in Physics, 2048, for his *General Theory of Subquantum Physical Interaction in Incipient Systems*.

"No. There's really nothing there, other than coordinates on a chart. Believe me, we've done sensor scans of the area. Eighty-seven thousand years of plate movement and weathering have done a fair job of completely obliterating any remains."

◆   ◆   ◆

Sara Ellsworth stared glumly out the window as the black taxi worked its way through the London traffic on its way to the temporary Gehunite Embassy on Wilton Crescent. The Gehunites had rented a house there, which had promptly been granted the appropriate extraterritorial status of an embassy by the Crown.

The Empress was installed in one of the bedrooms and officially recognised as both head of state for the extinct empire, and its ambassador to the Court of Saint James's, bringing with her a staff of 23. That number included a seven-member squad of Imperial Marines tasked with security, and four petty officers who took care of the cooking and cleaning. The rest were officers whose normal duties included taking on diplomatic functions any time the ship contacted a non-Gehunite civilisation.

These day, Marina had told Sara, that included most of them. The ship visited even colonial worlds so infrequently that they had all developed along different lines in the intervals.

"The only people who really share an identical culture," Marina had said, "are the crews of the three starships, as we all left here at the same time. But we haven't seen either of the other two since then, and quite possibly never will."

Sara took out her mobile phone and pulled up a message from Ellen. She had taken a considerable risk sending it, even using a secure web proxy.

"FBI took away your parents," the text said.

She wondered what that meant. Where had they been taken? Just to the Denver office, where they'd talk to them for a while and then send them home? Or somewhere else?

There was an area of a few square miles in Wyoming that didn't exist on any satellite maps accessible from an American internet connection. If you went onto the secure web, and used a foreign proxy, the area reappeared.

The story was that it was a classified military installation used for testing various secret defence technologies. She didn't think that held up once you got a close view from a British satellite. What you saw from above was a compound perhaps half a mile wide and a mile and a half long, surrounded by a triple fence and guard towers. Inside were row upon row of long, soulless apartment blocks. Barracks, she thought, might be a better term.

Interspersed amongst the barracks were other buildings. One of them was obviously a theatre. The stage house was visible in the satellite images. There were also at least five churches or chapels, along with warehouses, administration buildings, and more than a dozen buildings that appeared to be mess halls.

The satellite images also included people. Lots of people, of all ages, including children.

There were any number of suggestions as to the place's real purpose. The most common one was that it was a temporary holding facility for illegal aliens awaiting deportation. A somewhat darker suggestion was that this was where people sometimes disappeared to.

Everyone knew people like that. Individuals, or even entire families, that suddenly, overnight, decided to "move away" without really telling anyone. Oddly, these always seemed to be people considered "trouble makers." People who persisted in declaring that the world was older than the Bible allowed. People who had the nerve to claim that coastal cities were being slowly swallowed by the oceans because the world was getting warmer and the seas were rising and not, as official policy had it, because the coastal land was subsiding. Atheists. Homosexuals.

The law said homosexuals were to be executed, but there were rumours that this was ignored in the case of "useful" individuals. Scientists, mathematicians, that sort of people. The story was they'd be allowed to go on living, so long as they remained productive, but would also be removed from society and sent somewhere that no one would ever see them again.

Sara strongly suspected the darker implications were true. If it was a transient camp for deportees, she wondered, why was there such a large cemetery just outside the gates? No, she thought, the sceptics were likely right. The place was a concentration camp. A reasonably comfortable one, from the look of things, but still a concentration camp. Or perhaps a better term was relocation camp, such as rumour suggested were built to house Japanese Americans during World War II.

Those camps were mentioned in some old history books she'd seen. The current ones said that all Christian Japanese Americans had quickly declared their support for the United States, and that the handful of Buddhist and Shinto Japanese, who obviously remained faithful to Japan, had been exchanged for American civilians living in Japan at the beginning of the war. There had been no camps, the history books said. Establishing them would have been out of character for the deeply religious Franklin Roosevelt.

Sara wasn't so sure. The newer books just seemed to fit too neatly into the official picture of the government as a benevolent Christian parent bringing God's blessing to his favourite people.

"I hope they're alright," Sara muttered.

"Who?" Marina asked.

"My parents." She showed her the message.

Marina shook her head. "I can't read that," she said.

"It says that the FBI took away my parents. Why would they do that?"

"Who are the FBI?"

Sara frowned. "The federal cops," she said. "But my parents didn't do anything."

Marina nodded. If her parents hadn't done anything, then logically this FBI should let them go.

Logically.

Everything she had seen and read suggested that the United States was unfamiliar with the concept of logic.

"I'm sure everything will be all right," Marina said.

"I hope so."

The cab pulled up to the kerb in front of the embassy. The two Marine guards peered at it curiously. Sara noticed that they were armed with rifles of some sort. They looked like none she had ever seen. For a moment, she wondered if the British allowed them to have bullets, but then she remembered that the house and its grounds, including the pavement in front of it, was legally Gehunite territory. The British really wouldn't have any say in whether the rifles were loaded.

Marina exited the cab first, with Sara following. The guards snapped to attention and brought their rifles to present arms. Marina returned the salute and led Sara into the building.

Twenty

PRESIDENT WILL GORDON READ THE REPORT CAREFULLY. Sometimes, he decided, you had to wonder if people were capable of thinking. The Denver FBI office had responded to a kidnapping report. Normal enough. Kidnapping had been the province of the FBI since 1932. With a minor involved there was no waiting period. For adults, they couldn't take over until enough time had passed for the victim to have been taken across state lines. It didn't matter whether they actually were. There was a presumption that after a few hours it *could* have happened, and interstate crime was the FBI's department.

Then, it turned out, there was no kidnapping. At least, none that could be charged and prosecuted. The girl had gone away voluntarily, and the people who helped her appeared to be diplomats and consequently untouchable. The State Department would ask the British government to recall their military attaché in Denver. Probably, the man had done little more than make the initial contact, but his was the only name they had, so he'd be the one sent home.

The Brits would have to take the blame. Tough, but that's how it was supposed to work. They'd aided a hostile government—was government the right word? It would have to do. They'd aided a hostile government to kidnap an American citizen. That sort of action had consequences. Kicking out the only known responsible diplomat was one of them.

And that should have been where it ended. They'd put the parents on television, after carefully preparing them, and have them tell their story. Tell how the Brits had taken their little girl as part of their weird scheme to trick the world into accepting their elaborate space-returnee hoax. Have them plead with the English to return their kidnapped daughter, before she was subjected to brainwashing.

The American government would be sympathetic to their plight. They would vow to do everything in their power to see that young Sara was returned to her loving home.

Obviously, she wouldn't *actually* come back. He'd have someone in London take care of that. She certainly couldn't be allowed back into the United States.

Not if she actually met these space people. It was important that Americans accepted the government line, that it was all a hoax. Oh, sure, people could go into space. There were people living on Mars, weren't there? But people from eighty-odd thousand years ago? No, that wasn't possible. It didn't matter if it was true. The official policy of the United States was that Genesis was true in all respects. His brother could fudge the story with his multiple-creations myths, but that couldn't become policy. There was too much invested in the young-earth version.

Gordon wasn't stupid. He knew perfectly well that it was all probably true, and the space people were really earth people from a very, very long time ago. He'd been a fifth-generation evangelist before running for office. He knew perfectly well it was all a scam. But it was a very profitable scam, and perpetuating it required that the people, if not their leaders, maintained their faith. Policy, and law, was that the Bible was true and without error. If reality differed from policy, policy had to prevail.

The girl couldn't return, and her parents should have become the poster parents for the evils of perfidious Albion.

He smiled at that. He'd had a fairly good classical education. It was nice to see he remembered such things.

Except the FBI had screwed it up. This SSA Bennett, the boss out there in Denver, had arrested the parents. He didn't believe they were innocent in their daughter's defection. Or so he reported. They were already at Camp Antelope. The cover story was already being spread. The loss of their daughter had broken them and they'd moved away. They didn't want anything to do with their past. They'd just moved, and no one knew where they went.

There was no way they could bring them back home now. Not from Antelope.

A few foreigners got out, to be instantly deported with a stern warning about what would happen to them, and their families, if they ever said anything about their experience, which, in any case, would have been in a segregated section where the only Americans they'd ever encounter were the guards. But American citizens? No, once they were in, they stayed in. The camp didn't even officially exist.

It was a place for questionable people. People who'd shown they couldn't live in society without causing problems. Atheists, communists, the small percentage of gays who possessed skills that made them too valuable to execute. Or people like the Ellsworths, who shouldn't have been sent there, but now that they had been they'd have to stay until they died.

The FBI had already got the cover story in place. People would understand why the family had left. That sort of thing was part of the FBI's job. People sometimes had to disappear.

It had been a tough slog, getting rid of the Liberals, the bleeding hearts who failed to recognise that people shouldn't be allowed to think for themselves. They'd had to take over the White House and Congress, which had let them take over the courts.

The hardest part, really, had been taking over the Republican Party. It hadn't been easy to infiltrate that bunch. The oldline Republicans had still believed in personal autonomy. Converting them from the party of Lincoln, Teddy Roosevelt, and Nelson Rockefeller into the party of Jesus hadn't been easy. Not until the old leadership had died off, and been replaced by younger leaders, by leaders who'd never heard Barry Goldwater warn what would happen if religion was given a voice in politics.

Well, Goldwater had been a Jew, hadn't he? Oh, sure, he was an Episcopalian, but that didn't matter. He was still a Jew. And Episcopalians weren't strong Christians anyway. Hell, they ordained women. They'd even ordained gays for a while, until that sort of perversion was made illegal.

So the Ellsworths, who from all he could tell were merely a nice, middle-class Baptist couple with a rebellious daughter, would live out the rest of their lives at Camp Antelope. And someone in the UK would have to take care of their daughter.

Before that idiot Bennett had locked up her parents, he'd have just had someone tell her to stay in the UK. Or somewhere outside the United States, anyway. Only Bennett had included a bit in the cover story suggesting the girl had been taken by a serial killer. Now they'd have to not only make sure she didn't return, but make sure no one ever heard from her again.

It seemed a strange thing for a former evangelist to be doing, ordering a minor diplomatic functionary in England to kill an American citizen. He had a feeling Jesus wouldn't approve, even though it was being done to ensure His kingdom would soon come to Earth.

Twenty-One

SARA ELLSWORTH WAS AS NERVOUS AS SHE'D EVER BEEN in her life. After spending two days in a comfortable room in the Gehunite Embassy, she found herself waiting in the entry hall, looking through the faceted glass panes in the door as the police blocked traffic on Wilton Crescent.

"Any moment now," Marina said.

The cops all suddenly looked up. The Marines, Sara noticed, kept their eyes on the crowd gathered on the far side of the street. The shuttle wasn't going to hurt anyone. If there was any danger, it would come from one of those people.

The shuttle touched down in the middle of the street, making hardly a sound as it descended. It landed so that the door, when it opened, was facing the embassy.

"Let's go," Marina said, opening the door.

Sara followed her out. Marina motioned for her to climb aboard first, then quickly followed. Her escort pointed to a seat, then sat beside her. Sara was surprised to notice there were no seat belts.

The door closed and the shuttle lifted off. Sara could tell this only because she could see the street start to fall away outside the window. There was no sensation of movement.

She saw something bright rising from the narrow space between two houses opposite the embassy. "What's that?" she asked.

"What?"

"That." She pointed.

Marina's eyes opened wide. "Somebody," she said, "doesn't like us. That's a missile of some sort."

An alarm started blaring at the front of the shuttle. The pilot reacted and the shuttle changed attitude and dropped a couple hundred feet. The point of light changed course, following them. A moment later it grew suddenly brighter as the automated defence system engaged the missile with a concentrated energy beam, raising the two-kilogramme warhead's temperature to $3,000°$ in less than a second and blowing it up.

They descended rapidly. Sara's view was of nothing more interesting than some houses and other building, and the length of the street. The pilot, she presumed, would be able to see where the missile had been fired from.

She could see four Gehunite Marines running from the embassy and out of view. Perhaps a minute later they returned, dragging a dark-haired man. One of the Marines was carrying a stubby tube. The missile launcher, Sara presumed.

The shuttle dropped back to the street and the four Marines brought the man aboard. They took him to the back of the shuttle, which promptly lifted off.

"You can't do this to me," the man protested. "I have diplomatic immunity."

One of the Marines was examining the man's passport with a translator. "So you did," she said. "Unfortunately for you, this shuttle is officially sovereign territory of the Empire of Gehun. Diplomatic immunity only applies in countries where yours has diplomatic relations, and yours has made a rather public point of claiming we don't exist."

The man looked defiant. Despite the rather ordinary clothes, he had the look of a soldier of some sort. Sara immediately recognized the New York accent. Their attacker had been an American, and presumably connected with the embassy.

From all she had heard, this was the first time anyone had attacked a Gehunite, or one of their shuttles. Sara thought it unlikely the first attack happening while she was aboard the shuttle was a coincidence.

"I think this is about me," she told Marina.

Her escort nodded. "What makes you that important? You're a nice kid, but you don't strike me as being out of the average."

"I'm not. I'm just curious." She frowned. "Maybe that's the problem. Back home, they don't like curious people. You're just supposed to do as you're told."

Outside the windows, the sky was rapidly darkening as the shuttle gained altitude. Soon the city had ceased to be anything more than an indistinct blot on a mostly-green island.

The pilot came in at an angle that gave Sara a good view of the ship from her window. It was huge. The Sagan Space Platform, until recently presumed to be the largest man-made object ever to orbit the earth, looked like a toy beside it.

The landing bay doors opened, surprising Sara. It looked to her like the seamless silver skin of the ship removed itself to allow the shuttle to enter. It was only from the inside that you could see the doors when they were closed.

"We'll have to wait a few minutes while the shuttle bay is pressurized," Marina told her.

"What happens to the air when they open it?" Sara asked.

"It's evacuated into holding tanks," the Gehunite officer explained. "That's really the only practical option. If we just opened the doors and let the air out, not only would it push the ship around, but we'd eventually run out of air."

"How could opening the doors move the ship?"

"You're in space, Sara. There no air up here, so there's no friction to affect the ship. It takes very little thrust to move it. A couple of people in atmospheric suits using their manoeuvring thrusters could shift it."

Sara looked towards the rear of the shuttle. The Marines were keeping a close watch on the American. They'd searched him after bringing him aboard, and the female Marine corporal, who seemed to be the leader, was examining a wicked-looking folding knife. The man looked at Sara and smiled. It was not a friendly smile.

The shuttle pilot, a pleasant looking lieutenant with blond hair, came back into the passenger compartment and said something to Marina. He wasn't wearing a translator, so what Sara heard sounded like gibberish.

"Come along," Marina said, rising. "The shuttle bay's pressurised. You can go see the ship."

♦   ♦   ♦

They entered the airlock. The heavy door closed behind them, and the big compartment was flooded with an odd blue light. Sara looked curiously at Marina.

"Decontamination system," she said. "Don't want to bring anything contagious up from the planet. It's only a few seconds, then they'll open the inner door."

Romiwero was waiting for them just outside the landing bay airlock. She smiled as the girl almost tripped over the coaming. After years aboard a starship, or even an ordinary ship, you no longer noticed hatch coamings.

"Welcome aboard, Sara," she said.

"Uh, hi."

The captain was in her working uniform, which had a more utilitarian appearance than Marina's service dress uniform.

"I'll leave you with the captain," Marina told her. "My leave is up, so it's time for me to get back to work." She looked at the captain. "By your leave, Captain."

"Welcome back, Lieutenant. I believe you have the evening watch, so that should give you some time to readjust before taking over."

Romiwero watched Marina walk off down a passageway, then turned back to Sara. "So," she said, "you're the girl who gave us hope."

"Uh, what?"

Romiwero smiled. "Until you came on the radio and scolded us, we weren't entirely sure what to expect. There was a lot of electronic noise coming from this planet, but no one was responding to our message. We weren't sure what to expect, you see."

"I think so."

"We knew there were still people here. What we didn't know was the state of the contemporary civilisation. What we were picking up wasn't promising. And the only thing we were hearing on what used to be our primary traffic control channel was a lot of electronic beeping. Then you came on."

"I wasn't that polite," Sara said. "I mean, if I remember right, about all I did was tell you shut up and get off the channel."

"We didn't know that until somewhat later, after we'd learnt to translate your language into ours. What mattered to us at the time was that *someone* had answered. It's usually so long between visits to any particular planet that we can't reasonably expect the language not to have evolved into something we no longer understand. But your entertainment channels seem to run towards a lot of violence. That's never reassuring. You can't help but wonder if the violence reflects a mere propensity for action as a diversion, or the actual behaviour of the society that's watching it."

Sara laughed. "That depends where you are," she said. "Where I live, it mostly runs to ridiculous religious programming. Jesus is due back any second now, your neighbours are about to raptured, so don't be left behind. That sort of thing."

"I don't really understand that," Romiwero said. "But, come along. I'll show you around the ship. The part we live in, at least. The aftermost three quarters of this great beast contain nothing but engines and fuel storage."

The Marines were bringing out their prisoner as the Captain led Sara down the same passageway Marina had taken.

"It takes a lot of power to go faster than light, doesn't it?" Sara asked, as they rode a lift up to the command level.

"You can't do that," Romiwero said. "Not really."

"Isn't that what your, uh, jump drive is all about?"

"It only seems that way. We can go extremely fast. Full speed is 127,000 kilometres per second. Much beyond that and physics starts kicking in. Mass increases faster than power, so it simply isn't possible to generate enough thrust to overcome it."

"How does it work, then?"

Romiwero looked at the girl and smiled. The things she'd learnt about the United States had led her to expect someone quite different. She'd got an impression of a country where no one was curious about anything.

"The jump drive creates what we call an Arkhgaizim passageway. The name comes from Arigor Arkhgaizim, a physicist at the University of Balin, who worked out the maths that led to the jump drive. The passageway connects two points in spacetime and the ship jumps between them."

"So, a wormhole?"

"I believe that's what you call it, yes."

"I'd really love to see what that feels like," Sara enthused.

"You'd be disappointed. It doesn't feel like anything. You're just somewhere else all of a sudden. And you're suddenly much older, so far as the universe is concerned."

Sara nodded. "That's something else I don't understand."

Romiwero opened a door and led Sara into the wardroom. It was deserted, except for a chief steward, who was smiling and looking very attentive behind the bar. If she looked closer, the captain knew, she'd find the reading pad he'd slipped under the bar when he heard the door start to open.

She led Sara to a corner and indicated a comfortable, leather-upholstered armchair. Like all the other leather appointments aboard *Warrior*, the hide was cloned and had never adorned a cow. Cloned leather had considerable advantages over natural hides, not the least being the ability to make the cloned hide as large as needed. If you required a five by eight metre hide, you simply grew it that size, rather than trying to match natural hides from several steers.

Romiwero sat in an identical chair. "I am very nearly 87,000 years old, so far as the universe is concerned," she said. "And just over a month ago I celebrated my forty-fifth birthday. Ship time and real time are wildly out of synch."

"That's what I mean," Sara said. "Those numbers don't go together."

"Here's what happens," the captain explained. "Because nothing can exceed the speed of light, even with the Arkhgaizim passageway, it still requires, say, 220 years for the ship to travel 220 light years. What the passageway does — what it seems to do, at least — is insulate the ship and everything in it from the passage of time. From a universal point of view, the ship takes 220 years to travel through the passageway, but from our viewpoint it's instantaneous.

"Now, you could argue that this is a means of travelling in time as much as in space, but it's strictly a one-way trip. You can only move forward, never back. A ship like this one — and there are, or at least were, two others just like her — can only return to *where* she started. She can never return to *when*. As soon as we made our first jump, two days after we left orbit, we said good-bye to everyone we'd ever known. In a single moment, we went from a starship crew with large, extended families at home, to a crew whose immediate families had mostly been dead for over a century.

Sara nodded. It was starting to make sense.

"I wonder if I still have a family," she said.

"What do you mean?" Romiwero asked.

"From the messages I got from my friend, Ellen, my parents have disappeared. The FBI took them away and they never came home." She frowned. "I'm even wondering about Ellen now. Nothing from her in two days. Maybe they got her, too."

The steward materialised at the captain's side.

She looked at Sara. "Would you like something to drink? We have our own beers and spirits, made aboard ship, and we've been stocking up on our British friends' products as well."

"I don't drink. I'm not old enough. Unless you've got a Coke back there."

The steward looked at her curiously. He'd been warned about a probable visitor, so he'd worn his translator, but it didn't do very well with brand names. "What is Coke?"

"Carbonated drink, kind of brownish, fizzy, comes in a curvy bottle." Sara indicated the shape of the bottle with her hands.

The steward looked thoughtful, then smiled. "Maybe," he said.

He walked back to the bar and opened a refrigerated storage cupboard behind it. They'd been bringing up all sorts of things from the planet. Maybe, he thought. Yes.

The steward pulled a wasp-waisted bottle from the cooler and held it up. "This?"

Sara nodded. The steward opened the bottle and brought it over on a tray, together with a glass. A second glass, and a bottle of Callaaite ale, was for the captain.

Sara didn't bother with the glass, drinking from the bottle. Then she looked at the other two, suddenly wondering if she was breaking some sort of social taboo. Her Aunt May was like that. You didn't drink from anything but a proper glass or cup in her house.

As no one was paying any attention, she decided it must be okay.

"I never expected to find Coke aboard a starship," Sara said.

"We've brought up all sorts of modern things," Romiwero replied. "I'll admit I don't care for that one. Others seem to like it. You obviously do." She poured the ale into her glass and sipped at it. "You say you're too young to drink alcohol, though. How old are you, exactly?"

"Fifteen."

The captain nodded. "When we left, you'd have been old enough. I suppose you are now, so long as you're aboard this ship. Our laws apply here." She paused, took another drink. "How much education have you had, Sara?"

"I'll be a junior when school starts again. I'm just finishing up tenth grade. Two more to go."

"You'd have been ready for university in our system. Our children started school at three, graduated from secondary school—what you'd call high school—at about fifteen, then either started at university, entered an apprenticeship, or took a job that didn't require either of those. Other Ranks in the Navy, for example. Officers have to attend a service college before commissioning, but other ranks can join after secondary school.

Sara looked around the wardroom. It was a large room, with dark, carved oak wainscoting, and deep blue patterned wallpaper above. The table looked like it could seat at least thirty. More of the low armchairs, like the one she was seated in, were placed around the bulkheads, with small tables between them. From the length of the bar, and the number of bottles behind it, it was obvious the Imperial Navy maintained a traditional attitude towards alcohol.

"Needs windows," Sara commented.

"Easily managed," Romiwero said. She took a communicator from her pocket and spoke into it. "Maintenance. Viewport, 108–109, starboard, wardroom."

The solid bulkhead to Sara's right shimmered and disappeared above the wainscoting. It took her a moment to realise that the bulkhead was still there, its surface now transformed into a high definition screen detailed enough to pass for an actual window. Looking up—the ship was inverted relative to the planet—she could see they were passing over the United States.

"My parents are down there," she said. "Somewhere."

"Perhaps we should look for them," Romiwero suggested.

There was a soft buzzing sound from the bar. Sara glanced over, to see the steward pick up a communications handset and speak into it. He listened for a moment, then said, "*Osha. Ko zhintu.*"

Romiwero rose. "Excuse me a moment." She walked quickly to the bar and took the handset.

The captain listened for several minutes, intermittently commenting or asking a question. Sara took out her phone and started working a crossword puzzle while she waited for the captain to return.

"Sorry," Romiwero said, sitting down again.

"You have a ship to run," Sara said. "Probably keeps you pretty busy."

"It does at that. That was about you, though."

"Me?"

"My security people have been having a chat with the fellow who tried to shoot down our shuttle. They can be quite persuasive."

Sara looked at her narrowly. "You didn't torture the guy, did you?" It was the sort of thing her own government wouldn't balk at.

Romiwero laughed. "No, absolutely not. No, we just gave him a whiff of a chemical compound that affects the brain in a way that removes inhibitions and makes a person feel that cooperating with their new friends is absolutely the most important thing in the world."

"Some kind of truth serum?"

"I suppose you could call it that."

"So, he talked?"

"Told us everything. He's a very happy fellow at the moment, but complaining about his hands being restrained."

"Why do that? Would he attack someone?"

"As I said, the gas removes inhibitions. Unfortunately, besides making people talk, it removes some inhibitions we'd just as soon *not* be removed."

"Oh." Sara flashed on a totally uninhibited man, then wished she hadn't. "Uh, what did he say?"

"That he took the shot because you were aboard the shuttle. Apparently, someone high up in your government wants you dead. Or the American ambassador in London is interpreting it that way, anyway."

"I'm not that important. I mean, if it was up to me, I'd just come up here, visit with you guys for a while, then go back home and do normal high school stuff. I don't think I can now, though. I may have to stay in England." She shrugged. "Well, at least I already speak the language."

"After what happened today," Romiwero said, "I'm not sure that would be safe."

"I'm not, either."

She sat back in the chair, sipping her Coke, looking out the view-screen. All of the wallpaper was digital, she realised. The Gehunites had apparently managed to build screens that were completely non-reflective. It wasn't until you got very close that you realised that what looked like wallpaper was an image, and not something printed and pasted onto the wall.

"How did you stop the missile?" she asked. "I noticed your Marines were all armed with ordinary guns. I didn't expect that. I was expecting ray guns of some sort. But I didn't hear any gunfire during the attack."

"It's a different weapons system. Marines use normal firearms, very like what your own forces use. Our two cultures seem to have tackled the question of how to build a personal weapon and come up with essentially the same answer. A conical projectile, fixed into a tubular brass casing, and fired with a percussion cap primer. Ours use an 8-millimetre bullet, and the stocks and mechanisms are a bit different, but the principle is exactly the same. They're relatively inexpensive, easy to manufacture, and they certainly do the job. But they'd be a bad choice in the sort of situation you were in. Too dangerous to people on the ground, for one thing.

"Also, the shuttles operate outside the atmosphere, where recoil from firearms would cause all kinds of problems with steering. They're equipped with high energy laser and particle beam weapons, similar to what this ship is armed with, though nowhere near as powerful. When our new friend fired that little missile, it was just a matter of locking on and hitting it with the weapon. That heated up the missile enough to blow it up."

"Why don't your soldiers use these?"

"Too bulky. Hand-fired versions only exist in fiction. You'd need a forty-kilo power supply to make one work."

"What are you going to do with the guy?"

"Once the gas has worn off, we'll give him to our British friends. I suppose they'll send him home, as he *is* a diplomat."

Sara looked up at the planet. The east coast would be coming into view before long. "You said you might be able to find my parents?"

Romiwero took a drink of ale and nodded. "Possibly. We'd have to know where to start looking. And, they'd have to be where we can see them, which means outdoors."

"I have an idea of where. I can't say for sure, but there are rumours."

"Where?"

"Wyoming. There's a camp there that only shows up on satellite imaging if you're *not* in the United States. I think it's where the government puts people they don't like." She shook her head. "Or whose children they don't like. I had my doubts about being able to go home when I agreed to come here. After today I'm sure of it."

"It did seem a bit extreme."

"I got a visit from our ambassador while I was staying at your embassy in London. He told me, quite bluntly, that I was welcome to stay in England, but not to go home. I got the distinct impression that trying to go back home would get me killed."

"What did you tell him?"

"I told him to go to hell. I guess that anti-aircraft missile was the answer."

"Perhaps," the captain said, "it's just as well we had Lieutenant Fehmadaatin accompany you from Vancouver."

"Good fighter?"

"She's probably the most dangerous person aboard this ship."

"Really? She seems like a really nice person."

"She is. She's a really nice person who happens to know about 200 different ways to kill you with her bare hands."

"Well," Sara said, "I like her. But, you gave me a bodyguard?"

Romiwero laughed. "No, nothing like that. She'd gone there because she liked the travel brochure. I just decided that, since she was there anyway, she could stay over an extra day and accompany you to England. If I'd thought you needed protection, though, she'd certainly have been one of the people I sent."

Twenty-Two

ART ELLSWORTH SAT ON THE EDGE OF THE BED, looking out the second story window at the floodlit lawn below. He found himself wanting to call it a parade ground. That was what it reminded him of. These apartment buildings, as they were officially called, looked like barracks, so what was in front of them would be a parade ground.

They'd been there a week now. Things people said suggested it wouldn't be a short stay. "No one ever leaves," someone had told him.

He looked over his shoulder at Joanne, sleeping soundly, turned towards the wall. He felt sure she blamed him for their predicament. They hadn't had sex since they arrived. He wondered if that was because she was still mad at him, or because the FBI had found her birth control pills and confiscated them.

She wouldn't be able to get more in this place. Contraception was illegal unless a woman could get two doctors to agree that getting pregnant would kill her. Birth control pills were mostly smuggled in from Canada. They weren't that hard to come by on the outside. Inside the camp it was a different story. The place was full of young kids, most of them born there.

There were also a lot of teenagers, almost none of whom were born in the camp. They came in like the adults, after being caught doing something that, presumably, merited being removed from society.

What you didn't see were mid-range children. There were kids younger than two, and teenagers. Once a child reached the age of two he disappeared from the camp. Adopted out, was the story. Art figured it was true. Let the mothers raise them until they could walk and talk, and were mostly out of diapers. At two, they were still too young to form long-lasting memories. They wouldn't remember the camp after a few years on the outside. Or, if they did, the memories would be vague, for little children tend to be very self-centred, fixated on their parents more than their surroundings.

Art still wasn't quite sure why *they* were there. He'd told Sara to stay home. If she'd gone anyway, that was her decision. We're *victims* here, me and Joanne, he thought, not criminals.

Had anyone told him President Gordon agreed with him, Art wouldn't have believed it.

But no one was going to tell him that. Nor would anyone tell him that SSA Bennett, Supervisory Special Agent in Charge of the Denver FBI office, was now ordinary Special Agent Bennett, rather unexpectedly reassigned to the Nome, Alaska field office as junior agent in charge of old paperwork.

Art might have been happy to hear both of those things, but it wouldn't help his present situation. They weren't going anywhere. They knew too much now. It was the rumour of such places that made them effective, gave people something to be afraid of, even while the government vehemently denied any such camps existed. It wouldn't do to let people out. Sometimes illusion was more important than reality. Fear of something you weren't sure of kept you in line. If you knew—really knew—it could backfire, with the useful fear replaced by defiance.

◆   ◆   ◆

Jerry Kowalski sipped his tea and watched Nick and Maureen Harris as they sat together on the couch, in front of the big picture window in the living room of their Denver split-level. I should have grabbed the couch for myself, he thought. The house faced west, so the low early evening sun put the couple in shadow. A power position, Kowalski decided.

Kowalski looked at Special Agent Topper, who was sitting uncomfortably in the other armchair. We're both just a little out of place, he decided. With Bennett reassigned, Kowalski had been promoted to Supervisory Special Agent and placed in charge of the Denver office. Just luck, really. Kowalski and Topper had both advised against taking the Ellsworths into custody, much less sending them to Camp Antelope. So only Bennett had suffered the fallout. Considering he'd managed to piss off the president, Bennett was lucky he'd just been demoted and shipped off to the wilderness. Gordon could just as easily have made him join the Ellsworths in that miserable Wyoming limbo.

"We'll be doing whatever we can to find your daughter," Kowalski said.

"I don't understand why no one has tried to contact us," Maureen said. "Don't they usually do that?"

"Sometimes they wait a while," Kowalski replied.

"We're not even sure it *was* a kidnapping at this point," Topper added. "We're making that assumption just to be on the safe side, but we're not sure."

Nick Harris shook his head. He stood up and started pacing in front of the couch. "What else could it be?" he demanded.

"She's fifteen," Kowalski said. "Sometimes girls that age just run away."

"No," Maureen declared. "Not our Ellen. Somebody took her."

The doorbell rang. Topper went to answer it. He returned with Special Agent Alex Gorell. He was a big, impressive looking guy, with dark, deep-set brown eyes, and dark brown hair cut very short.

"Special Agent Gorell will stay with you for the next eight hours," Kowalski said. "Another agent will take over at that point, if we haven't learnt anything else by then."

"Ma'am," Gorell said. "Sir."

"Special Agent Topper and I will be going now. There are investigative avenues we can best follow at the office. Electronic forensics, that sort of thing."

"We've got some really impressive computers," Topper offered.

"Just find Ellen," Nick pleaded. "She's the only kid we've got."

Kowalski and Topper walked out to their car in silence. Kowalski got into the driver's seat. Topper got in on the other side a moment later. The senior agent started the car. "Go to office," he said.

"Going to office," the car's computer responded. It seemed to think about this for a minute, then said, "Estimated driving time is fourteen minutes."

The car pulled away from the kerb and headed into the city.

"I feel sorry for those two," Topper said.

Kowalski nodded. "So do I. We'll let them stew until around noon tomorrow, then give them the report."

Topper grimaced. "What's the story this time?"

"She used her ID to board a plane to New York. Security cameras show she was alone, so we have to presume she just ran away. So far as we know, she arrived there okay. After that, nothing. I guess we can say we figure she bought a fake ID in New York." He shook his head, staring at the navigation display. One of these days, he thought, he was going to try driving for himself. It had been too long.

"Damn shame when teenage girls run away, Jerry," Topper said. "Damn shame."

"Yeah. Well, she shouldn't have texted the Ellsworth kid. Not with what she told her."

"When are they shipping her out?"

"Later tonight. She'll be in Wyoming sometime tomorrow afternoon."

◆   ◆   ◆

"What do you plan to do?" Marina asked. They were in her quarters. She'd changed into shorts and a halter top, and let her long, blond hair hang down her back.

Sara shrugged. "I'm not sure. Live in England, I suppose."

"They seem good people."

"I thought about going with you guys, but what about my parents?" She gave a sad little laugh. "Anyway, I suppose I'm too young for that."

"You're fifteen, aren't you?" Marina asked.

"That's right."

"Then you're old enough. It's not like you'd be thrown into any complicated technical situations right away. I expect you'd spend the first year of so just learning the language. Translators are convenient, but it's much better to communicate without them."

"I'm not sure I could learn it."

"The grammar is simpler than yours. I didn't learn to speak Gehunite until I was very nearly your age."

"You didn't?"

"No. Well, I grew up in Callaahavn, so we always spoke Callaaish." She blinked and frowned. It was the first time she'd heard what the translator did to the name of her native tongue. Why, she wondered, did it turn the "nur" in *Callaanur* into "ish," but the "kili" in *Gehunkili* into "ite?" Both suffixes had the same meaning.

"Could you say something in your own language?" Sara asked. She was curious to hear what it sounded like without the translator.

Marina shrugged and touched a button on her translator. "*El kornii vim gutkimt da stiitsgropemechun unt hette kom,*" she said.

Sounds vaguely Germanic, Sara thought. Or Scandinavian. She smiled. Come to that, it probably *was* Scandinavian in a way. She'd seen maps of what earth had looked like when this ship started its journey. Callaa had been located on a peninsula in the general vicinity of modern Norway and Sweden.

"What's that mean?" she asked.

Marina switched her translator back on. "All manner of good luck for the United States girl and more to come." She shrugged. "Old Callaaite greeting."

Sara frowned. "Let's hope you're right."

They were in the living room of Marina's quarters. Like the others, her suite was a duplicate of her home. The walls were wood, time-worn pine logs, looking exactly like the log walls of her mother's house in Callaahavn. It was an illusion, of course. The logs were machine hewn wooden slabs with flat backs, attached to the metal bulkheads that defined the actual spaces. The view from the window was a hologram. It looked like a panoramic view of the ancient city and the mountains beyond. In reality, the space it was projected into was only ten centimetres deep.

A log fire—another hologram, this one coupled with appropriate sound effects and a heat source—was burning in a stone fireplace. A large oil painting hung above it, of a tall, strikingly fit middle-aged blond woman. She was wearing a body-conforming cuirass and backplate, a short, segmented leather and plate skirt, black knee-high boots with steel greaves, and black leather gauntlets. A broad leather belt circled her waist, supporting a sword and scabbard. Sara thought she could see a resemblance to Marina.

"Who's that?" she asked.

Marina looked up at the painting. "My mother. That's her ceremonial dress uniform. There's a helmet that goes with it, but she didn't wear it for the painting." She smiled. "She had that painted just before I left. Wanted me to have something to remember her by."

"Long time ago, huh?" Sara commented.

"A very long time." Marina picked up her glass from the table beside her chair and took a sip. "That's a problem with the way we travel. Going by the amount of time that passes for us, most of our parents and other close relatives should still be alive. We've only aged fifteen years since we left. But everyone we knew on this planet has been dead for millennia."

"That's why I wonder if I really want to go with you. From what the captain told me, when you leave, after you finish your first jump, everyone you know on this planet will have been dead for a couple hundred years.

"Very true."

"How do you handle that?"

Marina shrugged. "You just do.

Twenty - Three

THE LAST PART OF THE TRIP WAS IN THE BACK OF A BOX TRUCK. Ellen Harris wasn't sure how long they'd been travelling, or how far the truck had driven. Most of what she'd had with her when they picked her up had been confiscated. They had her phone, her tablet, everything that had been in her purse.

She was still wearing her school uniform. Trying to, at least. They'd taken her belt and shoe laces. If she stood up, the greenish-blue plaid skirt hung precariously from her hips without the belt to cinch it around her waist. Her white blouse was crumpled and dirty, and she'd unbuttoned the collar. They'd taken her tie as well.

The two FBI guys in Denver had been polite, business-like. They'd asked a lot of questions about Sara. How much did Ellen know of her friend's plans? Why was she still in contact with a traitor?

"Sara's not a traitor," Ellen had insisted. "She just wanted to see the spaceship."

"No such thing," FBI Guy One said.

"You can see the damned thing from my back yard."

"Nothing there. It's an optical illusion."

The way the FBI guy said that, it was obvious to Ellen that he was just repeating the official line. He'd probably seen the ship himself.

And it hadn't mattered. It was obvious no one cared about the starship. The government could officially deny it, claim it was a British hoax, but it was huge and even binoculars could show some detail. No, the problem was that she'd told Sara what happened to her parents. A text message saying, "FBI took your mom & dad," *was* a problem.

There was an official story. Sara's parents had been so broken up by their daughter's disappearance that they'd packed up and moved away overnight. The Feds had put out that Sara might have been kidnapped by a notorious serial killer they called "the Anaes-thetist," because he killed using hospital anaesthetics.

He'd topped the Most Wanted list for over twenty years. As she knew where Sara was, Ellen couldn't help wondering why the FBI had picked that particular story. Was it possible he'd never been caught because he didn't exist? What if the government was elimi-nating people and blaming a serial killer?

For that matter, what were they saying about *her* now? She didn't know where she was. They'd taken her watch, so she didn't know how long they'd been travelling. There'd been the drive from the FBI office to a small airport. A flight in the back of a windowless plane, landing in the middle of the night at another small airport. And then being stuffed into the back of a small truck.

She'd made herself as comfortable as she could manage on some old moving pads they'd tossed in with her. Now all she could do was wait and see where it ended.

She didn't think they were going to kill her. If that was the plan, there wouldn't be much point in the travel. They'd have killed her in Denver. She was sure the government had ways of get-ting rid of inconvenient bodies. How hard would it be for the FBI to arrange for someone to be buried in a proper cemetery under a false name? Or have a body cremated and completely remove the evidence?

The truck slowed and made a right angle turn. The tyres sounded different. Ellen supposed that had something to do with the pavement.

They drove for what seemed like another hour or more. She wasn't sure. It could have been an hour, or two hours, or twenty minutes. Without a watch, without a window to look out, time was meaningless.

Eventually, the truck stopped. It idled for some time, and then drove on, very slowly, for a short distance. This time the engine was shut off. Ellen wondered if they'd arrived, or were just stopping for gas.

The answer came immediately. There was the sound of latches being opened, and the rear door to the cargo box rolled up. Outside, it was a bright, sunny day. Too bright for Ellen's eyes, acclimated to the near complete darkness in the back of the truck, to take in clearly. Two men were standing behind the truck. They were just silhouettes against the glare.

"Come on," one of them snapped. "Get out of the truck. This is the end of the line."

Ellen pushed herself to her feet and walked carefully to the back of the cargo box. The glare was less now, her eyes adjusting. The men were wearing uniforms. Black or navy trousers, with a light blue stripe, and dark blue polo shirts. Badges were embroidered on the left chest. On the right were the initials USCPS.[11] The same initials were on the front of their black baseball caps. There were police batons, pepper spray canisters, and radios on their black web belts. The taller of the two was holding a large kraft envelope in his left hand.

"Where am I?" Ellen asked.

"You'll find out soon enough," the taller one said. "Come on, get down."

She sat on the tailgate and dropped to the ground, grabbing the waistband of her skirt with her left hand to keep it from falling off. There was gravel underfoot.

The two guards positioned themselves on either side of her and walked her up a gravel path to a two-storey brick office building. A sign over the door said, "Administration."

◆   ◆   ◆

Ed Hastings awakened in a small, nondescript room. He was lying on his back. He was in bed, but still had his clothes on. He lay there, confused, for a few moments. Where the hell was he, and how had he got there?

He started to sit up, then realised his wrists and ankles were restrained. What the hell?

The door opened and a man wearing a blue uniform came in. The man muttered something unintelligible, and a moment later

---

11   United States Consolidated Prisons System. Created as a part of the Homeland Police Reorganisation Act of 2037, the USCPS operated all penal facilities in the United States, from the smallest county lockup, to the largest maximum security prisons.

Hastings heard the translation coming from a small box on the man's belt. "Good, you're awake."

"Where am I?"

"You're aboard *Warrior*," the man said.

Why does this guy remind me of a cave man? Hastings wondered. "Why am I here?" he asked. "Why am I tied to this bed?"

"You're restrained because just before you fell asleep you kept trying to take off all your clothes."

"I did?"

"Not your fault. The anti-inhibitory drugs we gave you have that effect. We might have even let you do it, but you kept trying to kiss Lieutenant Borkavni and he didn't find you particularly appealing."

Shit! Hastings thought. "You can't hold me here," he protested. "I'm a diplomat."

"We're not going to keep you," Brynnazen replied. "You've told us everything we need to know. We'll be giving you to the British shortly. They tell us they'll be sending you back to your own country. It seems you're no longer welcome in the United Kingdom."

Hastings tried to look unconcerned. They'd presumed he'd be sent home after this mission, unless he somehow managed to remain undetected. His diplomatic immunity would have protected him from prosecution in England. The problem was, he couldn't remember what he'd told these people. He'd been drugged, obviously, but he didn't remember much after the shuttle took off with him aboard and the Ellsworth girl still in one piece.

"Uh, just what did I tell you?"

Brynnazen smiled. "Everything. That you had orders to kill Sara Ellsworth. That your government supplied the Russian anti-aircraft missile you used to try to shoot down our shuttlecraft. That your orders came directly from your president. You also said that using the missile against the shuttlecraft was your own idea, and the original idea had been to blow up the girl in the car on her way back to the airport."

"I said all that?"

"You also said you wanted to have sex with Lieutenant Borkavni."

"You're, uh, not going to tell anyone that, are you?" Screwing up the mission wouldn't mean that much. If it got out he'd made advances to a man, even drugged, someone might start asking questions. The kind of questions that could lead to a firing squad on the evening news. Some crimes were considered so heinous that public execution had been brought back, and being gay was one of them.

"From our point of view, the most important thing was that shooting at the shuttle was your idea. If that had been part of your orders, it would constitute an act of war. I don't think that's something your country would want. Not the way we fight wars."

Brynnazen smiled inwardly. The way we fight wars? *Warrior* was heavily armed, but had never fired her weapons in anger. Gehun hadn't fought a war in nearly 200 years at the time they left. Still, the policy existed, and it was calculated as a deterrent.

"We don't put big armies in the field," he explained. "We do small, confined strikes intended to kill the people in charge. We find that wiping out all the politicians tends to bring things to a conclusion in short order."

It would at that, Hastings thought. Wasn't the whole point of having a war that unimportant people would do the fighting and the leaders would reap the benefits?

He was a pragmatist. A lot of things his government did had always struck him as a little silly. On the other hand, his government job mostly consisted of killing people. There was nothing silly about that.

He didn't remember this Lieutenant Borkavni. But this guy had referred to Borkavni as "he," and Hastings could vaguely remember a good-looking fellow involved in the interrogation.

"I really made a pass as this lieutenant?"

"A very explicit one."

Could he be sure that would never get back to his bosses? They didn't have any trouble with him killing people. That's what they paid him to do. But they needed to be kept ignorant of other parts of his life.

"Tell me," he said, "what do your people think about political asylum?"

◆   ◆   ◆

Colquhoun received the news in an email from the British Ambassador in Washington. A note had been delivered by the State Department, requesting the expulsion of the military attaché in Denver. He'd be going home in a little over a week.

Johnson found him in his quarters. The British government owned a four-storey office building in Denver. The ground floor was use as the consulate. Everything from the first floor up was used as staff residence.

The Consul, Sir Walter, had the first floor. It provided a comfortable flat for him, his wife, and their three small children. Colquhoun had a four room flat at the front of the second floor. He was packing his few possessions when Johnson popped in, bringing a bottle of 30-year-old single-malt Scotch.

"Nearly packed are you, Charlie?" Johnson said.

"Not much to pack," Colquhoun replied. "The Army teaches you to keep things simple. Less to move that way."

"I thought I should bring something to take the edge off."

Colquhoun looked at the distinctive triangular bottle, with its deep amber contents. "Where in the world did you find that?"

"I have my connections."

"I don't make enough to buy that."

Johnson laughed. "Have you considered retiring and taking a different job? I believe my department is looking for a few older recruits with military backgrounds."

"Not for me, my friend. I'll be going back to Edinburgh to spend the next two years at regimental headquarters."

"I get to stay here," Johnson said. "For now."

"Lucky chap. You do all the work, take most of the risk, and it's *me* they send home."

"The Yanks tried to blow the girl up, you know, Charlie."

"So I heard. Didn't work."

"No. Our space-faring friends evidently have excellent defences on their shuttles."

"We're sure it was the Yanks, are we? They're stupid, but I didn't think they were quite that stupid."

Johnson nodded and poured two glasses of neat Scotch. He handed one to Colquhoun. "Here's to adventure," he said.

"And staying far from it," Colquhoun added, taking a sip. It was immediately clear why someone would pay £1,200 for a bottle of this ambrosia.

"They caught the guy who fired the missile. The missile was a Russian man-portable anti-aircraft type, but the chap using it was accredited to the American Embassy. There are some nasty notes emanating from Saint James's about that."

"I'm not the only one being kicked out of a country, then?"

"We don't have him. The Gehunites are keeping him for now. Seems he overlooked something. The United States is pretending their spaceship, and them, don't exist, so they haven't bothered to establish diplomatic relations with them. So far as our friends are concerned, the Yank is just a criminal apprehended on their soil making an attack on one of their assets." He shrugged. "And, anyway, the Yanks are denying they had anything to do with it and have revoked his diplomatic status. If our friends give him back, we get to put him on trial. No question whatsoever but trying to blow up any sort of aircraft a few hundred feet over Wilton Crescent is dangerous and illegal."

"Do you suppose we will?"

Johnson grinned. "I expect that's going to depend on how cooperative he is. Maybe we'll put him to work instead. Have him write a tell-all book or something."

Colquhoun walked to the window and looked out. The street was quiet now. Most people had gone home. Years ago, he presumed, there would have been crowds on the street in the early evening. There had been bars and night clubs back then, before the present lot took over and made them illegal.

The Yanks hadn't gone to the extremes of 200 years ago, when Prohibition was in effect, and you couldn't manufacture, transport, or sell anything alcoholic. That hadn't worked out well. These days you could do all of those things. What you weren't allowed to do was consume beer or liquor in public, or appear on the streets intoxicated. That had put all the bars out of business, and private parties in places like hotel banquet rooms and catering halls were necessarily dry.

"What have you heard on the girl's family?" Colquhoun asked.

"They've got them locked up in that camp in Wyoming. No one will ever see them again, I'm afraid."

"You've passed word on to London, I presume?"

"Naturally."

"Pity we can't do anything about it," Colquhoun said, taking another sip. "But no sense doing something that could start a war."

♦   ♦   ♦

Ellen was tired. In-processing had taken hours. There was a huge pile of paperwork to fill out, and Camp Antelope apparently still used actual paper forms. There were hardly any computers to be seen. It made sense, once she thought about it. No one could ever hack into a database if the database consisted of thousands of paper files in metal file cabinets. There was no internet for the residents.

That's what they called them, Ellen discovered. Residents. It sounded so much better than prisoners.

The first part was about what she'd expected. How old was she? How far had she got in school? Any health problems? What church did she attend?

After that, there was a battery of tests. She wasn't sure what they were supposed to measure. In some cases, she thought they might serve to confirm that her school placement on the outside matched what she knew. Others were obviously psychological.

The last was an interview with the Southern Baptist chaplain. That had been the church her family attended, so that was what she put on the form. He was a soft-spoken, pleasant looking middle-aged man she found herself instantly disliking. Partly, she was finding it difficult to like anyone who was involved in this place. The government made an absolute fetish of freedom, after all, though it didn't seem to care that much about actually implementing it.

Then, there was just something about Reverend Wallace that made her uneasy. The way he looked at her, perhaps? The man had a definite ephebophilic aura about him.

At last, she was taken to a warehouse for clothing issue, and then to the unaccompanied girls' dormitory. She'd stay there, under close supervision, until she was eighteen. They were apparently very careful about keeping the boys and girls apart except during classes.

Twenty-Four

IT WAS A LOVELY DAY IN LONDON. There were only a few feathery puffs of white cloud streaking the azure sky. The sun was high, but at this time of year still not too intense. The ancient buildings along the byways were lovely, reflecting an earlier, more refined era.

Sara had again spent the night in the Gehunite Embassy on Wilton Crescent. Today would be a time to play tourist in London. She'd wander about the city as she pondered her future. The Gehunites would depart eventually, so she couldn't stay at the embassy forever. Once they were gone it would be closed down. It wasn't as if they'd be coming back anytime soon.

She looked up at a sign hoarding. A handsome young man, wearing a mid-twentieth century shirt and tie with a grey Victorian frock coat and a fedora hat was smiling down at the street. A pretty blond, wearing an old-fashioned orange spacesuit with the helmet off, was looking apprehensively around his right side. "Series 121, starts 11th May!" the sign proclaimed.

"Series 121 of what?" Sara asked.

"I'm not sure," Captain Maniah replied. "Some television programme that's evidently been on forever."

Maniah was walking to Sara's left. Fehmadaatin was to her right. Romiwero, and the empress, were taking no chances with their guest. Not after what the American, Hastings, had tried to do.

The two older women were in civilian clothes. To someone who'd never seen them before, they could easily be a family group.

Three pretty blonds. Two close in age, one much younger. Mother, daughter, and aunt, perhaps?

"Have you decided what you're going to do?" Marina asked.

Sara shook her head. "I'd like to go home," she said. "But I obviously can't do that."

"No," Marina said. "Your people seem a bit upset with you. I still can't understand what's wrong with them."

"They're incapable of thinking things through, mostly," Sara said. She shrugged. "My opinion, anyway. For whatever that's worth."

Maniah pointed to a church. "I remember you blamed those places, but they've got them here, too, and these people are sensible enough."

"That's because people here don't take everything literally. Back home, they do. If the Bible says God created the world and everything on it in six days, then that's how it happened. And you'd better agree with that unless you want to end up in prison. Or worse."

"Odd people. We don't know exactly how the whole thing got started, but we know what happened from a millisecond or so after it happened, and it certainly didn't involve a supernatural being making people out of clay. We're carbon based, not silica based."

"We used to have gods," Marina said. "Now, mostly, we don't. Just the religious observances that used to be associated with them."

"For the most part," Maniah added, "the observances we kept were the ones that involved a lot of food. The ones where you were supposed to fast are mostly gone."

"The happy holidays," Marina said, "not the sad ones."

"Do you have a lot of holidays?"

"Not really. The most important have always been the two extra-calendrical holidays, the New Year's Holiday, and Reconciliation Day."

"The second one," Marina said, "only happens every four years."

"What's that mean? Extra-calendrical?"

"There are 364 days in a calendar year," Maniah explained, "but 365 days in a solar year. So at the end of each year we add an extra day, the New Year's Holiday. It's extra. Months always begin on the first, which is always a Firstday—you'd say a Sunday, I suppose—and always end on the twenty-eighth, which is always a Seventhday. The New Year's Holiday isn't a part of any week, so insert-ing it at the end of the year doesn't affect the arrangement."

Sara couldn't quite see how that could work. It seemed to her that if all the months were twenty-eight days long, they'd be miss-ing more than one day at the end of a year. "How many months do you have on your calendar?" she asked.

"Thirteen," Marina said.

"So this Reconciliation Day is?"

"The solar year is 365 days, plus roughly a quarter of a day. We stick an extra day in between Sixmonth and Sevenmonth in every year evenly divisible by four to compensate. It's not part of the week, either."

Sara nodded. She'd learnt something. The Gehunites had an odd, but simple calendar, and apparently neither their months nor their days of the week had names. Just cardinal numbers for the months and ordinal numbers for the weekdays. A very simple, logi-cal system, that couldn't possible work today. If they switched, the Christian Sabbath would start out on Sunday for the first year, but after that it would move back one day every year. The modern sys-tem relied on a seven-day interval and you couldn't stick an extra day in without fouling it up.

Well, she thought, the systems were incompatible in a lot of ways. They had a thirty-hour day, with hundred minute hours and hundred second minutes, and their version of a circle had three hundred degrees.

"I'm worried about my parents," Sara said, after a long silence.

"At least we know where they are now," Maniah said. "And that they're alright."

"Locked up in that camp isn't alright. It's just existing. You hear these stories. No one ever comes out of there alive."

They were approaching Knightsbridge, on the opposite side of the street from the Berkeley, when two men came out of Kinnerton Street. They were large men, with short, military style haircuts. Sara didn't think anything of it for a second or two. They were dressed casually, in tee-shirts and jeans, and appeared to be engrossed in conversation.

Then the taller of the two deftly changed course and bumped hard into Maniah, knocking her down. The other grabbed Sara and started to pull her towards the street, where a panel van had just pulled up to the kerb.

The taller man, out of position to body block Marina, swung at her instead. Marina dodged, letting her training kick in. The side of her right hand smashed into the side of his neck, while an instant later she leaned away from him, her right leg coming up and straightening, ramming her heel into his groin. He collapsed onto the pavement, sobbing.

Maniah was back on her feet by now and went after Sara. She caught up with the man as he was about to shove the girl into the back of the van. She might not be as proficient in unarmed combat as Marina, but she *was* a captain of Marines, with twenty years of military training to draw on. She produced a slim fighting knife from beneath her cardigan and slashed at the man's upper arm.

He screamed and let go of Sara, who instinctively backed away from the van, where two more men had been reaching out to take her. One of the men yelled something and the van bolted down Wilton Place and took a left onto Knightsbridge, provoking a great deal of tyre screeching and shouting from people whose cars had abruptly braked to avoid collision.

A small crowd had gathered by now. Londoners were as curious as anyone, and it wasn't often you saw a scene from a martial arts film play out in real life.

Two police constables arrived three minutes later.

♦   ♦   ♦

Empress Felia looked out her bedroom window onto Wilton Crescent. The usual crowd of curious locals and tourists were gathered across the street. "What in the world is the matter with your countrymen?" she asked, looking back at Sara, who was standing near the bed with Maniah and Marina. Colonel Brynnazen had joined them when they returned to the embassy.

"I honestly don't know," Sara replied.

"This is the second time their people have attacked us trying to get at you."

"Less force, though," Marina said. "I think their plan was just to knock the two of us down and grab Sara. Nothing as bad as trying to shoot down a shuttle. I doubt it occurred to them that the two women with her were trained fighters."

"Our British hosts were a bit unhappy with what happened to the fellow with the slashed triceps," Felia commented. "However, I was able to point out that the commanding officer of the embassy's Marine detachment had diplomatic status." She looked at Marina.

"You, on the other hand, don't, but as all you did was beat up the other chap, they were willing to look the other way."

"What's happening to those guys?" Sara asked.

"They're both in hospital. One recovering after having his arm muscles sewn back together, and the other with a severe case of traumatic orchiditis." She managed to suppress a snicker. "After recovery, they'll be given back to your embassy and sent home. I presume."

"Not like the guy who tried to shoot us down?"

"No, Sara, he gets to stay. He's changing sides and joining us. He's raised a reasonable argument that his life would be in danger should he be returned home. Something about having a lover in London and he'd face execution if it were known."

Sara smiled. "Must be another man," she said. "If it was a woman, all he'd have to worry about is a fine and a month or two in jail."

"I believe that's the case."

"One thing seems obvious," Brynnazen said. "The United States of America has decided it wants our young friend dead. Now, I can have one or two of my Marines with her at all times when she's in London, but that will only help while *Warrior* remains in orbit. Will the British protect her once we're gone?"

Felia sat at the small desk between the windows. "They say they will. Something about giving her a new identity and settling her in some small village where the Americans wouldn't be expected to look. They'll put out the story that she's gone with us. After that, they said they'd likely change her hair colour, have someone work with her and teach her a proper accent to go with her new identity, and so forth."

"What if I actually *did* go with you?" Sara asked.

The empress smiled. "It would save you a lot of trouble. By the time you came back here, everyone who'd have any interest in harming you would be long dead."

"But I'd end up in the Navy?"

"Most likely. On the other hand, I believe I do have a vacant position in the governmental liaison office." She picked up an onyx paperweight and turned it slowly in her hands. "How are you with computers?"

Sara shrugged. "I'm very good. With the type of computers we have here, at least. Yours look to be a lot more advanced, though."

"It's going to take you at least a year to learn the language. You can learn to use our computers at the same time."

"What's the job, exactly?"

"Personal assistant to me. As I suddenly find myself acting as empress, in addition to my normal duties as ambassador at large and a scientist, I now rate a second assistant."

"I do still have two years left before I finish high school," Sara put in. No sense building up her hopes. American kids—contemporary earth kids in general—started school two years later than Gehunites had done."

"Not to worry. Even the university graduates joining us will be taking lots of classes to catch them up from what's current knowledge on earth to what we know about many of the same subjects. You know more recent history, obviously, but we're well ahead in the science and physics departments. You'll take the classes with them. If you want the job."

"I think I do."

♦   ♦   ♦

Lieutenant Marina Fehmadaatin made a slight adjustment to the shuttlecraft controls. The shuttle was hovering at 47,000 metres over Wyoming's Great Divide Basin, examining the ground with a powerful telescopic lens. They were well above any airline traffic. At this altitude, the air was quite thin. Too thin to provide adequate lift for any normal transport aircraft.

"Anything yet?" Marina asked.

Just behind her, Sara was studying a view-screen. "Not yet."

Marina relaxed. The shuttle was on automatic. For now, this was just a surveillance mission. Unless they found what they were looking for. She presumed Sara's parents were somewhere in the sprawling internment camp below. That was the intelligence they'd received from the British.

The shuttle's computer was scanning the telescopic images from the camp, trying to match photographs of Sara's parents with anyone who was outdoors. Sara was watching the display. Marina suspected the computer would make the match first. It could compare everyone in a crowd at once.

"Hey! There!"

Marina looked back into the cabin. "Did you find someone?"

"Yeah. But not my parents."

Maniah came up from the rear of the shuttle. "What did you find."

"Right there. That's Ellen, with those girls."

Sara had locked the telescope onto an individual. It would stay that way until she released it to scan the rest of the camp again.

"Are you sure?" Maniah asked.

"Yes. I told you guys she warned me about the FBI taking my parents, and then I never heard from her again. This is where you'd expect her to end up."

Maniah zoomed in. The girl Sara called "Ellen" was in a group of fifteen other girls of a similar age. They were all dressed alike, in long-sleeved white blouses, buttoned to the neck, grey pleated skirts that ended just below the knee, white knee socks, and highly-polished black shoes.

"Okay," Maniah said, using the English word, which had been quickly picked up by most of the crew, "we'll keep an eye on her and resume the main search."

The Marine captain made an adjustment to the search software. It would now keep track of Ellen's movements while it resumed searching for Sara's parents.

"How do you feel about this?" Maniah asked. "We're trained for this sort of thing. You're not."

"I still have to go."

"True. Your parents know you. We'd just be a lot of strangers in uniform trying to tell them what's happening using translation software. No guarantee they'd even believe us."

"It would be easier if we could just beam them up."

Maniah nodded. "It would if that was possible. I suppose it makes a great convenience for motion pictures. Especially early on, when landing a spaceship meant doing it with models. But so far it's not possible in the real world. We'll just have to go down to the camp, grab your parents and your friend, and generally do what Marines are best at."

"What's that?"

"Making a lot of noise and blowing stuff up."

"The captain has suggested we not blow anything up, if we can avoid it," Marina said. "The Americans are likely to be annoyed enough."

"My boss said the same thing," Sara added. "It appears there's no chance of dealing with my homeland through diplomatic channels, but she'd prefer to avoid starting an actual war."

"Finc," Maniah conceded. "We'll just grab the people we're after and leave."

The monitor pinged twice. Sara looked closely. "That's them," she said.

The Marine officer studied the monitor, zooming it out so that it showed both Sara's parents and her friend, Ellen. They were roughly 500 metres apart, but getting closer.

"Time to get ready," Maniah said. She looked aft. "Geriadaatin!"

The blond Marine corporal who'd been in charge of the little squad that nabbed Hastings after the anti-aircraft missile attack trotted up from the stern. "Captain?"

"Get *Kurik* Ellsworth into her gear," Maniah ordered. "No weapons."

The Marine nodded, looking at Sara. "Come with me," she said.

Sara followed her to a small compartment at the after end of the shuttle's passenger bay. "Put these on," Geriadaatin directed, pointing to a padded jumpsuit, boots, and gauntlets.

Sara got out of her dress and got into the uniform-like jumpsuit. It was a snug fit. There were zip fasteners on the inside of the lower legs, to allow the tight garment to fit over her feet. The upper section zipped up the front, with a padded flap covering the fastener.

"Comfortable?" the Marine asked.

"Not particularly."

"You'll get used to it after a few minutes."

"I hope so."

"Trust me."

Sara's outfit differed from what the Marines were wearing only in colour. Their uniforms were dark blue. Hers was a metallic charcoal grey. Where Geriadaatin wore her corporal's chevrons on her upper left sleeve, Sara's uniform had a Gehunite flag, overlaid with a crown and some embroidered lettering. Felia had told her the words, in English, would translate as "Imperial Diplomatic Service."

The Marines wore web belts, fitted with ammunition pouches, first aid packs, and the other normal accoutrements of any combat soldier. Sara had the belt, but the only thing attached to it was the first aid pack. She was there to identify her parents, and her friend, not to fight.

"You'll want to be careful," Geriadaatin said. "This uniform will stop most small arms fire, but it's still going to hurt like hell if you get hit. And, of course, you'll still die if you get shot in the head.

The uniform covers most of you, but the most vulnerable part is still out in the open. And you have to presume that the enemy will be able to figure that out."

Sara returned to the forward end of the shuttle, re-joining Maniah at the monitor. The three dots that indicated their targets had merged in the long-range view. Now Maniah zoomed in again, the individuals resolving.

"Looks like your friend is with your parents," Maniah said.

Sara nodded. "Makes sense. Ellen knows them, and I doubt if there's anyone else there any of them can say that about."

"Now would be a good time, then," Marina suggested. "They're together, and out in the open. We can swoop in and grab them without having to go chasing them all over the camp."

"I agree," Maniah said.

"Let me call up the ship, then," Marina said. "If the captain concurs, we'll head down."

Twenty - Five

JOANNE ELLSWORTH WAS STILL MAD AT HER HUSBAND. He was adapting to life at Camp Antelope. She wasn't. She missed her friends, she missed shopping, and, most of all, she missed her daughter. It was obvious she'd never get any of those things back.

She couldn't decide how she felt about Ellen.

The girl was a reminder of Sara. But, she was at least someone she knew who wasn't Art, and the two girls were the same age. They'd been classmates, and best friends. And that friendship was why the girl was here. Telling Sara what had happened to her parents was the sort of thing any friend would do. Would be expected to do.

The government hadn't seen it that way. Who locks up a 15-year-old girl for the rest of her life because she texted a friend?

"How was school today?" Joanne enquired. It felt like a homey thing to say, despite being in what she was quite sure qualified as a concentration camp.

The government used the term relocation facility. The government, Joanne had noticed, used a lot of inaccurate terminology.

"Stupid," Ellen said. "The teachers back in Denver weren't very good, but the ones here are idiots. You'd think, in a place like this, the teachers would be smarter."

"Residents don't teach," Art interjected. "They bring the teachers and other staff in from outside."

Joanne looked at him reproachfully. "Mrs. Carlson, in the next apartment, is on the staff. She runs the kitchen in the Number 8 dining hall."

"I mean," Art said, "residents don't have the kind of staff jobs that matter. The doctors are doctors, cooks are cooks, like that, but nothing that can have an influence. Do you really think they'd let a teacher they'd locked in here for having heretical ideas into a classroom to keep spreading them?"

♦   ♦   ♦

"Something's screwed up with this 'scope," a technician said. He was monitoring the air defence radar. No one expected an airborne assault on the camp, but policy required keeping anyone from flying over it. With all the trouble the government went to in ensuring no satellite images ever appeared on the internet, it wouldn't do to have tourists pointing their cameras out the windows of Flight 307 to Seattle.

The shift supervisor ambled over. "What have you got?"

"I'm not sure. It's like something's there, but not really. Maybe a really big bird?"

"Could be a drone," the supervisor suggested. "What do we have on visual?"

The technician adjusted the roof mounted camera to point at the same coordinates. The image appeared on a monitor next to the radar screen. "Nothing," he said. "Just clear sky."

"Must be a glitch of some sort. Write it up and we'll get maintenance to check it out."

♦   ♦   ♦

Warrior's shuttle was hovering 4,000 metres above the camp. Had someone sent up a plane to investigate, they would have seen the shuttle clearly from above or at the same level. From below it was nearly invisible. Cameras on the top of the fuselage took in a complete image of the sky above the shuttle. The lower surface of the craft was covered by millions of imaging diodes that recreated the pictures from the cameras. Looking up from below, you saw an exact image of the sky above the shuttle, the brightness precisely adjusted to the same luminescence.

To someone on the ground, the shuttle simply disappeared. Earth's military had used a similar principle as early as the 20th century, mounting lights on the lower surfaces of aircraft and adjusting them to the same light level as the sky above. That worked by eliminating the contrast between the aircraft and the sky. The shuttle's system took that to a higher level, not just matching light levels, but reproducing an actual image of what was above the craft.

Radar was a little trickier, but manageable. The shuttle was made of materials that tended to absorb, rather than reflect, radar impulses. Complex electronic systems could be adjusted to further reduce reflected signal strength. The shuttle wasn't invisible to radar. It wasn't possible to do that. But the 18-metre long shuttle had the radar signature of a large bird, and no country's air defence system worried that much about an errant vulture loitering over a base.

Inside the shuttle, the monitor continued to show Sara's parents outside, still talking to her friend.

There were watchtowers close enough to present a problem. The camp was huge. Perimeter towers were of no concern on this mission. They were intended to prevent anyone from breaking out, not to control the inmates half a mile inside the camp.

Dozens of other guard towers were sited throughout the interior of the camp. Those were the ones that might present a problem to the raiders.

Maniah was studying one of them now. The shuttle was almost directly above the tower, and all she could see was the square, overhanging roof, and a shadow on the ground to the east of the tower. It was obviously on an open base, but the shadow didn't reveal any weapons. The roof overhang was enough to conceal the platform from above, and cast a shadow that obscured it on the ground.

She shifted her viewpoint to a more distant tower. Now she had an oblique view. "Four men," she said, taking notes on a small digital pad. "Looks like two heavy automatic guns. Personal weapons on the guards."

Marina looked back from her seat at the controls. "Are we ready, Captain?"

"I think so. You'll need to keep an eye on the guard tower at 128–442. Put the shuttle down between the targets and the tower, and be ready to return fire if necessary."

"Got it."

Maniah looked at Sara. The girl looked like a regular warrior in her armoured uniform. But she wasn't armed. They couldn't risk anything like that. She wasn't trained. Not only was there a risk that she'd accidentally shoot one of her own companions, there was also a risk that she'd start shooting when it wasn't justified. A big part of firearms training was dedicated to teaching the trainees when *not* to use a weapon. Leave the firearms to the Marines, who at least theoretically knew what they were doing.

Theoretically. They'd spent the last fifteen years aboard ship, drilling for the possibility of combat. That was all they'd done. The brief scuffle with the two American thugs had been the closest Maniah had come to combat in her twenty years of service.

Corporal Geriadaatin would keep an eye on Sara. They hadn't told the girl, not wanting to worry her any more than she already was, but the tiny blond Callaaite Marine was acting as her bodyguard. She didn't look particularly dangerous, Maniah thought. Only 152 centimetres in height, and weighing only 47 kilograms, she looked like a short, slender, and very attractive young woman.

Looks could be deceiving. The corporal was the only member of *Warrior*'s crew who would eagerly spar with Fehmadaatin. The two had trained under the same masters in Callaahavn.

Maniah glanced across the compartment at Sergeant Gnitschish. The Griknaite Marine nodded. Her squad would be ready for whatever came.

Well, Maniah thought, time to get at it. "Take her down," she ordered.

◆   ◆   ◆

To say the shuttle's arrival was abrupt would be grossly understating the event. The little craft's inertial damping system allowed it to drop 4,000 metres straight down in less than eighteen seconds. The last ten metres took nearly as long as the drop from altitude, giving time for several startled inmates to scramble out from under the strange craft.

The door burst open and the stairs deployed. Marines dashed down the steps and took up defensive positions, their eyes scanning their surroundings, looking for any potential danger. A moment later Sara was in the door with Corporal Geriadaatin.

Fifty-calibre slugs flattened against the far side of the shuttle as the guard tower opened fire. The machine-gun was ancient, but it still worked as efficiently as ever.

Inside the shuttle, Marina adjusted her aim and directed a three-second burst at the gun. The gunner leaped back as the old machine-gun glowed white hot. The barrel slumped, and the receiver blew up when the last round exploded in the chamber and the bullet had nowhere to go.

Marina shifted her aim to one of the four wooden poles that supported the guard tower. The heat was more than enough to vaporise a half-metre section, causing the tower to tilt alarmingly, and the guards to quickly decide they wanted to be somewhere else.

"Mom!" Sara shouted. Like everyone else, her parents had started running when the shuttle suddenly dropped into their midst.

"Mom!"

Joanne stopped. Art and Ellen nearly ran into her. All three turned around. She was a mother; she recognised the urgent voice.

"Mom! Dad! Ellen!" Sara shouted. "Come on! Get aboard!"

The three began to run back towards the shuttle. Sara was in shadow, but who else could it be?

The moment the three were aboard, the Marines dashed back up the steps, the steps retracted, and the doors closed. Marina put the shuttle into a vertical ascent and shot straight up to 1,800 metres in just under a second.

The alarm started screaming. The shuttle's sensors indicated fast-moving aircraft heading directly for them. There was an Air Force base twenty miles from the camp. It hadn't taken them long to scramble interceptors.

Under orders to keep any damage to the minimum necessary—she would have left the guard tower unmolested if it hadn't started shooting—Marina switched over to horizontal flight and started climbing at 8,000 metres per minute, with a speed over the ground of 6,000 kilometres per hour. They'd be long gone before the interceptors could reach the camp perimeter.

In the passenger compartment, Sara was still hugging her mother and father. Finally, she got them settled into seats along the starboard side.

Her mother was looking at her with tears in her eyes. "What in the world are you wearing?" she asked, eventually.

Sara looked down at herself, dressed in the charcoal grey, form-fitting uniform. "It comes with the job," she said.

Now Ellen looked at her. "You have a job?"

"Deputy Personal Assistant to Her Imperial Majesty Felia VII," she said.

Her mother looked at her as if she'd said something incomprehensible.

"Sounds important," Ellen said.

"Mostly," Sara replied, "it means I spend the bulk of the working day in school, learning the language so I don't have to rely on an automatic translator to communicate. After that, I'll do other stuff."

"How can you have a job?" Art asked. "You're not even done with high school."

"I think I am, Dad. It's not like I can go back to Denver."

"No, I suppose not." He thought for a moment. "None of us can."

"Where *are* we going?" Joanne asked.

"Right now, we're going up to the ship. Doctor Vordik will check you out, make sure you're still healthy after being in that camp. After that, I've been told you can go anywhere you like. The British have offered asylum, but so have several other countries."

"What about you?" Ellen asked.

"When the ship leaves, I'll be going with it."

"Will we see you again?" Joanne asked. "If you go with these people?"

Sara shook her head. "No. They tell me the first jump will probably be toward Iridalazhik, one of the colony worlds. That's located 342 light years from earth. I'm told it will just seem like a second or so for anyone aboard, but when we come out of jump space it will be 2468 here. Everyone we leave behind will be long dead."

Art looked around the cabin. The Marines were conversing loudly, looking quite pleased with themselves. He had no idea what any of them were saying. He wondered if Sara did. How much of the language had she learnt in the short time she'd been with these people?

One of the Marines glanced over in their direction and Art involuntarily flinched. He turned back to his daughter. "Who's the, uh, green one?"

Sara followed his glance and smiled. Her father's world was expanding in unexpected ways. There had been quiet whispers about aliens when *Warrior* first arrived. It had come as a bit of a surprise when it turned out there were a few actual aliens in the crew.

"That's Sergeant Gnitschish," Sara explained. "She's a Griknaite. They're from a planet nearly 3,000 light years from here."

"That's a she?"

"You can tell by the double row of yellow scales that start at the brow line and run up over her head and down her back. The males don't have that. Their heads are all green."

"Dangerous?"

Sara shrugged. "Well," she said, "she's a Marine."

"On approach," Marina shouted.

"Look out the windows," Sara advised. "This is really cool."

Joanne started to turn. "You understood that?"

"No," Sara said. She tapped her right ear, touching the nearly invisible earpiece. "This translates it for me."

"Holy crap!" Ellen exclaimed, as the shuttle lifted above the Sagan Space Platform and *Warrior* came into view.

◆   ◆   ◆

It was well past dark, and the drapes were drawn in the Oval Office. President Will Gordon sat in an easy chair, looking across the low coffee table at the gold-upholstered sofa where the Secretary of State, the Secretary of Defence, and the Air Force Chief of Staff were looking back at him. The Director of the Department of Internal Security was seated in an armchair to the right of the sofa.

"How much damage was done?" Gordon asked.

"Minimal," the Director replied. "An internal guard tower was knocked down, two guards suffered minor injuries."

"What's 'minor?'" SecDef asked.

"One of them sprained a wrist. The other had some cuts and bruises."

"Nothing else?" Gordon asked.

"They melted a .50-calibre machine-gun."

The Air Force general looked at him curiously. "Melted?"

"Melted. Then it blew up when a round cooked off in the chamber with the barrel blocked."

The president nodded. This was just confirming the reports. "And they took the Ellsworths with them, correct? And some other resident?"

"That's right, sir," the Director replied. "The girl was Ellen Harris. She's the one who sent the illegal text to the Ellsworth girl after she defected."

"What's your opinion on this, Nick?"

The Secretary of State was reaching for his coffee. He sat up instead. "Honestly, Will, it might be best to just forget the whole thing. There was very little damage. They pulled out two inmates that probably shouldn't have been there to begin with, and another who really presents no threat to anyone. No one knows about the raid, other than the group of residents who saw it happen."

"They can't talk to anyone outside," the Director added. "So it shouldn't be a problem."

"But it is a problem," Gordon said. "I never wanted the Ellsworth's there, as you say, but that idiot SAC in Denver screwed that up. Once they were there, though, there was nothing I could do about it. We can't let people out. Not ever. The real question is, what do we do about the residents who witnessed this?"

"There weren't that many. Keep them where they are. The staff can have a quiet word with any witnesses. It's not like anyone is going to do this again. All three of the residents that were extracted have a direct connection to the Ellsworth girl. They didn't try to take anyone else."

"So, you figure those three were all they were after?"

"Seems likely."

Gordon nodded. He picked up a coffee cup and took a sip. It was cold. "And what about the girl? We've tried to eliminate her twice. One of the men you sent after her defected, and the other two were kicked out of England, after having the shit beat out of them by a couple of women."

SecState frowned. "The defector turned out to be a pervert, so no loss there. The other two misread the situation. They spotted the girl with two women in street clothes. They were just women. It shouldn't have been a problem. Not for those men."

The DIS Director snorted. "You should leave this sort of thing to the experts, Nick. We did some checking after those two beat up your boys. Those women? One of them is a Marine officer. Now, whatever you may think about some other country's military, a Marine is a Marine, and even the women are pretty tough. As for the other one? The reports I get say she's a naval officer, and has apparently been taking time out from playing tourist to give unarmed combat tips to the fucking SAS. Maybe if you'd sent a SEAL team, but your guys never stood a chance."

"Be that as it may," SecState said, "I think the best thing to do now is leave the girl alone. The Gehunites have given her diplomatic status, and she'll apparently be going with them when they leave. So the problem will be removing itself before too much longer."

"Can they do that?" Gordon asked. "She's an American citizen."

"They can," SecState said, "and they have. All countries have their own criteria for granting citizenship, or for covering non-citizens working for their diplomatic corps under immunity."

"What did they do here?"

"They've informed Ambassador Miller that Miss Ellsworth has been accredited to their embassy in London and issued a diplomatic passport."

"But we don't have relations with them, do we?"

"No, sir, we don't."

"So we're not required to recognise that immunity, then," the Director suggested.

"No. But neither are they, which is why the first man we sent after the girl was arrested and taken up to their ship instead of just being let go."

"That's the one who defected?" Gordon said.

"Correct. Turns out he likes other men." The Director lifted his coffee cup and sipped at the dark, sweet brew. He liked his coffee with six sugar cubes. "No loss, except he may tell them some things we'd prefer to keep quiet."

"I feel like we should do something," the president said, sounding peeved. "You've seen the pictures from the security cameras." He took one of the eight by ten colour prints from the stack. It showed the shuttle, with the fugitives being rushed up the steps into the craft and the Marines still deployed in front of it. "These guys claim to be from this planet, but the one to the right of the door is sure as hell not human."

"Intelligence says that one is from a planet called Grikna, sir," General Curtis said.

"Where's that? Do we need to worry about *these* guys showing up and causing trouble?"

Curtis shook his head. "From what we've learnt, Grikna is located 2,850 light years from earth. If they sent a 'come help us conquer this place' message today, we'd have been dead longer than King Solomon before they even received the message. No, we obviously need to worry about the people on the ship, but we're still protected by distance from anyone else."

Gordon sat back in his chair and looked at the painting hanging above the sofa. It depicted Adams, Jefferson, Hancock, Franklin, and that lot lining up to sign the Declaration of Independence in 1776. Jesus looked down on them, smiling beatifically, from the portrait over the president's desk, giving his approval to the new country. Copies of the painting appeared in most American history textbooks now. If you travelled to Philadelphia, you could see a full-sized copy of the painting in the Assembly Chamber at Independence Hall.

What would those men have thought of the current situation, he wondered? There was no longer any question that these Gehunites were godless heathens. Among the books they'd published in their brief time in orbit was a religious history of their culture. They'd been religious, certainly, in various pagan ways, but apparently all that was left of their original religions were a few holidays and some meaningless rituals maintained out of a sense of tradition.

"Carl," Gordon said, "what have you got in your arsenal that could deal with these people?"

Curtis looked thoughtful. The proper answer, he was sure, was not a damn thing. But that wasn't what the president would want to hear. "I suppose we could nuke them," he said.

"They're parked next to the Sagan Space Platform," SecState pointed out. "Blowing them up is likely to piss off the Brits and the Russians."

"Have you got bombs big enough to handle a ship that size?"

"I think a couple of 350-megaton nukes should do the job, sir," Curtis replied.

"Director Marsh," the president said. "We'll need a *reason* if we attack them."

The Director shook his head, feeling strangely out of place in the role he felt compelled to take on. "Are you sure that's such a good idea, sir? We know how powerful their weapons are. Do we have any idea how they'll react if we attack them and it doesn't work?"

Gordon frowned. "Just come up with a reason, Director."

"Okay. I suppose we can dress some special ops troops in Gehunite uniforms and have them blow up a church or something."

"An empty church, I presume?" SecState offered.

"Be more effective if there were people in it," Gordon said. He smiled suddenly. "How about we fill a church with the witnesses from Camp Antelope? Take care of two problems at once?"

The Director nodded. "Possible," he said.

"How long would it take to organise?" Gordon asked.

"A few days."

"Do it."

Twenty - Six

WORK HAD STOPPED FOR THE DAY WHEN SARA LED ELLEN into her future home. The basic construction was complete, with walls in place, doors hung, and flooring laid. The walls still needed painting. The windows were framed, but the holographic displays, and the glazing, had not been installed.

Offered the option, Sara had decided not to duplicate her parents' Denver house. She'd opted to have the place she wanted to live in after school built instead. When it was completed and furnished, she'd have a ten-room, single-level flat, with a balcony in the living room overlooking Central Park from the tenth floor. It didn't duplicate any particular real flat, but was an idealised representation of a New York luxury apartment home.

The view would be real. They'd used a tiny drone to get a holographic camera onto the balcony of a real building on Central Park West. It would have been easier if they'd been able to go there openly, but that wasn't possible. So they had a week's worth of imaging to work with. Weather and seasons would be computer generated.

"I like this," Ellen said. "They're doing all this just for you?"

Sara nodded. "They're very nice people, really."

"Everybody lives like this?"

"You're going away forever," Sara noted, a little wistfully. "The captain told me that, this way, everyone gets to take something of their home with them. People brought things from their homes.

The brought their furniture. They brought pictures, knickknacks, souvenirs. They brought their pets. They brought their dietary quirks."

Ellen stepped out onto the balcony. It looked like a film set, she thought. "How *is* the food, anyway?"

"Pretty good. The meat's cloned. They don't kill any animals, they just grow a steak. Watch out for the salads, though. Some of the green stuff isn't edible."

"Huh? Why would you put something in a salad if it wasn't edible?"

"Edible for us. Apparently, these people can digest cellulose. On the other hand, there isn't an adult Gehunite on this ship who can drink milk, so we have that over them. There's 86,000 years of evolution between us and them."

"They don't look any different. Well, except the Neanderthals."

Sara sat on the balcony rail. She planned to do that often, particularly once the imaging system was set up and she could feel like she was being a daredevil, risking a hundred foot drop when, in fact, there was a solid deck no more than six inches below the balcony.

"I guess we're different inside."

"Aren't you worried about that? What if you get sick when you're off roaming the universe?"

Sara laughed. "I don't think we're *that* different. We just don't have a foot-long, inch-and-a-half-thick appendix full of bugs that like wood fibres, that's all."

"You're going to have an adventure."

"You could come along. There are several people from our time joining the crew, not just me."

Ellen thought about it. She obviously couldn't go back home. Not unless something drastic happened there. She'd have to live in a new country. England was certainly a possibility. Or maybe Canada, or one of the formerly-British Caribbean islands, where she wouldn't have to learn a new language. That would be a downside to going with Sara. She'd have to start speaking the same language as everyone else aboard, and that meant learning a language from scratch. Not an easy one to pronounce, either, from what she'd heard.

"I'll have to think about that," Ellen said.

◆   ◆   ◆

Joanne Ellsworth was finding life in her new home a little confusing. That morning, taking the short walk to the village centre to explore the shops, she'd nearly been run down by a police car as she tried to cross the street. The constable had been pleasant enough about the incident, and "almost" was more or less the norm for auto-pedestrian accidents in any case, with automotive computers having much faster reflexes than human drivers. How much longer, though, she wondered, would it be before she started looking to her right first when crossing a street?

For that matter, why did the English still drive on the wrong side of the road?

Art, at least, had a job already. The USRRA, the United States Refugee Resettlement Agency, had found him a position with a London engineering firm. He'd become a commuter for the first time at the age of forty, taking the train the ninety kilometres from the little village to King's Cross Station and back five days a week. The work was a bit different from what he'd done at home. There he'd mostly worked on highway projects. His current project was a small hydro-power dam planned for a remote highland area in Scotland.

For now, Joanne was taking things easy, adjusting to her new country. She'd be spending most of the next year in school. It seemed her degree from the University of Colorado wasn't considered sufficient for entry on the British nursing registry. She'd have to re-qualify, and that meant going back to school.

Someone knocked on the door. Joanne switched on the camera and relaxed. It was just Mrs. Davison, from next door. They'd been warned to be careful. American agents had made two attempts on their daughter's life. Having been sprung from Camp Antelope, it was reasonable to presume someone might have it in for them as well.

Not a 78-year-old retired school teacher, though. She was just a dear old lady with a great love of gardening and gossip, and a remarkably impenetrable accent that Joanne was slowly getting used to. Joanne could look forward to spending the next hour or so discovering what everyone in the village had been up to, and watching a rapid drop in the level of the single malt. Mrs. Davison was very fond of a wee dram—or four.

She opened the door to admit her visitor.

♦   ♦   ♦

The Second Methodist Church had served the tiny village of Kirkdale, Wyoming since 1897. The present building went up in 2064,
in a brick neo-gothic style that called the original to mind, but
eliminated most of the problems. It looked old, but the masonry
concealed a steel frame, and the building had been designed with
central heat and cooling in mind. In the old church, both had
been something of an afterthought.

The village of Kirkdale was located eight miles from Camp
Antelope. Of the town's 3,208 residents, all but 278 were connected
with the camp. Most of the guards lived there. So did the bulk of
the admin staff. The 'civilians' were mostly on staff at the small
local hospital, or worked in the businesses downtown.

That Sunday morning, the church had an influx of visitors.
Eighteen strangers joined the congregation, taking seats in a group
along the northern side of the sanctuary. They sat quietly, listened
to the service, participating at the appropriate times, and managed to convey a sense of extreme nervousness without ever saying
anything.

All the visitors shared a common sense of foreboding. There
were dozens of chapels inside the camp. Why were they being
taken to a church on the outside? Whispered conversations made
them even more nervous. It seemed that every one of them had
been there when the Gehunites raided the camp. They'd seen it
happen, all of them.

The biggest surprise was when they actually arrived at the
church. Most of them had expected it to be a ruse, and they were
really being taken away to another camp. Or to be killed.

The preacher was in the middle of his sermon when the doors
burst open and a half-dozen men in Gehunite uniforms rushed
into the sanctuary. Things became very noisy after that. Bullets
were flying everywhere.

Many parishioners were armed, being camp guards. The ones
on the ends of the pews started shooting back at once. Apparently,
none of them were good shots. The attackers remained unscathed.
So did the parishioners, though bullets whizzed over their heads
and did a lot of damage to the 19th century stained glass windows
behind them.

The preacher was cowering behind the lectern. The polished
walnut wouldn't stop a bullet, but if no one could see him, he rea-

soned, there was a good chance they wouldn't be shooting in his direction.

The visitors weren't as lucky. All eighteen were killed, some by the raiders, others by stray bullets fired by the worshippers.

♦   ♦   ♦

Warrior monitored all broadcast channels within range of her antennae. These included cable channels, which were relayed from point to point via geosynchronous satellites orbiting the equator at 35,786 kilometres. GNN was one of these channels.

Officially, the designator stood for General News Network. Most Americans conceded that it might, more appropriately, be styled the *Government* News Network. Bad as it was, and prone as it was to report everything through a government-tinted filter, it was still the only real source for international news, or for breaking news around the country. Local stations covered local events, and occasionally ran national stories, if they were important enough.

Sara was still in her temporary quarters, talking to Ellen, with the television on in the background. She wasn't paying that much attention to it until the headline bar flashed, "18 Killed in Alien Raid in Wyoming."

The visual showed a Gehunite shuttle touching down in a small town, and a squad of naval officers in dress uniforms piling out, carrying automatic weapons.

What the hell is this? she wondered. That couldn't be right.

"Early reports indicate that an alien raiding party attacked a church service in the town of Kirkdale, Wyoming, shortly after 9:30 this morning," the anchor reported. "Eighteen local residents were reported killed in this unprovoked attack."

"What in the world?" Ellen gasped.

Sara continued to stare at the screen. "No," she finally said, "that can't be right."

"You just saw it."

"That's the trouble," Sara said. "I just saw it. The uniforms are wrong."

"They look just like what I've seen here," Ellen objected.

"Right. Exactly. But do they look anything like what we were wearing when we came to get you and my folks? Those people were wearing dress uniforms, not battledress. Hell, Ellen, the cops back home wear more armour than those guys."

An insistent buzzing from the phone interrupted. Sara picked up the handset. She listened for a moment, said, "On my way," and hung up. "I've got to go," she said, turning back to Ellen. "Think about it. And ask yourself who'd gain anything from this? The people here, or the people who put you and my folks in that camp?"

Sara hurried out and sprinted along the corridor to the lift. Reaching the command level, she turned left out of the lift and hurried to Felia's office.

The Empress was already there when Sara arrived. So was the captain, Colonel Brynnazen, Commander Oshrorehno, Lieutenant Commander Zhvassich, and Hastings, the American defector. The view-screen was showing the same GNN news programme Sara had been watching in her quarters.

"Have you see this, Sara?" Felia asked.

"Yes."

"What are your thoughts?"

"My thoughts are that I'm 15-years-old, and this is way over my competence level. I'm only a diplomat by default; I still need to get the training."

Felia nodded and fiddled with the keyboard on her desk. The live broadcast was replaced by a still photo, obviously taken during the Camp Antelope raid. Sara could see herself, standing in the doorway with Corporal Geriadaatin, but someone — she presumed someone at GNN — had drawn a red circle around Sergeant Gnitschish.

"They're showing this one a lot," Felia said. "The gist of it is that our human appearance is a masquerade, and this is what we really look like."

"Which is ridiculous," Zhvassish said. "As if a starship couldn't *possibly* have crew members from more than one planet."

"What's your opinion, Mr. Hastings?"

"My opinion, your Majesty, is that they're setting something up. I worked with these people. They're relying on the fact that most Americans are conditioned to just accept whatever they see on television as accurate." He looked around the room. "My opinion? They're creating an excuse to attack you."

Romiwero raised an eyebrow. "How? Are they even capable of it?"

"You really haven't retaliated. Not when I took that shot at your shuttle. Not when two of my former colleagues tried to kidnap Miss

Ellsworth in London. All you did was drop into Camp Antelope, take three people out, and otherwise act as if nothing had happened. They're going to take that as weakness."

Felia frowned and leaned forward. "I prefer to think of it as exercising restraint. Captain?"

"We put the ship on alert, certainly," Romiwero said. "Might be a good idea, no one goes planetside unless it's in a group."

"You might want to leave the uniforms on the ship," Hastings suggested. "In street clothes, you'll pass as contemporary people." He glanced at Brynnazen and Zhvassish. "Well, most of you will, anyway."

"Why am I here?" Sara asked.

"You're American," Romiwero replied. "You know how things work there."

"I only know what they put on the news. And I'm not sure how accurate that really is. GNN says one thing, but what you get from other sources online says something else."

"Do you think they'll try to attack us, Sara?" Felia asked.

"Maybe. Can they?"

"Not easily," Brynnazen said. "We're mostly up here, and they're down there."

Felia gestured towards the view-screen. "Are people down there going to believe that? The shuttle images have obviously been manipulated."

Hastings grimaced. "Americans are remarkably gullible," he said. "They'll believe just about anything. Particularly if you make it seem frightening. We're an odd people. We love to talk about liberty, and everyone being equal, but we also want to think we're better than everyone else. If you put something on the news that reinforces that sense of superiority, the majority of Americans will automatically believe it.

"And we love to be threatened. If you want to get people to do what you want, you tell them something is threatening something they value. The people who run the country are mostly young-earth creationists. At least, officially, that's what they are. Because of that, the world can't be more than about 6,000 years old. You say you lived here more than 80,000 years before that. Therefore, you either can't exist—which you obviously do—or you're lying. Either way, you're a threat."

"But we don't really believe that," Sara objected. "That whole young-earth thing, I mean."

"Gordon does. Or he says he does. In either case, it's official policy."

Felia leaned forward in her chair, resting her elbows on her desk. "That's what I find so difficult to understand. Many years ago, one of my ancestors claimed to be a demigod, and based his right to rule on that claim. By the time we left here, no one believed that anymore. We saw gods as things our ancestors made up to explain things they couldn't understand. Observation, science, later explained most of them, so belief in gods dwindled. They just weren't necessary."

"They are to Americans," Hastings said. "Though most Americans wouldn't like the plural very much. There's only one God, so far as we're concerned. And a very high percentage of Americans fervently believe that a belief in God is the only reason people are capable of behaving morally."

"I don't think this has anything to do with whether the Americans are planning to attack us," Romiwero commented.

"It might," Sara said. "Why have they generally suppressed news of your arrival? And put out that you're aliens, from another planet? As long as you're from somewhere else, it doesn't contradict their basic philosophy. There's nothing in the Bible that says there *are* other planets and life forms, but there's nothing that says there *aren't*, either."

"I think," Felia said, "that about all we can do is wait and stay alert. I'll be going down to London in two hours. Sara, you'll be coming along, so pack enough for a week. Oh, and if your friend asks what's going on, just tell her that the news reports are incorrect."

"I already did."

♦   ♦   ♦

Ambassador Miller arrived at the Gehunite Embassy in London three hours after the shuttle dropped off Felia, Sara, Ellen, and a half-dozen others. He was dressed in a conservative blue suit, and carried a leather portfolio under his arm.

Felia greeted him from behind her desk. After a minimal exchange of formalities, Miller unzipped his portfolio and extracted a single sheet of paper. The official communication was short and formal. It accused the government of Gehun of conducting an attack on a church in Kirkdale, Wyoming. This, the document declared, would be interpreted as an act of war unless certain conditions were met, the most important of which was the immediate departure of *Warrior*.

"We're not going anywhere," Felia said. "Not for a while."

"You have three days," Miller said. "After that, I'm afraid, I can't be responsible for what happens."

"What makes you think you can dictate to us?"

Miller fidgeted in the guest chair. "This is my government talking, not me."

"You stage an attack on your own people," Felia said. "You then fake evidence to put the blame on us, but you don't do a very convincing job of it. The image manipulation is childish. Then you use that as an excuse to threaten us? Do you actually expect my government to do what you demand?"

"Your government? Isn't your government just you and a few hundred people aboard your ship? Considering there are 342,000,000 Americans, I don't see that you have much choice."

Felia slowly shook her head. "When we left this planet, there hadn't been a war in well over a century. Since that time, we've been involved in exactly one minor skirmish, on a planet far away from this one. But, that doesn't mean we can't fight. On a one-on-one basis, there's not a lot of difference between our weapons and yours. Metal projectiles propelled by chemical reactions.

"Escalate, though, and we can use weapons that are well beyond anything you possess. You know what happened in your concentration camp. We fired only to disable your weapons, not to harm your people. Imagine that same weapon scaled up by a magnitude of a hundred."

"Are you threatening us?" Miller demanded.

"Not at all. Just pointing out that a mouse is well advised not to make hostile advances to a lion. Bravado is fine, but it's unlikely to go well for the mouse."

Miller stood up. "As I said, you have three days to leave orbit and go away. Today is Monday. That means you need to be gone by Thursday at noon Washington time. After that, something could happen."

Twenty-Seven

LIEUTENANT MARINA FEHMADAATIN SAT in the captain's chair on *Warrior*'s bridge, reading *Beowulf.* The story reminded her of some old Callaaite sagas. The translation into Callaaish emphasised the similarities. Of course, in a Callaaite saga, it would have been a woman ripping Grendel's arm off, not a man.

She looked up at the clock. Nine earth hours until the American deadline. *Warrior* was just passing over the west coast of the United States, on a standard west-to-east orbit. Most low earth satellites orbited west to east for purely practical reasons. The planet was already rotating in that direction, so launching a satellite in the same direction added planetary rotation speed to launch speed, requiring less thrust to reach escape velocity.

Everyone was still using chemical rockets as launch vehicles. The gravity manipulation system used by *Warrior*'s shuttles had been forgotten after Emthemlu deorbited and not yet rediscovered. They were paying the rent on the London embassy by ferrying Sagan Space Platform crew, saving the British government a fortune in the process. It was a simple solution for adapting a Gehunite culture where money had long since disappeared to a modern earth culture where it was still used.

Crew members were provided with local currency—an available balance on a credit chip, really; no one used actual money anymore—when they went down to the planet. There were tons of gold and gemstones aboard the ship that could be exchanged for credit.

It was dark on the planet below, just past midnight in California. The city lights were subdued. Sara had told her there was little in the way of night life. Hardly surprising, Marina thought, if there were no bars or night clubs. Americans went to bed early.

What would happen in nine hours? she wondered. The Americans couldn't be so foolish as to attack, could they?

A loud horn interrupted her speculation. She put down her reading pad and concentrated on the readings on the view-screen.

"What's going on?" Romiwero demanded, rushing onto the bridge.

Marina hopped up from the captain's chair and moved to her normal position at the navigator's console. "It seems the Americans were serious. And early. Defence system reports two missiles launched from a complex in, uh, Montana."

Romiwero dropped into her chair and flipped up the left arm-rest. Feeling terribly disappointed, she pressed the red button at the front. The alarm horn was replaced by a clanging bell and a recorded "All hands to action stations" announcement.

On the main view-screen, the earth view was revolving as the ship automatically rotated to present its lower section to the planet.

The rest of the bridge crew had appeared within three minutes. "Systems coming on line, captain," the gunnery officer reported. His title was a nod to tradition. There were no guns aboard, other than personal weapons for the Marines.

"Do we have a readout of what they've fired?" Romiwero asked.

"Working on it."

"Almost has to be nuclear," Marina said. "They can't think a conventional bomb would do much damage to us."

"Confirming," the gunnery officer reported. "Sensors indicate fissionable material present in the warheads."

"Lock your weapons on the missiles," Romiwero ordered. "If they get within a hundred kilometres, destroy them."

"Aye, aye."

"She was going to give the Americans every possible chance to abort the attack. One hundred kilometres seemed close enough. Whatever they'd sent up, it couldn't do any damage at that distance. At an orbital height of 400 kilometres, a thermonuclear detonation would cause little or no blast damage even at a hundred *metres*. There was no atmosphere for a pressure wave to propagate. The nukes would need to be in physical contact with the ship when they detonated to hurt them. The intense heat, upwards of

$100,000,000°$, and the massive gamma ray emissions, were another matter entirely.

"Getting closer, Captain," Guns reported.

Felia's image appeared in the lower right corner of the viewscreen. She was still in London, and would have been alerted as soon as the alarm sounded.

"Everything in order up there?" she asked.

"We're tracking their missiles," Romiwero replied. "Weapons are ready."

"I'm trying to get through to their president, but he doesn't seem to be answering his phone."

Romiwero shook her head. "Do you think he has any idea what he's done?"

"I very much doubt it," the Empress replied. "I have no doubt he knows he's just started a war. I'm sure there are people advising him on the potential consequences."

"Two hundred kilometres," Guns reported.

"Does he know what he's doing to himself? It's very likely those nukes are going to detonate. They'll do a lot more damage on the ground than they will to us."

"I don't think he's thinking at all," Felia said.

"One hundred fifty kilometres, Captain."

"Safeties off," Romiwero ordered. "All weapons free."

"In range in twenty, ten, five, four, three, two, one. Firing."

One hundred kilometres from *Warrior*, and still accelerating, a pair of Dominator missiles homed in on the giant starship. As the starship fired, the missiles began to glow. It required less than a second for the warheads to heat up to over a thousand degrees.

The core of each warhead was a plutonium sphere, surrounded by a high explosive shell. The shell was designed so that each section would detonate at exactly the same time, compressing the plutonium sphere to slightly less than half its original diameter. That would be sufficient to start a chain reaction in the compressed sphere.

But that would be just the beginning. The sphere would detonate in a fission reaction, which would then detonate the secondary materials in a fusion reaction. The resulting explosion would be the equivalent of detonating a pile of TNT weighing 350-million tons.

The instant heating from *Warrior's* high-energy weapons did precisely that, detonating the high explosive shell of the primary as efficiently as the trigger would have done. Both warheads exploded in a massive thermonuclear blast.

Had the warheads exploded close to the ground, there would have been little that remained standing for a 93-kilometre radius. The blast effect would have reached out more than twice as far. Air is compressible, but only to a certain degree. Most of the blast would have been expended in creating a massive pressure wave.

But these warheads detonated above the atmosphere. Lacking air to contain and dissipate the thermonuclear blast, the whole force was converted into energy, radiating out in all directions, largely as gamma rays. When it hit the atmosphere, this energy created a massive electromagnetic pulse.

Looking down from orbit, Romiwero could see the lights blinking out across North America. It was exactly what she'd predicted. The electromagnetic pulse had created a massive power surge in the electrical grid, blowing out transformers, frying computers, and knocking out most forms of communication. There would be very little containing transistors that still worked unless it was hardened to resist an electromagnetic pulse. Other than a few government systems, it appeared that very little down there was.

The explosions had no noticeable effect aboard *Warrior*. Designed to operate in deep space, the ship was heavily shielded against all types of radiation. No one would survive very long otherwise.

"Space platform has gone dark, Captain," the communications officer reported. "No lights, and no emissions."

"Get someone over there. See what we can do to help."

One of the shuttles had been fitted with a docking ring shortly after they arrived in orbit. It was more convenient than using the individual travel pods and having to enter and leave the platform through the airlock.

Marina looked up from her console. "I'm surprised that affected them. Their systems should have been protected."

"That was a rather spectacular explosion," Romiwero replied. "Have we got an estimate on the yield?"

"Looks to be roughly 2.9-million terajoules," Guns reported. "They weren't just trying to damage us. They wanted to vaporise us."

"Someone," Marina said, "needs to remind them of our philosophy of war."

Romiwero nodded and turned back to the view-screen. The danger apparently over for the time being, she put Felia on the main screen and switched the planetary view to the inset. "We seem to be alright here, your Majesty," she reported. It still felt a little odd. She'd been on a first-name basis with Felia since before *Warrior* first left orbit all those years ago. She still was, really. But this situation seemed to call for formality.

"I'll be paying a call on Ambassador Miller at 1300 hours local time," she said. "I'm going to suggest an immediate apology."

"His Majesty's government may want to join the queue," Romiwero said. "It looks like the explosion knocked out the power systems on the space platform. If the missiles had hit us, I doubt the space platform would have survived."

"Does Saint James's know this?"

"Unlikely. I've sent a shuttle to retrieve Captain Sebastian and his crew. I imagine they'll make a report once they're aboard and have access to a radio."

"Any damage to *Warrior?*"

"None reported. Looks like extensive damage to the enemy, though. There aren't a lot of lights on down there at the moment. Likely their power grid has been cooked."

"Most of their electronic communications are down as well," Communications reported. "No radio or broadcast television. Nothing in the microwave spectrum. About all we're getting is some of the same code communications our young friend likes to play with." He shrugged. "A lot of amateur radio enthusiasts apparently like to use old equipment that uses valves instead of transistors. They're not as vulnerable."

"Anything official? Military?"

"Not that we can monitor. They may be using land line instead of wireless, but there's a good chance those lines are down as well."

Felia smiled. "Good. If they've messed themselves up badly enough, they'll have too much to fix to be causing more trouble for us."

"I'm sure they'll find a way to *blame* us, though," Romiwero said.

"Undoubtedly. All their communications are down. It will certainly be our fault. They attack their own people and say we did it. They'll say it was our bomb, too."

◆   ◆   ◆

Captain Charles Sebastian checked the final three crew members off his list and swung through the airlock door into the shuttle. It felt odd, gravity suddenly returning as he crossed the coaming.

He looked back, through the small window in the inner airlock door, and into the darkened passageway beyond. He pulled the outer door closed and spun the locking wheel. With the platform closed off, he stepped back as one of *Warrior*'s crew closed the docking hatch door and sealed it.

The shuttle eased away from the platform for the short ride over to the starship. Sebastian found himself looking aft. He wasn't sure how to feel. His command was growing smaller as he watched, dark and dead looking. The electromagnetic pulse from the exploding warheads had destroyed the vast array of solar panels that powered the platform. Worse, it had wiped out all the batteries. There was no way to generate power, and nowhere to store it even if they could.

The electronic equipment inside the platform was likely salvageable. It might even be just as good as ever. Until power was restored, there was no way to tell.

Jenkins walked over to him. She was moving uneasily. After months of zero gravity she was having trouble walking in normal gravity. Unlike Sebastian, she had never visited *Warrior*. It was all very strange to her.

"It was my people, wasn't it?" she said. "Those idiots have gone and started a war they can't win."

Sebastian nodded, shrugging. "It seems possible. But they may not be complete idiots. These people aren't interested in fighting a war." He looked towards the front of the shuttle, where a pair of officers were guiding the little craft into a landing bay. "Think about it. Your former country fires a couple of big nukes at them, and their first concern is to come evacuate us, not to shoot back."

"How much damage do you think there was?"

"To *Warrior*, I'd say none at all. To us? Substantial. If this was a military operation against the platform, I'd call it a mission kill. We always knew the panels were vulnerable to this sort of thing. It was just the sort of risk you had to take. Solar panels don't do much good if you hide them behind a lot a shielding and light can't get to them. The batteries were a bit more of a surprise. They should have been shielded."

"Are we sure they're destroyed?" Jenkins asked. "Could it have just burnt out the wiring, and the power's there, but we can't get at it?"

"Possibly. Whatever it was, it's going to take months to repair. My time will be up. So will yours. When the platform comes back on line, she's likely to have an entirely new crew."

"What do we do?"

"Write reports. Probably hitch a ride back home. I suppose the sponsoring countries will try to convince the Gehunites to hang around a bit longer than they'd originally intended. They can haul repair parts and personnel up here a lot easier than we can."

♦   ♦   ♦

President Will Gordon looked out through the Oval Office windows. His office was dark behind him, the only light coming from an old oil lamp on the corner of his desk. At one time, he thought, they could have used the White House's old gas fixtures, but those had been removed when Truman gutted the building and rebuilt the interior back in the late 1940s.

It was ridiculous, he thought. The White House had an emergency generator, and it was up and running. EMPs had no real effect on diesel engines. The problem was the lights. Like most other solid-state electronics, the light-emitting diodes in the lights had been fried. It had never occurred to anyone to harden the light bulbs.

There was a similar problem with the computer system. The computers themselves, tucked away in the White House basement inside a Faraday cage, had handled the EMP just fine. The monitors, mice, and keyboards, scattered about the building, had not. The computers were no doubt digesting lots of useful data, but there was nothing to display it on.

"I did warn you," General Curtis pointed out.

"Shut up, Carl." Gordon went back to his brooding. It was dark outside. Darker than he had ever seen it in Washington.

How were the police doing? he wondered. Did their cars still work? Probably not. With the onboard computers fried, about the only cars that could be expected to work were pre-1980s antiques. And where would you get petrol to fuel them in a world where all the cars were electric? The street lights were out, as was the power to any building that didn't have its own generator. Most that did would be having the same problem with fried LED bulbs.

A Secret Service agent entered the room. "Another 147 dead, sir," he reported.

Gordon turned to look at him in the dim light. "How?"

"Another airliner, sir."

"Where?"

"New Mexico. It was flying from Los Angeles to New Orleans when the pulse hit. Crashed a few miles outside Roswell."

Appropriate, Curtis thought. Attack a genuine space ship and planes crash near America's UFO epicentre. Why hadn't anyone thought to ground all flights? Even if the missiles had hit the ship, there would still have been a massive electromagnetic pulse to contend with. Not to mention problems with the Brits, Russians, and Indians, whose citizens manned the Sagan Space Platform. In the vacuum of outer space, those two warheads detonating a few hundred yards away wouldn't have created any shock wave, but the heat and gamma radiation would have destroyed the platform anyway.

"Get Sustern in here," Gordon ordered. "We're going to need to get a proper news release out."

"Yes, sir."

It's probably past time for me to retire, Curtis decided. We have fucked up on a massive scale. Reports coming in were saying the EMP damage covered most of the country, and extended into northern Mexico and a good portion of southern Canada. Given population distribution in Canada, that would mean the parts where most of their citizens lived. People are going to want someone to blame. If the truth gets out—which it very likely would—there was going to be trouble. Could they fight a war with Gehun, Canada, and Mexico at the same time?

Walter Sustern, the White House Press Secretary, entered the Oval Office and walked to where the president was standing by the windows.

"Oh, good," Gordon acknowledged, "you're here. We need to get something out to the press."

Sustern nodded grimly. "Naturally, sir."

"Put something together. Blame the aliens, naturally."

"Of course, sir. We'll say it was a follow-up to their raid in Wyoming. Not satisfied with killing a small number of our citizens, the so-called Gehunites launched a massive electromagnetic pulse attack on the United States, with the intention of destroying the electric grid and communications facilities in preparation for invasion. Something like that."

"Excellent. Put it together, then bring it to me for final approval before you release it."

"Yes, sir." Sustern left for his office. He was wondering what he was going to write the release on. His computer was fried. Was there an antique typewriter stuck away somewhere?

"They did it, eh, Will?" Curtis asked.

"Couldn't have been us."

"Do you think people will believe that?"

Gordon smiled. "Of course, they will. Who's going to say otherwise?"

◆   ◆   ◆

Technical Sergeant Edward Hiller looked down at the dead FBI agent and shook his head. Now what? All three of the Feds were dead, and he was still alive. The question was, would he stay that way once he went back to the surface? He thought he was safe enough, locked away in the silo complex, but he couldn't stay there forever.

It was pure, dumb luck he was alive as it was. The three FBI agents had shown up while he was in the latrine. Hearing the shooting, he'd cautiously made his way to his quarters and retrieved his sidearm.

After that, he'd done his best to become the phantom of the missile silo. Not an easy task. There weren't many places to hide down there. But he knew the complex better than the FBI guys, and after killing the men in the control room, they'd spread out to look for the missing man. Him. They'd expected a crew of five, and only found four, so someone else had to be down there.

They should have stuck together, Hiller thought. He'd caught the first one in the galley. No time for questions. The Fed had taken a snap shot that missed, and Hiller had taken an equally quick shot that caught the guy in the middle of the chest. He was dead before he hit the floor.

He felt a little guilty about the second guy. It seemed a bit unsporting, shooting him in the back before he realised he wasn't alone in the passageway. Well, it wasn't sport, was it? These three guys had murdered the rest of the missile crew for some reason. That wasn't how it was supposed to work. You don't kill heroes, do you?

The third was the hardest. They spotted each other at the same moment and both opened fire. Bullets were caroming off the concrete walls of the passageway. Hiller caught the FBI agent in the right arm. Not a fatal wound, but the agent dropped his gun and Hiller put another round into his leg, just to be sure he didn't try to pick it up again.

"What the fuck are you doing here?" Hiller had demanded.

The agent looked at him coldly. "I'm just doing my job," he replied.

"Your job is murdering Air Force missile crews?"

"Nothing personal. You know too much, that's all."

This surprised the thirty-one-year-old NCO. "I don't know shit, to tell you the truth. I just follow orders. We pointed the missile at coordinates that came down from HQ and fired it when the president said to fire it."

"Like I said, you know too much."

That was when it hit him. The only thing he really knew was that the missile had been fired. If he knew too much, and that was all he knew, then apparently the official line was going to be that *no* missile had been fired.

Someone had obviously fucked things up.

"Nothing personal," the FBI agent repeated.

"Yeah," Hiller said. "Neither is this." He put a nine-millimetre round into the agent's forehead.

◆   ◆   ◆

Sir Charles Vickers waited for the interviewer to finish her conversation with the camera operator. It had been a full day since the missile attack on *Warrior*. The most important thing that could be said was that, so far, it did not appear to have started a war.

He had spent a good part of that morning at Downing Street, meeting with the Empress, who was acting primarily in her ambassadorial role. Put simply, the people on *Warrior*, despite being predominantly military, weren't interested in fighting. She'd made it very clear that they could, if it became necessary, but equally clear they'd prefer to avoid it.

The interviewer took her seat, shuffling her notes in her hands. She wasn't as pretty close up as she always appeared on the screen, Vickers decided. The makeup was more obvious in person.

"So, Prime Minister, the world has been a very interesting place for the last 37 hours. What can you tell us?"

Vickers smiled grimly. "Well, Elizabeth, I'd like to start with some good news. We were worried that the American attack might have destroyed the Sagan Space Platform. It appears those fears were unfounded. With some help from our Gehunite friends, power has been restored to the platform, and the crew are back at their posts."

"The Americans," Elizabeth said, "are saying the Gehunites were the ones who detonated an EMP device, attacking them."

Vickers nodded dismissively. "The Americans, as usual, are spinning things for their own population. President Gordon is a theologian, not a scientist. His government decided to attack the Gehunites and the attack backfired, causing tremendous damage to his own country without hurting his target."

"What about the attack on the church?"

"Elizabeth, you might just as well ask, what about the Polish attack on the German radio station at Gleiwitz in 1939. Both were carried out by the so-called victims for the purpose of providing an excuse for military action. Both aggressors bit off more than they could chew once they tried to take advantage of that excuse. The difference was that it required five years for the Germans to realise that, but only a few hours for the Americans."

"Do you know what the Gehunites plan to do?"

"I spent a good part of this morning speaking to their empress. They don't actually plan to do anything. Not in the way of military action. They're offering logistical support for the areas outside the United States that were affected by the attack."

"Logistical support?" the interviewer asked.

"Transportation, mostly. Their own computers and technology are largely incompatible with ours, but their shuttles are significantly faster than our planes, and they can fly outside the atmosphere, so there's no problems with going supersonic over populated areas. They're bringing in new computers and other electronics from unaffected areas."

"What about the United States?"

"Unless they ask for help, they're on their own. So far, they haven't asked."

◆   ◆   ◆

The door to the Oval Office was made to look like part of the wall. It was the sort of trick that was popular in the early 19th century. It wasn't quite a "secret" door. There was a knob, after all, and the outline was clear enough.

Gordon was rather surprised when it opened. He hadn't been expecting anyone. He was even more surprised when the first person through the door was General Allen, the chairman of the Joint Chiefs of Staff. He was followed by six more senior officers, General Curtis, the Air Force Chief of Staff, the Navy's Admiral Wallace, the Army's General Harrison, the Commandant of the Marine Corps, General Berry, and Admiral Mumford, of the Coast Guard. They were, in turn, followed by a dozen junior officers and enlisted men from all the services.

Gordon didn't remember a meeting on his schedule. And why hadn't they been announced? Where was his Secret Service detail?

"What's going on?" he asked.

Curtis stepped forward. "Something has come up, Will," he said. "There's someone here I think you should meet." He turned back to the group behind the senior officers. "Hiller? Come up here, son."

A tall, well-built young man in an Air Force dress uniform stepped up.

"This is Technical Sergeant Edward Hiller," Curtis said. "He was a missile technician assigned to silo 47Mike–XRay3."

Gordon shrugged. It didn't mean anything to him.

"That was the silo that fired the second missile," Curtis explained. "Sergeant Hiller is the only surviving crew member. The others were murdered by the FBI agents you sent to eliminate any direct witnesses. Hiller killed the agents and reported what happened to the commanding general at Malmstrom. He reported it to me. We've since confirmed what happened at Sergeant Hiller's silo, and at the other one, where the entire crew was murdered."

"I'm afraid that doesn't leave us much choice," Admiral Mumford said. "I'm placing you under arrest, sir."

Gordon glared at him. "You can't do that. A president can't be arrested. The Attorney General's office can prepare charges, and Congress can decide on impeachment, but the military has nothing to say in these matters."

"Sorry," General Allen said, "but the Constitution no longer applies. The entire country has been placed under martial law. Congress has been dissolved, and there will be new elections in November. Including a special election for President."

"Just about now," General Harrison added, "four companies of the 117th Military Police Battalion are taking over from the DIS and USCPS people at Camp Antelope. That facility is closed, as from now, and the inmates will be going home. I expect they'll have some interesting stories to tell their old neighbours. Other units are presently raiding DIS headquarters, FBI headquarters, and any other Federal law enforcement agencies to ensure records aren't destroyed before charges can be brought."

"No," Gordon said. "You don't have the authority."

"Oh, but I do," Admiral Mumford declared. "The Coast Guard is legally a Federal law enforcement agency, as well as a military component. Coast Guard personnel have arrest powers under Federal law, and that includes the Commandant. You're being charged with treason, Mr. President, along with conspiracy to commit murder, being an accessory to murder before the fact, illegal imprisonment of American citizens, and conspiracy to wage an undeclared war."

"Some of you were involved with that," Gordon protested.

"Those who were have been granted immunity. In any case, it's obvious you acted against the advice of the Joint Chiefs. The problem with being able to rule by decree," Mumford said, "is that only one opinion counts and only one man is ultimately responsible."

Twenty - Eight

ART ELLSWORTH STUDIED THE TICKET FOLDER with mixed emotions. The American diplomat who brought it was used to the reaction. A year after the attack on *Warrior*, things had settled down back home, but you could hardly say they'd returned to normal.

The military officers who'd deposed Gordon and his government had been true to their word. New elections were held on 5th November 2126. A new Congress was in place, and a new president was in the White House. Gordon would spend the rest of his life in the old Army prison at Fort Leavenworth. Gordon was only 71, so he could look forward to a long confinement.

Before elections, the states had ratified six constitutional amendments. The most important restored the religious freedom guaranteed by the previous Constitution, so that government employment, or holding political office, was no longer limited to Christians. Others restored judicial review powers to the Supreme Court, and stripped the president of his power to impose law by executive order.

Things were going to be a lot more transparent in the future. If reality happened to disagree with something in the Bible, from now on reality would have the upper hand.

"We can really go home?" Art asked.

"Absolutely. You can move right back into your old house, and your old company is ready to put you back on the payroll in your old job. There's still a lot of rebuilding to do."

"What about our daughter?" Joanne asked.

"If she wants to go with you, she can. She was at our embassy a few days ago, with Empress Felia."

"I don't think she'll come back," Art sighed. "Roaming the universe is a lot more exciting than going back to Denver to finish high school."

"I suppose," Joanne agreed. She still wanted her daughter back. Not just the weekly visits they'd been having, but really back.

"We're going to have to think about this," Art said. "I'm not as trusting as I used to be."

The diplomat nodded. "Can't say I blame you."

♦   ♦   ♦

Lieutenant Commander Marina Fehmadaatin sat in a small pub near Trafalgar Square, watching the television suspended behind the worn oak bar. On the screen, a blue box was spinning through a void. Must be nice, Marina thought, to be able to go back to the time you started if you wanted to. She liked the English, but still felt that her own country had been better. Being able to go back there was a dream that could never be fulfilled, except in fiction. As she'd done for the last sixteen years, she'd just have to settle for the *faux* Callaa in her quarters.

Time was growing shorter. They'd been there a little over a year now. The original plan had called for half that. *Warrior's* crew had shrunk by fourteen, who had decided to remain behind. All but two were older crew members, who had been ready to retire in any event. They'd be trading the *faux* hominess of their shipboard quarters for the somewhat more authentic hominess of a British country village. The other two had met someone and opted to stay behind to be with them. Love, Marina noted, made you do strange things.

Despite that loss, they'd leave with a net gain of thirty-seven. Of the new crew, 42 were enlisting in the Imperial Navy. After completing language training, thirty-six would spend several more months qualifying for a proper naval rating, and six more, all former Royal Navy officers, would be commissioned in their old ranks. The other nine were scientists or technicians, including Anne Jenkins, the American expatriate astrophysicist from the Sagan Space Platform. She'd spent her relatively brief career studying the stars. Now she'd spend the rest of it studying them a bit closer.

Sara was probably with her parents, Marina thought. They'd been offered a chance to go home and pick up their lives where they'd left off. Sara was staying with the ship.

The girl had come a long way in the past year. Her translator was tucked away in a drawer in her bedside table, only to be taken out if she had to communicate with a modern earthling who didn't speak English. Other than the odd unfamiliar word or idiom, she was fluent in Gehunite. She was even proving to be a rather good writer in her new language. The girl had a wild imagination.

Her friend, Ellen, was having more trouble with the language, but she was getting there. Both girls were going with the ship when it departed. She expected to see quite a bit of Ellen in the future. She'd expressed an interest in striking for quartermaster once she started her naval training, and that would put her in Marina's department. Sara was already well established in her job in Felia's diplomatic office.

♦   ♦   ♦

Nick Harris returned his mobile phone to his shirt pocket, smiling. Ellen was doing fine, enjoying her training, and looking forward to exploring the universe. Things would be harder then, he thought. Until the ship left, he could call his daughter whenever he liked. Once it was gone, all he'd have would be memories.

Still, at least he would know where she was. That she could be expected to live for what, from his earthbound viewpoint, would be thousands of years. Not like before, when the FBI had blatantly lied to him and Maureen, told them Ellen had run away when they knew exactly where she was.

Nor had Ellen tried to contact them after she was rescued. Better they be left wondering, she'd argued, than that she told them what happened, potentially putting them where she'd been. It wasn't until after the EMP fiasco, and the military coup that took the power to govern back from those who'd held it for so long, that Ellen felt safe in letting her parents know she was still alive.

Nick was where he was for just that reason. Emptying Camp Antelope, and at the same time allowing the news media to report the facts without the filter of government censorship, told him he was not unique. Thousands of parents across the country thought their kids had run away, then discovered they'd been taken by the government. Nick had found himself speaking out about it, which led to starting a charity, which led to putting his name forward when it became clear the generals and admirals were serious, and that elections really would be held.

He could just make out the top of the Washington monument, peeking over the trees, from his office window in the old Russell Senate Office Building. The name was still on the building, even 105 years after the senate had ceased to exist.

Nick had one of the nicest office suites in the old building. Traditionally, those had been assigned based on seniority. After the last election, office assignments had been by lottery. Out of the 692 members of Congress, only 28 had previously held office. The Temporary Governance Committee had summarily fired every politician in the Federal government. Most of those eligible for a pension had taken it and retired from politics. One hundred eighteen had been indicted once the Committee took a close look at their finances. Some had tried to run again and been defeated in the primaries.

Except for those 28 returnees, there was no congressional seniority to speak of. The whole thing was simply tossed out the window, with everyone starting out as equals. The Ninth Amendment had insured that.

His office door opened. "Your three o'clock appointment is here, Congressman," his assistant said.

"Thank you."

♦   ♦   ♦

"This is nice," Joanne Ellsworth said, looking around the big living room in Sara's flat. "Big."

"There's a lot of room available," Sara told her. "The ship was designed to have room for 800 colonists, plus the crew. Without the colonists, that leaves a lot of space to expand crew quarters, or add other facilities."

"You're sure about doing this?" Art asked.

"Yeah, Dad, I'm sure."

"I feel like I should be able to make you come home with us," he said. "You're still only sixteen, after all."

"On this ship, that's an adult." She hugged her father. "Don't worry, Dad. I'm not going to forget you two. And I'm not going to be getting into any trouble, either."

"Not while we're alive, you mean?"

Sara laughed, walking across the room to the balcony doors.

"Okay," she said, "you've got me there. A couple days from now I'll be nearly three hundred years in the future."

"I hate that part," Joanne said.

"Look at it this way, Mom. You'll never have to worry about outliving your daughter."

"Cute."

"Come on. Take a look at this view."

"That's really a hologram?" her father queried.

"Sure is. Look."

Sara hopped over the railing, standing half a metre in front of it. From her parents' point of view, even from her own, she seemed to be standing in mid-air, floating over Central Park West. Her mother looked for a moment, then turned back.

"I cannot look at that," she declared. Even knowing it was an illusion, it was too much for her to handle.

Sara jumped back over the rail onto the balcony. "Relax, Mom. It's not real. If I'd moved a couple more feet from the railing I'd have run into a bulkhead. They go to a great deal of trouble to make the crew comfortable. But it's still an illusion."

"I know, honey. I just hate the idea of you leaving."

"It was going to happen eventually. This is just a little sooner."

"Doesn't mean I like it."

♦   ♦   ♦

Captain Kimewe Romiwero sat back in her chair and studied the main view-screen. The view of earth was slowly rotating around the ship's axis. The navigation computers would be calculating the basc vector, drawing an imaginary line from the centre of the sun, through the centre of the earth, and out into space.

The ship continued to rotate. Romiwero glanced over at the Sagan Space Platform. Only a few of the people she'd originally met over there were still aboard. The rest had rotated back planetside. You could remain aboard *Warrior*, with her artificial gravity system, for years at a time. You could only stay aboard the platform for a few months before you started losing strength and bone mass.

"In position, Captain," Marina reported.

Romiwero glanced over at her, for the moment sitting at the helm, as she always did on departures. She still wasn't used to seeing the extra, thin stripe just above the other two. The promotion, she thought, was well deserved.

"Elir?"

"Ready to proceed, Captain," the engineering officer reported.

"Ring down ready."

"Ring down ready, aye."

"Stand by the leave orbit," Romiwero ordered.

"Course for jump point calculated," Marina reported.

"Very well. Ahead slow. Break her out of orbit, and set course for jump point."

They were on their way again.

What will this place be like next time we return? Romiwero wondered. The first jump would be 300 light years, a round trip of 600 years if they turned around immediately. It had been nearly 87,000 years between their original departure and their return. It could easily be as long again before they came back.

She smiled, looking at the screen. Lots of time to figure that out, she thought.

Acknowledgements

THANKS ARE DUE TO SEVERAL PEOPLE, who contributed in various ways to this book. First, thanks to all the science writers who provided a source for the physics, astronomy, and what not that provide a background for the story. I'm not mentioning names, because I've probably got some of it wrong and that's my fault, not theirs, so I'll take the blame.

Thanks of a sort are due to President Trump and the modern GOP. When I started writing this story, a ridiculously long time ago, the idea of a religio-fascist dictatorship in the United States seemed ridiculous. Now, with the banishment of science and culture from government, a president who seems determined to ignore the Constitution and rule by executive order, and a cabinet composed mostly of extremists who have spent years working to destroy the departments they now head, the country planned by the Gordon's and their real-life counterparts seems frighteningly possible. Americans are a resilient people, and likely will survive, but this may be the first time in American history when it won't possible to say, "We've survived worse."

Special thanks are also due to Kevin Scott, John Beahan, and Doug Estes, whose support during the writing of this little tome is greatly appreciated.

www.ingramcontent.com/pod-product-compliance
Lightning Source LLC
Chambersburg PA
CBHW050520260626
47157CB00004B/1406